THE SECRET SHE KEPT

CATHRYN GRANT

INKUBATOR
BOOKS

Published by Inkubator Books
www.inkubatorbooks.com

ISBN (eBook): 978-1-83756-068-4
ISBN (Paperback): 978-1-83756-069-1
ISBN (Hardback): 978-1-83756-070-7

PROLOGUE

NADIA

Rich people love their private parks with huge trees and smooth paths where they can go for long morning runs. Just the fact they have time to run for miles proves how they live in a different world from everyone else. Normal people don't have time to put on silky leggings and tops the color of ice cream, plug sci-fi buds into their ears that cost half a month's rent, and breathe in the clean air of suburbs protected by comforting foothills.

Normal people have to drag themselves out of bed when the alarm goes off and get dressed for work and show up on time, so their paycheck is the full amount at the end of the month. Even working from home, providing customer support, I'm controlled by clocks and apps that track when I'm using my keyboard. If I'm not already logged in at six a.m., points are deducted from any positive ratings I get from customers. And with plenty of customers giving one-star ratings just because they don't like my truthful answers to their crazy questions, I can't afford that.

Dr. Flaherty went for her run at five in the morning. I knew this because I'd watched her leave her house every weekday for three weeks. While I waited for her, my phone said 4:58, then 4:59, then 5:00, and her front door opened. Every day.

Then I followed her along those peaceful, curving paths.

Sometimes there were other runners, but never more than two, maybe three, because in February it was pitch dark at five a.m. I also picked a day when it was raining, which wasn't hard to do in the Pacific Northwest in the winter. Watching her had told me that rain didn't keep her from her run, but I figured it kept other people snuggled under the blankets, and I was right.

She was the only person, the only living, breathing thing I saw at all that morning. Even the birds and squirrels were smart enough to take shelter from the water that still dripped from the trees when the rain paused to take a breath.

This would be Dr. Flaherty's last day running. It would be her last day getting into her shiny white Mercedes. It would be her last day driving to the medical center. It would be her last day lying to her patients and telling them they didn't need a follow-up until six months later—*if* the problem persisted. It was the last day she would give that condescending smile and say, "But truthfully, if you ate a healthier diet, you wouldn't have so much abdominal distress." That's what she called it—abdominal distress.

It would definitely be her last day telling someone that working with insurance companies was too much trouble. She would provide better care—*boutique* care—if they could pay for it. Only seven thousand dollars up front, and then pay for everything yourself. A doctor for rich people.

When cancer cells are eating away inside your abdomen, but they aren't attached to a specific organ, doctors don't always notice right away. Or something. Flaherty never made it clear why she didn't look harder to figure out what was wrong with my mom. I guess she was too busy setting up her *boutique* medical services. Because then it turned out my mom didn't have enough money to deserve to be her patient. The doctor didn't say it that way, obviously. She said that with fewer patients, each one would get more attention; they would get better *quality* care.

When my mom finally found a new doctor, and the diagnosis was finally made, and treatment finally started, it was way too late. Way, way too late.

This was the last day that *dedicated* doctor would sleep peacefully in her enormous Mediterranean home.

My mom was nothing but a pile of ashes in a ceramic jar, waiting to be scattered in a forest. No more soft pillow and downy comforter for her. I had no idea when her ashes might settle into the woods, because my dad couldn't manage to drag his own tired, broken self out of the easy chair in our living room.

Dr. Flaherty was going to pay for what she'd done.

I increased my speed, moving closer to Dr. Flaherty in the thick, soupy rain. The sound of my footsteps was drowned by the splash of water. Besides, with those white buds in her ears, she was oblivious. She felt safe. I didn't even need to get that close.

I raised the gun and fired at the back of her head. I was close enough, and steady enough, that she collapsed instantly. But more than the reverberation of the gun through my bones, I felt the shock of what I'd done. The sight of her collapsed on the ground, blood turning her hair into something ugly and disgusting, made me feel sick. I bent over, trying to breathe. I thought I might throw up, but the feeling evaporated the minute I remembered how far the sound of the gunshot must have carried.

Shoving the gun into the pocket of my hoodie, I ran, following the same path she always took until I reached the edge of the park. I ran the extra half mile to my ten-year-old car parked alone in a small lot.

Dr. Flaherty was the first person I needed to punish. The next was Ruth Monroe. But Ruth was different.

Death would be too merciful for Ruth.

1

RUTH

ondays aren't a drudge for Cameron and me like they are for so many people. We feel lucky every single day of our lives. Loving what you do, knowing that your work has meaning, that it helps people, is an indescribable pleasure. So when I settle at my desk on Monday mornings and look through the window of my office across the hallway into Cameron's office at the back corner of the Second Chance Wellness Center, I'm always smiling. My smile broadens as he grins back at me.

We conceived of the wellness center after the car accident that fractured Cameron's pelvis and put him into months of painful recovery. Now we offer a new lease on life to people who have chronic pain and to those who are simply tired of feeling drained by general physical malaise.

On this Monday, there was a young woman waiting for me in the lobby when I arrived. She was my nine o'clock appointment, but it was only quarter to, so I smiled and told her I would be out to meet her in a few minutes.

She stood as if she meant to follow me anyway. She was about my height, with long hair dyed bright red with streaks of black. On most girls it would look cheap, but she was quite stunning because it was nicely cut and styled. She wore subtle makeup and a gold ring through the side of one nostril, which drew my attention away from her eyes and eager smile.

"I'll be out to meet with you at nine," I said.

"I'm here, you're here, so why wait?"

I smiled kindly. "Just give me a few minutes." I walked quickly across the lobby and down the hall to the small café, ordered my usual latte, and took it and a banana to my office. I opened my computer and responded to a few emails, looked at our financials, and then closed my eyes and enjoyed a few sips of coffee before I brought in the new client.

Her name was Nadia Fairchild. As she lowered herself carefully into the chair in my office, I brought up the profile our new clients fill out online before their first appointment. I'd already read it, but I wanted it for easy reference.

She took a sip of water from the bottle I'd given her.

"So you aren't aware of any injury that first caused your back pain? Even something minor?"

She shook her head.

"That's unusual."

"That's why my doctor up in Washington said it was stress."

I nodded.

"I heard about this place because I saw your interview online—you and Cameron—for the ten-year anniversary of the Center."

I smiled.

"It looks even more beautiful in real life than it did in the clips they showed."

"Thank you."

"Very swanky."

"I don't know if I'd use that word." She laughed. "We try to create a tranquil atmosphere."

She turned her attention to my desk. "That heart is beautiful."

I had an impulse to cover the glass emerald heart with my hand as if to protect it from her. Cameron had given it to me when we opened the Wellness Center. Looking at it throughout the day grounded me. I loved it, and I loved touching it.

"Thank you. Are you settling permanently in California?"

"It looks expensive." Her gaze met mine. "The heart."

I ignored her and typed a note into her profile for the rest of the team that she was scattered, and there might be psychological issues behind her back pain.

"You and Cameron have been married twelve years?"

Her question unsettled me. I didn't recall mentioning our marriage in the interview. How would she know that? Why did it matter to her? I gave her a cool smile and a brief nod.

"Do you like working together?"

"Let's talk about your back pain."

"And I guess you've lived here for all that time—in the Bay Area. You're really well known in the community. It's amazing how you helped him through his injuries. After the accident."

"I'm glad the interview inspired you. But we're here to talk about your back. Did you see a primary care physician or a specialist of some kind?"

"Primary care. He wouldn't refer me. He said I needed to strengthen my core and manage stress better."

"Both points are true, if somewhat limited. But it's a good starting point."

"How did you and Cameron meet?"

She was staring directly into my eyes, hardly blinking. It seemed as if she was more interested in me and my husband than she was in discussing how we could address the pain that she claimed was interfering with her job. "How long have you been experiencing pain?"

"I forget, exactly. A few weeks, I guess. How many people work here?"

"That's not important. We'll set you up with—"

"It must cost a lot to run this place."

"We think our fees are reasonable. Nearly all insurance plans cover six physical therapy sessions. And many plans cover acupuncture and massage therapy as well."

"I haven't checked with my insurance."

"Our office staff can help with that. I see you filled out all the information for us to contact your provider. No need to worry too much about that."

"It's interesting that you and Cameron aren't doctors, but I guess you explained that in the interview. Cameron seemed a little defensive about it, though."

"He's not defensive." I was annoyed with myself for even acknowledging what she'd said.

"Maybe it wasn't defensive, exactly. But I sensed ... something. Maybe it was that you two weren't quite ..." She extended her hand and wiggled her fingers slightly.

"We're not here to analyze your interpretations of a casual interview that's already ancient history. If you're interested in addressing your back pain, the first step will be to schedule an introductory session with one of our licensed physical therapists."

"Cool." She put her hand on her hip, pressing her fingers into the small of her back. "It's killing me. I think a massage would be good too."

"Let's see what the physical therapist says first." I began typing notes into her profile. The instructions would be automatically fed to the PT team and also available for the rest of the staff. Each service area we offered received the details for every new client we brought into the center.

"I'm really looking forward to making this a big part of my life."

I smiled.

"Everyone here seems really great," she said. "I got really good vibes the minute I walked in the door."

"We're all focused on helping our clients find optimal health."

"When will I be meeting Cameron?"

"That's not necessary. He and I share the orientation of our new clients."

"That's too bad. He seems like a great guy."

I gave her a tight smile and turned back to the computer to print a summary document for her. She was making me increasingly uneasy, but I'd never told a prospective client to leave. It seemed unprofessional. Maybe she was just immature. "I've arranged a tour of the facility for you in about ten minutes. One of the yoga instructors will show you around. Her name is—"

"You won't be giving me the tour?"

"No."

She asked if I would reconsider, but this was our standard process, and when I repeated my answer, she finally accepted it.

That evening, while Cameron opened a bottle of wine and I sautéed vegetables and tofu, I told him about Nadia. "It was a little creepy." I laughed, wishing I'd found a better way to describe her. It sounded extreme to call her creepy when she was a very pretty, mostly pleasant-seeming girl in her early twenties. She was full of energy despite the pain she described. There was nothing about her clothes or her demeanor that was anything close to creepy, but her fixation on me and Cameron was ... weird.

"What's so funny?" Cameron asked.

"I don't mean she's a creepy person, but it felt creepy, the way she kept steering the conversation back to personal questions about you and me."

"Like what?"

"She wanted to talk about that interview we did for the anniversary. Asking how long we've been married, as if she already knew the answer."

"So? It seems natural that the interview would come up. That was the whole point—PR."

"But why did she care about our marriage? And I don't think we talked about that in the interview. Did we?"

"We must have, if she knew about it."

"I'm almost certain we didn't."

"There's a lot of public information about us. She's just being diligent."

"It makes sense to want to know about the history of the Wellness Center and maybe to search out testimonials and reviews, but not personal information about us."

"I think it shows she double-clicks on things, doesn't take what people say at face value. There's nothing wrong with that. It's a good thing."

Everything he said was right. I couldn't argue with him, but I still felt unsettled. I'd never had a client ask such personal questions. I'd never had a client who wanted to talk more about me and my husband than about their own health issues. Usually, people in pain are very focused on how they can find relief as quickly as possible. To Nadia Fairchild, restoring good health seemed to be an afterthought.

2

NADIA

The physical therapist said my back seemed healthy, and my experience of pain was inconsistent. She actually repeated the lie I told from my made-up doctor—that I needed to deal better with stress. She recommended strength training, which I said I'd never done in my whole life, which was the truth, and yoga and Pilates. She also recommended massage therapy. I thought it was clever that even though they'd discovered I didn't need physical help with pain, there were still a lot of services for me at the Second Chance Wellness Center.

That's how I met Justine, one of the massage therapists.

I knew it was important to meet Justine because I'd seen her go into Ruth's office two minutes after I left. She closed the door, but from where I was standing partway down the hall, I could see them laughing and talking. It wasn't just a meeting between a staff person and one of the owners. They were friends. Good friends. And any friend of Ruth's was definitely going to be a friend of mine.

During my massage, Justine told me it was better to be quiet, because talking, even softly, activated muscles that she was trying to work into a subdued state. I ignored her. It wasn't as if I was talking that much. I was asking questions.

"It's also hard for me to work if you keep talking because it breaks my concentration," she said.

"I'm all alone in California. I don't know a single person here. So I guess I'm a little lonely." I let my voice quiver on that last part, and I could feel the pressure of her hands on my lower back soften, telling me I'd gotten to her.

After that, she didn't complain about answering my questions. I found out all about her eleven-year-old daughter, Kellyn, who Ruth let hang out at the Wellness Center after school every day because Ruth was *the sweetest person on the planet* and a *spectacular boss, if you could even call her that*. I found out Kellyn's daddy left when she was two, and that Justine had just broken up with the love of her life a few months ago after six years together. I found out both her parents were dead. I found out Ruth was her mentor and someone she admired very much and was *almost like a big sister*.

"It's really awesome that you're raising Kellyn all by yourself. You must love her so much."

"With all my heart," she said.

"I really admire you for having a career and taking care of your child."

"There's nothing really to admire," she said.

Justine found out absolutely nothing about me. She didn't seem to notice.

"You're lucky to have such a good friend at work," I said. "Working from home, like I do, it's hard to make friends. We only know each other from our chat app and video calls. My so-called friends are all over the place. Some of them aren't even in the US. We've never met each other in real life."

"That would feel strange." She took her hands off my skin. I could hear her squirting lotion onto her palms. "Please relax. And you really should try not to talk. Your entire upper body tightened while you were telling me about your job."

I sighed and pushed my face harder against the head-support ring. I sighed as she pressed her thumbs slowly along my spine. "That feels sooo good. It is lonely sometimes. It must be awesome working at a place like this. It feels like you're all one big family."

"Please don't talk, Nadia."

"Maybe we could get a smoothie after you're done with my massage. So we can talk then."

"I have another client."

"Oh." I let the word come out in a whisper, almost like I was starting to cry.

"If you don't mind hanging around, I'd be ready for a break after that. But no more talking right now, okay?"

After she was finished, I sat quietly as I was told and drank the required glass of water to make sure I was hydrated. Then I went to the café, which sold coffee and smoothies and healthy snacks. Justine's daughter was sitting at one of three small booths along the back wall. She was filling out a worksheet of math problems that looked like something I might have done after school a long time ago. That girl who used to solve math problems seemed like a different person. She seemed like someone who wasn't really me at all. I'd only been out of high school four years, but sometimes, it felt like that part of my life had never happened, because so many things had changed since then.

For a long time right after high school, I took care of my mother while the cancer gobbled up the inside of her body. And then I kissed the bone that used to be her cheek good-bye. Doing that turns you into a different person. For one thing, it makes you a person who doesn't worry at all about what someone might think of you. After you learn that your life can be over without any warning, no matter how hard you try to do things right, you realize you might as well do whatever you want.

I bought two cups of hot chocolate and two oatmeal cookies. I walked directly to Kellyn's table. "Ugh. Math homework," I said. "Is it busywork?"

She looked up at me. "Yeah."

"I'm Nadia."

"Oh."

"I just had the most amazing massage in the world from your extremely talented mom. She said you were doing homework and you love hot chocolate." I put the cup on the table.

"Thanks."

"Can I sit here?"

"It's a free country," she said.

I slid into the booth and handed her one of the cookies. "This is for you too."

"Mmm. Thanks." She took a bite. "How did you know it was busywork?"

"I graduated from high school, like, yesterday." I laughed. "Not exactly, but it feels like it was yesterday. Or last week. And trust me, homework is busywork. Like ninety-nine percent of the time. Teachers don't want to work until five o'clock because then they have to grade papers at night. But people want to make sure kids have stuff to do to keep them busy all day. Sooo ..."

"Busywork."

"Yup." I took a sip of my own hot chocolate.

"Are you a new client?" Kellyn asked. "I haven't seen you before."

"Yeah. Back pain."

"That sucks."

"Your mom's awesome hands really helped. I feel great right now. I can actually walk without limping." I took another sip of chocolate. "Do you know the owners very well? Ruth and Cameron?"

"Yeah."

"What are they like?"

She shrugged. "They're nice."

"Does your mom like working for them?"

She laughed. "Why are you asking me?"

I smiled. "Your mom seems like she loves her job, so I just wondered. This is a cool place."

"I like it. Sometimes if there are only a few people in the yoga classes, I get to join the class as long as I stay in the back."

"Are you into yoga and natural food and all that?"

"Kind of. I love ice cream, though. And hot chocolate."

"Who doesn't like ice cream?"

She laughed.

"I'm going to be doing all the things here," I said. "So I might see you in a yoga class."

"How did you hurt your back?"

"Who knows. I woke up one morning, and I could hardly stand up. Some people think it's stress."

"Do you have a lot of stress?"

"Probably. Do you?"

"Not really."

"How's school going for you?"

"Good. School is easy for me. I have straight A's, except a B in art. How can I get a B in art?" She rolled her eyes.

"That doesn't seem right. Art is about being yourself. You can't grade who you are."

"That's what I think." She grinned. "Maybe you should talk to my teacher."

"I doubt she would care about my opinion."

"Probably not." She took another sip of hot chocolate.

"How come you're talking to me? Usually everyone here ignores me."

"You look like a smart person, and we're practically the same age."

Kellyn giggled. "We're not the same age at all. I'm eleven. You're an adult."

"Barely."

We smiled at each other and finished our cookies.

It's so easy to make friends with people. Most people take you at face value. They assume you want to be friends. They assume you like them. If you ask questions and act interested, they assume you're interested in them. Even with all the stories of con artists constantly being documented for TV, no one ever imagines someone might be conning them. Even if it's just a little bit.

I didn't want to con an innocent eleven-year-old girl, obviously. I just wanted her to like me. I wanted everyone Ruth cared about to like me because then I would have more power over her life. Each person who liked me was one more person who might help me get closer to her and find out more about her. *Knowledge is power.* That's what I've heard, and I think it's the truth. It was turning out to be a lot easier than I'd thought to get knowledge about Ruth Monroe.

3

RUTH

Cameron and I had just finished the quarterly meeting with our accountant. I stepped out of the conference room to find Justine waiting for me. She glanced at her phone, swiping away a calendar reminder, then looking at me with her eyes wider than normal, not quite meeting my gaze. "I have a, um, medical appointment. I was going to take Kellyn with me, but I decided it's not a good idea ..." She looked at her phone again, but the screen was dark, so I wasn't sure what she was checking for.

"Do you mind keeping an eye on her?" She was still staring at her phone.

"Of course not."

"I hate asking you. I know it's—"

"Don't worry about it. She'll do her homework and be her usual quiet and charming self. It's not anything serious, is it?"

She shook her head but still wouldn't make eye contact. I was pretty sure it wasn't routine, but it was obvious she didn't want to give me any details. Probably because Kellyn didn't know.

"I should be back by four thirty," she said. "At the latest."

I found Kellyn in the café, where she liked to hang out doing homework on the days when her after-school homework club didn't meet, or she wasn't being carpooled by one of the other moms to her weekly dance class. "Do you want to hang out in my office?"

"I like it here," Kellyn said. "I can watch people."

"It's not too distracting?"

She laughed.

"Okay. Text me if you need anything and I'm not in my office."

She nodded and picked up her water bottle. She took a long swallow, then gave me a smile that told me she would be fine and didn't need me hovering in some misguided attempt at babysitting.

After ordering supplies for the massage therapists, I was standing just outside the yoga studio, watching a group of seven clients unroll their yoga mats. The soft voice of the teacher was barely audible over the recorded sounds of bells and trickling water that was playing from speakers in the ceiling. All those beautiful sounds were obliterated when a piercing alarm shot through the building. I pressed my palms against my ears in a futile effort to dull the shriek of the fire alarm.

I turned and hurried toward the offices, looking for Cameron. He was already in the main hallway, talking to the general manager about executing the evacuation plan. The staff knew what to do. We held training sessions every six months, so I knew the evacuation would go smoothly. I hurried to the lounge and found Kellyn packing up her things.

"It's probably a false alarm," I said. "But we need to go outside until the fire department comes and gives us the okay."

She nodded, shoving papers into her backpack.

"Now," I said. "Leave your backpack."

As we started toward the exit, Nadia Fairchild, the new client, appeared, coming from the physical therapy rooms. "Hey, Kellyn," Nadia said. "It feels like someone's ripping your brain out of your skull, doesn't it?"

Kellyn laughed and poked her fingers into her ears.

"Do you want me to keep an eye on Kellyn while you deal with this?" Nadia asked.

"How do you know Kellyn?" I asked.

Nadia gave me a friendly smile. "We both love smoothies and hanging out in the café."

"She's fine," I said. "We'll just wait in the designated area." We walked toward the exit, instinctively doing our best to keep our hands over our ears, which didn't actually provide much relief.

Outside, we stood at the far end of the parking lot with the rest of the staff and clients. We'd never experienced an evacuation before, and I was glad to see that the massage therapists had done an excellent job in quickly distributing sweatpants, sweatshirts, and Crocs for their clients so they could leave the building quickly and in comfort.

A moment later, Cameron was beside me. "The fire department is less than a minute away."

When they arrived, several firefighters went directly into the building, and one came to speak to Cameron and me. As we talked, I could feel Nadia edging closer. When the firefighter finished explaining their procedure, Nadia touched my arm. "There are a lot of people, and it would be so easy to not notice where Kellyn is. I'll stay with her, and then you don't have to be distracted."

"Okay. Sure. Thank you."

Nadia was right. Before I knew it, another fire truck arrived, and firefighters were swarming around the building. Some of our clients who had managed to grab their gym bags were saying they might as well leave, and Cameron was working with the receptionist to get a headcount for who had been in the building.

When all the chaos had settled and we were back in the building, we learned that they hadn't identified a malfunction in the system. All they could locate was a plastic cover over one of the alarms that had been cracked and a wedge of plastic removed. Cameron and I stared at each other, wondering who would want to disturb the health and well-being of the more than thirty-five people in the building with something as juvenile as a high school prank.

I found Nadia and Kellyn in the lounge. They were nibbling their way down to the points of their ice cream cones.

"Nadia took me to Bruster's." Kellyn licked her lips. "Awesome."

"Thanks so much for watching her. You were right, there was too much for me to keep a close eye."

Nadia smiled knowingly.

"I appreciate your help," I said. "But you shouldn't have—"

"It's nice to be appreciated. It would be terrible if something happened to her when you were distracted."

I nodded. "But I'm not sure it was a good idea to take her—"

"It's fine," Nadia said. "I didn't take her in my car, if that's what you're worried about. It's only three blocks. It's such a nice day, perfect for a walk."

"Thanks," Kellyn said. "Awesome. I haven't had a cone in forever."

"I'm glad I could help. I like being useful," Nadia said.

The conversation was wearing on me. I appreciated what she'd done, but Kellyn was eleven years old. It wasn't as if she couldn't take care of herself. And Cameron and I had been there. She wasn't in any danger. Nadia seemed to imply an unexpected fire alarm was a threatening emergency. She seemed to want more from me than a simple thank you.

"It's really hard being alone in a new city," Nadia said. "I really like knowing I'm already building my own little community." She grinned, chocolate ice cream making her lips look bruised, so she had a slightly ghoulish appearance. Her eyes were glassy, as if the whole experience had moved her to tears. "People can be so unfriendly to newcomers," she said.

"Sometimes, maybe." I took a few steps away from her. "You should get back to your homework when you finish that, Kellyn."

Kellyn nodded. "Absolutely."

I turned. "Thanks again, Nadia."

Nadia gobbled the rest of her cone and stood. She walked up beside me. "If you're not sure how to thank me, I would love an invitation to have dinner with you and Cameron. I'm living alone at an extended-stay motel. The ramen and take-out routine is getting old, and a little sad, to be honest. Eating in front of the TV. And not very healthy." She laughed. "I'm supposed to be getting healthy, right?"

"I—" Her aggressive request had shocked me into silence.

"So tomorrow night? At your house? I just need your address."

"I don't think—"

"I don't know anyone here. It's kind of lonely, to be honest."

She gave me such a pitiful smile. It was possible I'd misread her loneliness as something else. One dinner wasn't a big deal. It would make her feel welcome. "Okay. It won't be anything special."

"Just the company will be fabulous." She gave me a huge grin; then her expression sobered. "Looking after children is such a huge responsibility. Twenty-four seven. You can't let up for even half a second. That's why it's a good thing I was there for Kellyn. Do you have any children?"

I stared at her blankly.

She smiled and glanced at my narrow hips and flat abdomen. Sometimes, people said I was too thin, but Cameron and I had switched to a vegetarian diet after his accident, and I'd lost about fifteen pounds that stayed off throughout my late twenties and now well into my thirties.

"Too personal?" Nadia asked.

It was far too personal. But not answering would make me feel like she knew even more about me, because I was putting my feelings and pieces of my relationship with Cameron on display. It was a tangled web of emotions after Cameron's accident that led to our decision not to have children.

Even before his accident, Cameron had been uncertain. He'd watched his mother pour her entire soul into her children and had seen the ever-widening chasm between his parents until they were polite strangers sharing a house, and his father was rarely home for dinner. As he and I walked slowly together down the long, painful road of his recovery, our vision for the Wellness Center took shape. We spent hours talking about how children fundamentally altered a relationship, even when it was good. We observed other couples and the way their lives were consumed by the tiny people they'd created.

Cameron and I decided we wanted something else. We wanted to affect the lives of people already in existence. Maybe there was an element of selfishness, but it was also satisfying. Despite our long hours and dedication to the Wellness Center, we had the space and time to become entwined with each other in a way couples with children did not. And I secretly believed that remaining a twosome would make us immune to the stagnation I saw in other couples. Our shared passion for the Wellness Center would bond us and keep our relationship vibrant.

For the most part, all that was true. But a few shadows had crept over our little paradise. Sometimes I wondered if inviting my mother to live in the granny cottage had affected me in ways I didn't fully recognize. I wondered if her presence had bled into our marriage and caused small bruises that were now becoming visible.

"Maybe in a few years you'll have a baby?" Nadia asked. "Or is the subject painful for you?"

"Not at all," I said. "Cam and I decided not to have kids. There's nothing painful about it at all."

She gave me a condescending smile, and I regretted agreeing to having her come to dinner.

4

NADIA

It was cool to watch how fast the Wellness Center jumped into action when I pulled the fire alarm. I'd thought it might turn into chaos, not the chaos I tried to make Ruth imagine, but a little chaos. I'd pictured naked people running from the massage tables, wrapping towels around their bodies. I'd pictured Cameron trying to save the day by turning off the alarm himself. I'd wondered if Kellyn might freak out, afraid she'd be trapped in a burning building. None of that happened.

Still, it worked out anyway. I took Kellyn off Ruth's hands. I made myself useful, and I found a way to invite myself for dinner so she couldn't say no without being rude to a client and a vulnerable girl who was all alone in a strange city.

The Monroes' house was as huge and gorgeous as I'd pictured in my head—all on one floor, all glass and tile and bifold doors opening onto small gardens. The master bedroom looked out onto a pond with its own waterfall.

Ruth's mother lived in a so-called granny cottage in their gigantic backyard, which was funny because Ruth said they didn't want kids, so she might not ever be a granny. This *cottage* had two bedrooms with walk-in closets, a living room as big as a studio apartment and a breakfast room plus a counter for eating in the kitchen.

Ruth made dinner, and I had to admit, she was a fabulous cook. She made a spicy tofu dish that tasted like something from an authentic Chinese restaurant, saffron rice, the most delicate green beans I'd ever seen, and a salad with raspberries. They served white wine in glasses I was almost afraid to touch. The stem on my glass was so long and thin I was afraid it would break when I picked it up.

It was my first chance to really look at Cameron and to talk to him, so I took full advantage, even though Ruth's mother, Cheryl, was across the table, staring at me as if she hadn't seen anyone under thirty in the past ten years. Maybe it was my dyed hair. Or my nose ring. A lot of people her age obsess over piercings. It was a good thing she couldn't see my tattoo.

I ignored her for now and looked at Cameron. "I heard you tell the story of your accident," I said. "On a webcast interview about the tenth anniversary of the Wellness Center."

Cameron gave me a bored smile. I guess he got tired of talking about it.

"You're so in shape. It's hard to believe you had such terrible injuries. Hearing about it totally sold me on moving down here. I knew the Wellness Center was the place for me if I was going to get any relief for my pain."

"Glad to hear it," he said.

"You're, like, the same age as my dad, I think, but you look way younger."

He laughed. "Thanks."

"I'm not trying to embarrass you." I reached across the table and tapped his wrist bone. "It's a compliment. You're really inspiring. Your whole story. And everything you've accomplished." I looked up at the ridiculously high ceiling and the chandelier that was made of different-sized teardrop bubbles, giving the room a shimmering sparkle that made it feel like sunlight more than electric lights.

"Ruth and I did it together," he said.

"But it's your story. And your inner strength that made it happen. Someone supporting you can only do so much. The person healing has to want to get better, isn't that what they say?"

"That's very true," Cheryl said.

I smiled at her, then stabbed a few delicate green beans and ate them.

Ruth poured more wine into her glass but didn't offer any to the rest of us. She took a sip. "Cam was the only man I ever loved," she said.

I looked at her. I wanted to laugh. She thought I was flirting with her husband, and she didn't like it. I was, a little, but it was more flattery than flirting. I'd said he was as old as my dad—did she honestly think I was hot for the guy? I just wanted him to like me. I wanted everyone she loved to think I was amazing. That's all. He wasn't anything special to me.

"I fell for him when I was fourteen," Ruth said. "There was never anyone else. I went out with other guys when he was first away at college, but no one ever clicked. It was always him." She gave him a sappy smile and took a few more swallows of wine. I thought she'd better slow down on the wine, or she was going to say something embarrassing.

"And he only had eyes for me." She kept smiling until it looked like her lips were going to drip off her face, but Cameron was looking at his plate, carefully removing a bit of stem from one of his green beans. "It's unusual to find your soul mate when you're so young. We were really lucky."

Cheryl stood up, walked around behind Ruth, plucked

the wine bottle out of the chiller, carried it back to her place and refilled her glass. She thumped the bottle down on the table and took a long swallow. It looked as if mother and daughter were going to get into a drinking contest. I felt as if I'd stepped into something, but I couldn't figure out what it was. I wondered if there was some chilly, silent battle between them that could help me deliver the punishment Ruth had brought upon herself.

"Delicious as always," Cameron said.

"Thank you." Ruth smiled at him and raised her glass as if they were going to have a private toast, but he left his glass on the table and returned his attention to the food.

This was followed by a long silence with forks clicking on plates. Cheryl looked grateful to be eating dinner with them but upset at the same time. I couldn't say why I had that impression. Maybe because she kept looking around the enormous dining room in the same way I was, as if she hadn't been there in a long while. And she kept smiling at Ruth. She looked happy to be in her daughter's presence, as if that was the only thing that mattered.

Maybe Ruth and Cameron's happy little twosome without kids didn't have room for a mother-in-law either. It was kind of sad, looking at how Cheryl was careful not to say much except how good the food was. Almost every bite, she said *mm*, or something like that.

"How long have you lived in the little house out back?" I asked.

"Five and a half years," Cheryl said. "I'm very lucky to have such caring children. It's a beautiful house. So much space—almost more than I need."

"You are," I said. "And Ruth is lucky to have her mom so close. My mom died." I felt tears coming into my eyes. I didn't want to cry in front of them, but there they were, no matter how hard I tried to keep them behind my eyelids.

"Oh. Oh, I'm so sorry," Cheryl said.

Cameron and Ruth made sympathetic noises and words at the same time.

"Sorry." I wiped my eyes. "It's only been five months ... so ..."

"You poor thing," Cheryl said. "That's so hard. No one should lose her mom at such a young age."

I put a large bite of tofu and rice into my mouth and chewed it slowly. Glad that the spiciness took over the feelings inside my head and made the tears go away.

"Your doctor in Washington wasn't entirely wrong," Ruth said. "That could be a factor in your back pain. All the complicated feelings that come with grief can lodge themselves into the body in unexpected ways."

I nodded.

"Was it cancer?" Cheryl asked.

I nodded.

"Usually when someone is too young, it's cancer." Cheryl took a sip of wine.

I picked up my wineglass, still afraid of that stem that seemed like it wanted to break into a deadly spear. I took a tiny sip and put it down carefully on the table. "It was awful. The doctor thought she was just having some diet issues or something—not eating right. She kept telling my mom if it got worse to come back, prescribing drugs for digestion and heartburn and stuff like that. She didn't think it was anything serious."

"Oh dear," Cheryl said.

"It was awful. Then her doctor decided to become one of those boutique doctors. All the patients who wanted to stay with her had to pay seven thousand dollars a year up front. You're supposed to get more one-on-one care or some bullshit. But my mom couldn't afford that. And you still had to have insurance for the hospital and stuff. The doctor just didn't want to deal with the hassle of insurance claims, so only rich people who could pay for insurance and thousands extra could afford her. It's like she didn't even care if poor people died. And my mom did die because of her!"

I realized my voice was louder than it should have been. I took a sip of wine, pinching that deadly thin stem too hard.

"Oh. Oh, that's just awful," Cheryl said.

"By the time she found a new doctor and they figured out it was cancer, it had spread all over," I said, making my voice sound calm and sad instead of furious.

Cheryl let out a pained whimpering sound.

"I'm so sorry." Ruth's voice was soft. It sounded as if she really was sad, but Cheryl looked more upset, like she was going to cry. She looked like she was thinking about getting out of her chair and coming around the long table to give me a hug.

"Thanks," I said. "At least she got to be at home. And I took care of her."

"That's a lot for someone your age," Cheryl said. "Was your father there?"

"Yeah. But he had a hard time dealing."

Cheryl nodded. "How is he now?"

"A mess."

"Is he upset that you've moved away?"

"I have two older sisters and two younger sisters and an older brother. So he's not by himself unless that's what he wants."

Ruth picked up the wine bottle. She stood and walked around the table, refilling all the glasses until the bottle was empty. "I'm so sorry to hear what you've been through, Nadia. It would be useful to discuss that with one of our staff counselors."

"Okay. Maybe," I said.

Ruth went into the kitchen and came out a few minutes

later with a fancy chocolate cake that was very thin and had frosting that looked like a chocolate shell. It turned out to be as amazing as it looked.

The entire dinner couldn't have gone better if I'd planned every word of the conversation, which I hadn't. Not all of it.

5

NADIA

I logged into my work portal at five in the morning. That gave me time to take a two-hour lunch break. I could spend one hour at the Wellness Center getting a massage, then show up at Ruth's office just in time for lunch.

When Justine was finished making my body feel like spaghetti, I drank my water, then bought a latte and walked down the hallway to Ruth's office. Her office window looked across a sitting area into Cameron's. Both offices were equally huge—each with a big glass desk, a sitting area, bookshelves full of paperbacks, and the walls cleanly decorated with framed photographs of nature. Her photos featured wild birds, and his were wildcats. I wondered if that meant anything.

On Ruth's desk was a glass vase as big as one of those old-fashioned jugs for milking cows. It was filled with white roses. I wondered if Cameron sent them to her as an apology for not being more devoted at dinner the night before, for not telling her she was his first and only true love. It was so obvious she wanted him to, and it was so awkward when he didn't. Maybe she *was* his first love, but she wanted to hear him say it. Which was a little pathetic.

Her office door was open, so I went in and closed it behind me. I said hi. She looked surprised to see me. She glanced at the door. "Is there a problem?"

I sat in the armchair that was angled to face the two-person couch and the edge of her desk. "I was wondering if you want to grab lunch at the Thai place or—"

"Lunch? I—"

"Do you already have plans?"

"I have to ... I usually eat ... Look, Nadia. I invited you to dinner to thank you for looking after Kellyn. Although truthfully, she didn't really need looking after. She knows how to take care of herself. And the situation wasn't dangerous. But the point is, we need to keep our relationship professional."

"What does that mean?"

"It means you're a client here, and I don't socialize with our clients."

"That's cold."

"It's not cold. This is a business, and I—"

"I thought the Wellness Center was about nurturing the whole person."

"We are, but that doesn't mean—"

"So all your friendliness was just a fake act to get me to spend money here?"

"No. That's not what I mean."

I put my latte on the table and pressed my hands over my face. I took several slow deep breaths, then took my hands away. "I thought you liked me." I raised my voice. "I thought you honestly cared about me. I opened up to you at dinner because I thought you were concerned about me as a person!" I stood and moved closer to her desk.

"Don't get so upset. Please take a seat so we can discuss this calmly. I didn't mean to—"

"How can I be calm when you betrayed me? You pretended you liked me, and now you're kicking me into the gutter. You don't eat lunch with clients. Like I'm a total stranger. Some weirdo who just walked in off the street. Thanks a lot. So much for caring about the whole person's well-being."

"I think you're misinterpreting the meaning of that."

"Am I?"

She pulled open her desk drawer. "Maybe Second Chance isn't a good fit for you. If this is the only place you visited, it's probably a good idea to compare us to other similar offerings. I can make some recommendations." She opened a little box and pulled out three business cards. "All of these have outstanding reputations. All of them can help you with your pain and will be attentive to getting you on the road to optimal health."

"Without lying to me that they're concerned about me."

"I don't think I lied to you. I'm sorry if you had a different belief because of the dinner invitation. But you're the one who suggested it. You put me on the spot. I shouldn't have agreed to that, and I'm sorry."

"Isn't that lovely? So you not only think you're too good to eat lunch with me, you wish you hadn't done anything to make me feel wanted. You wish you didn't even know me." I could see her recoil a little more each time I opened my mouth. I remembered the worried look on her face when I'd lost it for a minute and exploded over the so-called doctor the night before. She was definitely scared of me now.

"Please don't twist this into something it's not. We're here to offer healing for your body and to offer services for emotional support if that's needed, but I don't personally interact with every client. I'm sure you realize that no healing center is going to provide that type of relationship. I don't have the bandwidth for that. You must realize—"

"The *bandwidth*? What kind of bullshit word is that? Are you a human being or a robot?" I turned around and picked up my coffee cup. I took a sip and put it on her desk. "So all that motherly concern about my back and maybe I have grief that's causing my pain and maybe I need this and that—all of that was just you doing your job?"

"I care about all our clients, but I cannot have a personal friendship with clients."

"I'm not everyone. You acted like I was someone you connected with. That there was something between us, and now you're telling me that was an act."

"If you feel you were misled, I'm happy to discuss a refund." She pulled back even more, trying to move away from me as I leaned over the desk.

"This isn't about money." I did wonder if it might become about money, but it wasn't yet. "Don't you get how cruel that is? I thought you liked me, and now you're telling me I mean nothing to you."

"Please don't put words in my mouth." She pushed her chair away from the desk, putting more space between us.

I straightened and took my hands off her desk. Then I reached for my coffee cup and knocked it over. The plastic lid stayed on, so only a small amount trickled out of the tiny slit.

She grabbed the half-empty cup and put it upright. "Careful."

She opened another drawer and took out a few tissues and mopped up the spilled coffee. She moved the emerald heart to the side and patted all around the spot where it had been sitting, even though the coffee was nowhere near it.

"I think it's better if you find another health facility." She picked up the cards and handed them to me. "As I said, all of these are excellent resources. We'll be happy to offer you a full refund."

"Too bad there's no refund for pretending to be a friend.

I'd like a full refund on that. A trade-in for a decent human being." I moved close to where she was standing.

She couldn't meet my gaze, and I could see the fear in her. Everything about my behavior announced that I was somewhat unbalanced. I could feel the anxiety in her short, quick breaths and her repeated glances between the door and her phone lying at the edge of her desk as she tried to decide whether she should call security.

I gave her a smile that communicated nothing. "Thanks." I opened the door and stepped out. I shoved the cards into my purse and started walking toward the lobby. The smile spread quickly across my face. In my head, I was talking to Ruth—*You are not in charge here, Ruth Monroe. You do not get to decide how this goes for you. I do.*

6

RUTH

The emotional assault from Nadia Fairchild shook me badly. I'd never experienced anything like that with a client. I partially blamed myself. I was angry at myself for giving in when she'd invited herself to my home for dinner. I was angry with myself for asking my mother to join us for that meal, which had clearly made more out of the evening in Nadia's mind. It had opened the door for Nadia to talk about her mother's death, which resulted in her feeling irrationally close to me and my family. I was annoyed with myself for serving dinner in the dining room, for opening a bottle of wine, for using our nicest glasses, for the exotic cake from a pastry shop.

Everything I'd done had sent the wrong message to a clearly unstable person.

I should have followed my first instinct—that crawling feeling in my belly when I first met her and discovered she knew things about Cameron and me that she'd had to dig around to find. Clients are never interested in our backgrounds beyond the story of Cam's accident and how we started the Wellness Center. There were tiny red flags all over the place during that first meeting, and I'd allowed my husband to talk me into ignoring them.

I closed the window blinds after Nadia left my office. I locked the door and lay on the couch. I closed my eyes and tried to settle my thoughts. After a while, I got up, gathered my things, and left out the back door. I texted Cameron from our home office and told him I was working there for the rest of the day. I needed space, I told myself. I didn't allow myself to feel ashamed for running away from a twenty-year-old girl.

Cameron and I were busy all weekend—a wine-tasting party with our neighbors on Friday, sailing in San Francisco Bay on Saturday, and Cameron had a 5K race on Sunday. We hardly had time to talk about the logistics of our plans and critical business at the center, much less an unstable client. By Sunday evening, Nadia's outburst had faded to the back of my mind. I felt in control again. I'd stopped chastising myself, and I decided I didn't need to unload my mild fear onto Cameron.

I liked to believe Cameron and I told each other everything. I did believe that. But I also didn't want to get into the blame game of telling him he'd undermined my instinct and persuaded me not to trust my gut. It was best to let it go. She was gone, and he would forget all about her. As I should.

On Mondays I liked to go in extra early to do a general status check after the weekend. I make sure the towels are well stocked, the locker room toiletry supplies are replenished, and the aromatherapy dispensers are functioning at the right levels. I want to ensure the crowded atmosphere of the weekend hasn't left the Center feeling tired or worn around the edges. I like getting a sense of the atmosphere myself because I want to feel the tranquility we intend to provide for our clients. If I don't feel it when I walk through the empty rooms, they won't feel it when the place is busy with clients and staff.

The doors were unlocked, and the receptionist at her desk. I could see down the hallway to the weight room that someone was already there using the equipment at six thirty in the morning. Dedication always thrilled me. It meant our clients believed in what we'd communicated. Commitment and dedication were the qualities that had enabled Cameron to achieve a full recovery, and it made the difference for over eighty percent of the people who utilized our services.

When I turned away from the weight room, Nadia was standing a few feet behind me. I hadn't heard the doors and hadn't been aware of any change in the atmosphere of the room. A wave of fear washed over me. I told myself not to be silly. The receptionist was sitting right there, less than ten feet away from me. Someone was in the weight room. Other staff would be arriving in minutes.

"Hi, Ruth."

"Nadia, I thought I made it clear you needed to find another health center. You agreed that—"

"You thought you were rid of me."

"I gave you several recommendations. If you'd like me to call and make personal referrals, I can—"

"I don't need a referral. I need to talk to you." She glanced at the receptionist. "In your office."

"We can talk here."

"It's private."

"We don't have anything private to discuss. I'd really like you to leave."

"That's not your call." She began walking across the lobby, headed toward the offices.

I followed. "Nadia, there's nothing for us to talk about. If you don't leave, I'm going to have to call the police."

Her laugh was sharp and loud, echoing through the empty building like something disembodied. "I only need a few minutes unless you decide you want to take longer. We'll see. But I think you owe me five minutes."

"I don't owe you anything."

"You owe me five minutes." Her voice was sharp and so loud, I flinched.

She was walking faster now, the heels of her boots clacking on the tile floor, her short skirt swaying across her bare legs, her bright red hair moving as if a breeze were blowing down the hallway. She was moving so quickly. I was taking long, impatient strides to keep up with her.

At my office door, she pressed the handle. When it didn't give way, she stepped to the side. "So, you don't trust your employees to stay out of your office?"

"We can talk right here."

"What I have to tell you is extremely private. It's about you, Ruth. I think you'll want to be in your office, with the door closed."

I thought about the way she'd flirted with Cameron at dinner. Telling him how hot he was, how young he looked, and how tough he was. Cameron ate it up, although only for a moment. I didn't think he ... I felt slightly ill as I looked at Nadia's unblinking eyes with their thickly mascaraed lashes. She stared at me as if she wanted to eat me alive. I took out my key, unlocked the door, and ushered her into my office.

She didn't bother to sit down.

"It's not going to be as easy to get rid of me as it was the last time," she said.

I put my purse on my desk chair. "What's going on?"

"I'm the little baby you didn't want. All grown up."

I felt my chest tighten. The air seemed to stop moving inside my lungs.

"I'm your daughter, Ruth. The baby you gave away twenty-two years ago."

"You ... your mother ..." I felt like I might faint. I grabbed the back of my desk chair.

"I know about all the promises. That she said she'd never tell me who you were, and you vowed you wouldn't ever try to get in touch with her. I guess you really, really, *really* did not want me to find you. Not ever. But she didn't expect to get cancer. She didn't want to die and leave me without a mother, so she broke her promise. Shit happens, right."

"I don't ... I can't ..." I pushed my purse off the chair. It fell sideways onto the floor. My wallet and a tube of lip gloss slid out. I collapsed into the chair, staring at her, searching for something of myself. "I never ..."

"Don't make this worse by lying. I know you had a baby. I can tell you anything you want to know about Lisa and Barry Fairchild to prove who I am."

My heart was beating so hard, it was difficult to hear my own voice. When I spoke, blood thundered in my ears. "I don't know anyone by that name."

"Oh! That's right. My mom said you didn't know them. But you could have tried. You could have tried to find out how your little girl was doing, you could have at least checked in on her over the years, but nope."

"I can't believe—"

"My birthday is February third."

I stared at her. She had the correct date. And her face. Her lips, and her hairline. Especially her hairline. For half a second, I felt like I was looking in the mirror; then the feeling dissipated.

"You must remember the date, even if you've forgotten all about *me* for twenty-two years. Or pretended I never existed. *Did* you forget the date?" She stared at me, her eyes and smile full of defiance.

I didn't pretend. It was never that. It was more like ... a slow dissolving into a sense of unreality. A dream, almost.

Things fade with time, especially things that happen when you're a child, a teenager, even. Some events stand out sharply, and parts of it did that too, but giving birth? The baby? Sometimes it seemed like it never even happened. Or that it happened to someone else, a girl who wasn't really me.

Did Nadia want me to hug her? Did *I* want to hug her? Should I tell her I loved her? I had no idea what I was feeling. Scared. Mostly scared. And so confused. I felt as if I'd been falling from the moment she said she was the baby I'd given up. It was never going to stop. I was going to keep descending for a very long time, and no one was there to catch me.

Cameron cannot find out about this!

How was I going to get her out of here? I had to keep her from telling Cameron.

Not telling him had been the worst mistake of my life. I'd had a hundred chances, a thousand. First, my mother wanted me to keep it to ourselves. It would make people look at me differently, especially Cameron, the son of close family friends. And then Cameron and I were falling in love and having fun together, and I didn't want to spoil that. After his accident, it was too much. He needed to focus on getting well. I was sure I would tell him before we were engaged, and then I thought I would immediately after, but I never found the right time or the right words.

The more time passed, the more impossible it became. The fact that I hadn't told him was its own secret with the power to hurt him more than the fact that I'd had a child and given it up for adoption.

From the beginning, I'd craved the kind of intimate relationship in which Cameron and I shared every facet of ourselves with each other. Instead, I'd spoiled it all by keeping this huge thing from him. Now it was too late. He couldn't know, and he absolutely couldn't know why I hadn't told him.

Nadia laughed. "You do not look like this is the best news you've heard all week. I guess no one knows? Obviously, your mother does. But I'm guessing the love of your life has no clue you have a daughter? The man you promised you wouldn't have children with?" She laughed again, and her laughter turned shrill. "It's ironic. It's really *so* ironic, don't you think?"

Did she want me to tell Cameron? Did she want to become part of our lives? Did she want him to *adopt* her? Why on earth was she here? Was she planning to tell my mother?

"I knew you would be shocked. I knew you didn't recognize me. How could you? Ignoring me for my entire life. But I did not expect you to look like you were scared out of your mind."

"Of course, I'm ... you've grown into a beautiful woman, and I ..."

She curled her lips into a smile. "How generous of you. But it's really obvious you haven't told anyone I exist. Especially not that good-looking husband of yours."

I swallowed hard. My throat felt as if it were filled with glass. The twist of her lips and the way her eyes burned into mine told me she wasn't looking for warm words and a welcoming kiss after all. Why had she come looking for me? It seemed as if she hated me.

"If you don't want Cameron to find out you have a child, despite your silly promise to remain child-free, you need to pay me fifty thousand dollars."

A loud, choking sound came from my throat. I coughed. "I ... I don't have fifty thousand dollars."

She laughed. "Of course you do. You have quite a lot more than that. You started this chic little wellness center with that twenty-two-mil wrongful death settlement. I think you can swing a tiny little fifty thousand."

"Not without Cameron finding out."

"I'm sure you'll figure it out."

My skull felt like iron bands were wrapped around it and she was slowly tightening them. I couldn't think. I needed her to leave me alone so I could absorb what was happening, so I could figure out what I should say to her, so I could figure out how I was feeling. It was too much. My whole body, every organ felt ready to explode. "I can't. It will take me time to—"

"Not a problem at all. I can stay at your house. I saw you have not just one, but three—I could hardly believe it, *three!* —beautiful guest rooms. I'll stay with you so you don't forget about me again while you're figuring it out."

"But how will I explain that to Cameron?"

"Not my problem."

"Or my mother?"

"Still not my problem." She smiled. "I'll check out of my hotel this afternoon and be there in time for dinner. If you could get me a key made by tomorrow, that would be awesome."

"But I—"

"Unless you want to write me a check this afternoon?"

"I can't." My voice was a hoarse, raw whisper. I felt like there was nothing inside me but the sound of a fierce wind howling through my bones, tumbleweeds blowing, scraping against my heart and lungs.

That night, when I told Cameron that Nadia would be staying with us, he looked at me as if I'd lost my mind.

"A week ago, you told me she made you uncomfortable, that she was fixated on you. Then you invite her to dinner, and now you've invited her to move in? That makes no sense."

"My feelings about her changed. She's so vulnerable—her mother's dead. She can hardly afford the fees for her program at the center, and she's been commuting over an hour every day for her sessions, which is aggravating her back pain ..."

"She's a client. It's totally inappropriate to have her stay here. Not to mention she's a complete stranger."

"Please, Cameron. She's really hurting. We won't even know she's here. We have plenty of room, why not share some of it? My heart really goes out to her. I'm afraid if I don't do something above and beyond to help her, she might end up in trouble."

"What does that mean?"

"Her father seems to have checked out ... she ... I just think it would really help her, and it wouldn't affect us at all."

He sighed. He rubbed the back of his neck. He took my hand in his and looked at me with a steady gaze. "If you feel that strongly about it. But it seems so ... You caught me by surprise. Are you sure it's a good idea?"

I nodded, maybe too eagerly.

"Okay. I guess." He studied my face. "But you need to run a background check on her. Tell her if she can't agree to that, she can't stay here."

"That's fine. I'm sure she'll be happy to do that." I felt like I might throw up. With every word he spoke, I manufactured a new lie. They came out so quickly, so easily, it disgusted me. I hadn't known I was capable of making up so many at once.

In a single evening, I'd built a steel cage around myself, and I couldn't imagine how I was going to get out.

7

NADIA

I wasn't sure what I expected from Ruth when I told her I was the little baby she'd abandoned. I don't think I ever pictured her crying and wrapping her arms around me, covering my cheeks with kisses. But apparently that is what some tiny piece of me, hidden so deep I didn't know it was there, was imagining for me. My usual thoughts weren't aware of that fantasy, but there it was.

Because when she collapsed into her chair and looked like I was holding a gun to her head and was going to plant a bullet in the center of her brain, it was the worst feeling in the entire world. And I've had a lot of awful feelings before that.

For half a second, I did want to kill her. But I also wanted her to hug me and tell me she missed me and how very, very sorry she was, and every minute of her life she'd regretted giving me away. And then I hated her more for not missing me and not crying and telling me how beautiful and precious I was. I didn't know what I wanted from her.

All I knew was that she never wanted me. Not for one single second. She never even wanted to know how my life turned out because she made my new parents swear they would never tell me who she was, that they would never say a word about her.

And there she was, sitting on top of twenty-two million dollars because Cameron's mother died in that car accident. That money could have saved my adoptive mom's life. She could have had platinum medical care, not kicked out the door onto the sidewalk and told to find a new doctor right when she had to have tests and find out what the hell was going *on* in her body! If Ruth Monroe had lifted one tiny little finger to find out how my life was going, she would have found out my mother was sick, and she could have helped.

Instead, the mother who did love me was dead, and the mother who didn't want me was living in an exotic, Instagram-worthy house, patting herself on the back, and doing slick interviews about her Wellness Center that existed to fill everyone's life with bliss.

I bought a bottle of vodka and had two shots before I started packing to move out of the extended-stay motel. That took the edge off. I was smiling as I put stuff in my suitcase, folding everything carefully so it would all be nice when I hung my clothes in that amazing walk-in closet at Ruth's house. I was smiling because it had worked out alright after all.

When I saw that Ruth was scared out of her mind, the fifty thousand number popped into my head without me even thinking about it. The minute I said it, I wished I'd asked for more, but fifty was good, for now. Enough to make her upset. Very upset. Obviously, she was more worried about being caught lying to her one true love than she was about how her daughter was feeling. Telling her I would move into her house was another awesome and spontaneous idea. The good ideas kept coming.

I'd never thought she loved me, not for a single minute,

and I wasn't sure why that little girl still living deep inside me was so hopelessly naïve. Of course, she didn't love me now, either. And I didn't love her, but I needed to see her. I needed to know what she was like. I couldn't help myself. I needed to punish her for taking my true mom away from me. And it was going to make me feel better watching her squirm and sweat, worry and lie, trying to save her skin.

When I walked through the front doors of the Wellness Center the next morning, I felt like I owned the place. And maybe I did, in a way. I was Ruth Monroe's only heir. It's just that no one knew that.

There were several therapies I was supposed to be following for the care of my back, but of course there was nothing wrong with my back. I had a strong, healthy back. It hadn't ached a day in my life. But I did love those massages. The yoga classes were nice too. Working out was also good for me, so overall I liked hanging out at the Center. It was getting me into shape, making my body feel supple and strong. Best of all, I could keep my eyes on Ruth and Cameron.

The massage was my first choice. Justine was a magician with her hands. They felt so good my bones turned to liquid, and my mind settled into this place where none of the ten thousand thoughts racing past could take hold. They floated by like leaves and broken twigs on a river.

Justine was not smiling when I stepped into the room.

"I heard you took my daughter out for ice cream," she said.

"I did. We had a great time. She's a smart girl."

"I know she's a smart girl. I don't like her going places with people I don't know, and I'm upset that you took her without talking to me first."

"We only walked three blocks—"

"You should have talked to me."

"You were at the doctor's."

"Even worse. Ruth was watching her."

"She was busy with the fire alarm thing."

"Please stop dodging the issue. You owe me an apology."

I laughed. "For what? For taking your kid to get an ice-cream cone? How is that a crime?"

"I don't even know you."

"Kellyn was perfectly comfortable with me. We've talked before. It's not like I'm a stranger."

"To me, you are."

"I thought you were my massage therapist. I let you put your hands all over my body. That makes me feel extremely close to you."

"You need to stop arguing with me. You're a client. Not someone I know well enough to supervise my daughter. I'm her mother, and I'm the one who decides what's best for her."

"Ruth trusts me." I looped my purse strap over one of the hooks on the wall, took off my jacket, and hung it on the hook beside it.

"I won't be doing your massage today."

"Why not?"

"I'm referring you to someone else. Maddy in room seven can see you in half an hour."

"I feel comfortable with you. Yours are the best."

"It's better if you see Maddy."

"Because I took your daughter out for ice cream without getting a permission slip?"

"Don't mock me." She turned to the sink and began washing her hands. "And don't take her out again without my permission."

"Why are you so upset? Ruth knows me. She trusts me."

She turned off the water and dried her hands.

"I had dinner at her house, you know. I met her mom.

What do you need in order to understand that I'm someone you can trust around Kellyn? A copy of my birth certificate?"

"You're not making this better by turning it into a joke. I like to know who's watching her."

"She's almost a teenager. You should probably be careful about not being too overprotective. That can push kids into being rebellious, did you know that?"

"I don't need parenting advice from someone who is barely done being a teenager herself," Justine said.

I left my coat on the hook and walked toward the changing room. I sat on the little chair outside and unbuckled my left sandal.

"I told you, I'm not doing your massage, Nadia."

"But you're so good. I'll give you a great tip."

"This isn't that kind of place. We don't take tips. This is a medical—"

"Why are you so upset? You sound like you're ready to cry. Is this only about Kellyn, or is something else going on here? Are you scared I'm stealing your friend?"

"What are you talking about?"

"Getting invited to dinner at Ruth's, knowing how close she and I are getting. Do you feel like you're being shoved aside?"

She rolled her eyes, but she didn't do a very good job of it. "I have no idea what you're talking about. But you need to go check in with Maddy pretty soon. I have another client coming."

I put my sandal back on. "Whatever. This is not very professional of you." I walked toward the door, grabbing my jacket and purse off the hooks. "Don't worry, I won't steal your friend. But you should probably keep in mind, she's not really your friend. She's your boss. At the end of the day, she's going to put her business before you, so ..." I smiled. "Keep in mind what I said. Start thinking about ways to give Kellyn a little more freedom. She really needs it."

She looked so worried when I left, I almost felt sorry for her, but I felt sorrier for me because she really gave such awesome massages. It was very petty of her to abandon me as a client because I took her daughter for an ice cream without getting permission.

8

Justine and I were sitting at the juice bar, drinking smoothies. I looked at the smooth skin on the backs of her hands, her surprisingly delicate wrists and fingers, for someone who was our most skilled massage therapist. The words she was speaking wouldn't penetrate my brain. They were disconnected from her dark, almost black shiny hair, her rosy cheeks. She was only thirty-two years old. A biopsy? For a lump in her left breast? The thought was impossible to believe. The idea of something cancerous growing inside her healthy-looking body was outrageous.

"I couldn't tell you the other day ... when I was going for the biopsy. I thought I might start crying, and then I might not be able to stop. I didn't want to cry in front of Kellyn. Or anyone. And I ... anyway. So now—"

"Oh, my god!"

At the sound of Nadia's voice, I turned so fast my arm bumped my drink, and it started to slide. Justine grabbed it. As I turned, I saw Nadia standing a few feet behind us. She must have been there for several minutes, for the entire conversation, but I'd had no awareness of her presence. I shivered, thinking how oblivious I'd been to someone standing so close to me, about her ability to sneak up on me without my noticing.

She moved closer, her expression equal parts concern and something less altruistic. "Have you thought about what would happen to Kellyn? If ..." Nadia's voice trailing off was ominous, allowing me to think the worst. I saw the fear flicker in Justine's eyes.

"I'm not assuming the worst," Nadia said. "I don't want to do that. But you have to consider it. You can't stick your head in the sand. If the unimaginable happens, who would take care of her? Are your parents around?"

Justine gave her a despairing look. She picked up her smoothie and put the straw between her lips.

"Don't be scared. I'm sure you'll think of someone," Nadia said.

"We're having a private conversation," Justine said.

"I'm waiting for a smoothie. I couldn't help hearing you. It's not like you were whispering."

"Well, don't stand so close." Justine's voice was cold.

"Sorry." Nadia wiped her eyes. "I'm really sensitive to things like this. Did Ruth tell you my mom died of cancer?"

I wondered if Justine heard the way Nadia emphasized the word *mom*. I wondered if Justine heard the syrupy tone in her voice that filled me with dread. The smoothie felt uneasy in my stomach, and I wasn't sure I'd be able to swallow another sip of it.

"I'm just giving you something to think about, that's all. And of course, not everyone dies. Lots of people are cured. My mom was just one of the unlucky ones. But I'm sure being a single parent, it rushed into your head right away. Being positive is important. They say it helps." She smiled. "I should get my smoothie." She edged away from us.

When she was far enough away that she couldn't hear, Justine put her hand on my wrist. "I'm still really upset with her. I don't like her, but she said what I was thinking."

"What's that?" Even though Nadia was standing well away from us, my stomach continued to sway. All I could think about was that night twenty-two years ago. The blurred, painful memories that she'd yanked from the furthest corners of my mind into glaring sunlight. The things my mother had said about my pregnancy. In some ways it all felt like a dream. Some pieces of it were so sharp in my mind, they often pierced their way into my consciousness despite being buried under thick layers of time and thousands of other thoughts placed deliberately on top.

I remembered the baby screaming. I remembered the smells of my own body. I remembered trying to catch a glimpse of the baby's face and that woman telling me it was best if I didn't look. It was easier that way.

And I thought about my lies of omission to the man I loved—a million tiny little lies over the years.

Laced between the memories were thoughts of the fifty thousand dollars Nadia wanted to keep my secret—our secret now.

I hadn't slept all night, knowing she was just a few steps down the hallway from our bedroom door. I felt as if I'd invited a ghost from another part of my life, an unfamiliar entity, into my home. It felt as if my entire life had been turned inside out. I was now aware of how blatantly I was lying right to Cameron's face every second of the day.

Of course, I'd been doing that since our first kiss, but I hadn't been so utterly conscious of it until now.

I closed my eyes for a moment and saw myself in my mother's bedroom, a rubber sheet beneath the cotton one, pillows behind me, whimpering as each wave of pain washed through me. A woman I'd never seen until that day reminded me how to breathe through the contractions. Mostly, I ignored her. At fifteen, I was used to ignoring what adults told me.

"I wanted to talk to you about it," Justine said.

"What?"

"Are you listening?"

"Yes. Of course." I tried to smile. I put my hand around the bottom half of my smoothie glass, but my fingers slid on the moisture created by the cold contents. It felt slimy and made me think again of delivering my baby.

Nadia.

I hadn't named her. No one asked me about a name. No one even told me she was a girl. I saw only a glimpse of her red face all scrunched up as she screamed her little head off. I saw her arm and tiny hand before it was wrapped in a blanket, and that woman—she'd told me to call her Nancy, but it was clear that wasn't really her name—took her out of the room.

I hadn't cried. I'd known before I had the smallest suggestion of a bump that I wasn't keeping her. My mother told me it was the best thing for the baby, the best thing for me. A fifteen-year-old girl couldn't raise a child. I would ruin her life, and she would ruin mine. It was the greatest act of love to give her to someone who could take care of her properly. The baby would always know, deep in her heart, that I loved her enough to give her a stable, loving home.

I'd believed my mother. Why would she lie? But now I wondered—how had she known that? Was it a story she told me to make me feel better? Had she even believed it herself?

"Anyway, Nadia is right. I'm ... terrified." She stopped, her voice strangled. "And I—"

"I wish you'd told me right away."

"At first, not talking about it made it feel less scary. Now I'm just scared all the time, so it doesn't matter."

"You need to tell your friends when things are going on, that's how we cope." I felt hypocritical saying those words, but they came out because I knew they were the truth. Still, a voice whispered inside—*hypocrite.*

"I need to ask you something," Justine said.

My stomach lurched again. I held on more tightly to my glass. I looked at Justine's half-empty one and my nearly full one. If I didn't drink some, she would ask what was wrong, but I couldn't manage even a tiny sip. My mind was descending into the past with the same liquid ease with which my fingers were sliding up and down the glass.

I saw myself in the weeks before the baby came, standing in my bedroom, looking at the shocking size of my abdomen in the mirror on the back of my door. I hardly recognized myself—my face was round and full, my breasts were twice their regular size, or so it seemed.

I hardly left my bedroom.

Staying home, doing schoolwork under her supervision was the best thing for all of us, my mother said. Don't tell anyone about the baby. It will be as if it never happened. We'll heal faster that way. We can get on with our lives. If people know, they'll mention it from time to time, and you'll never be able to move on. Like picking at a wound. She and I would share the secret alone. We would take it to our graves.

I remembered *Nancy* telling me she would love the baby as if it were her own. She had three older children, but there was always more love in her heart. It was her belief that the human heart grew without limits to accommodate more children. This little one would be as beloved as her others, as cherished as any others she gave birth to or adopted farther down the line. She was young, she said. I looked at her. To me, she seemed old—but probably no older than Justine, now that I thought about it. I remembered her smooth hands gripping mine as she told me to keep my attention focused on her, urging me to mimic the slow, measured breaths she was taking.

It felt like my body was being torn in half. I couldn't believe women did this every day, that they'd done this throughout history. I couldn't believe women gave birth to child after child, enduring such pain.

"Are you okay?" Justine asked.

I jerked my head around. Justine was leaning forward, her face turned toward mine, her hair dragging on the counter. "It feels like you're not listening to me."

"I am."

"I don't think you are. You seem like you're a million miles away. Your face is white as a sheet. And you haven't touched your smoothie. This is really important, and you're not even paying attention."

"I'm sorry. What did you want to say?" I pushed the glass away from me. "I don't know why I ordered this. I had a huge lunch, and it's too much." I laughed, but it sounded fake. Justine didn't seem to notice. Maybe she was equally distracted.

"I haven't asked anyone to be Kellyn's guardian. I was with Brent for all those years, and we never did anything legal, but I always knew he would be there for her. And after we broke up, I was just trying to hold things together, so I wasn't thinking about anything like that. Anyway ... I want to know if you would be Kellyn's guardian."

I felt an immediate rush of love that she trusted me so completely. I felt honored, and so many other things I couldn't describe. But Cameron. We'd promised. We'd absolutely promised—no kids. Being a guardian is not at all the same thing, of course. It's nothing like having children of your own. And the chances that her biopsy would reveal cancer, or that she wouldn't beat it if it did, were so small, but still ... I couldn't make such a promise, I couldn't have that attitude.

"So ... what are you thinking?"

I gave her a smile that I hoped was warm, not absolutely terrified, because what I was thinking about was the child I'd never mentioned to Cameron. The child who was already in my life, who was living in our house and demanding an outrageous sum of money from me. I was thinking about the Wellness Center and that Cameron and I both knew every detail about the finances of the Center as well as our personal investments. I couldn't take a thousand dollars out of our joint account without him knowing. Fifty thousand dollars made me want to laugh hysterically until I cried.

Those were my thoughts. I couldn't begin to give space in my mind to Justine's request right then. "I need to talk to Cameron. I can't just—"

"Oh." She looked surprised and slightly hurt. "But I can't see why he would say no."

I gave her another stiff, awkward smile. "I'm sure you'll outlive both of us."

"But you'll ask him? Even though the result will hopefully be negative, I keep waking up thinking of all these other disasters where Kellyn could be left alone. It's terrifying. Probably nothing ever will. It's mostly for my peace of mind, I guess."

"Peace of mind is important," I said.

"I feel like a bad mother, that I've never done anything about this until now. And it's not for very long." She laughed. "She'll be eighteen in seven years."

"It's hard to believe," I said.

She took the last few sips from her smoothie.

"Maybe you should put that in your travel cup." She pointed at my drink.

"I know it's wasteful, but I think I'll just toss it. It's been sitting out, and I don't know when I'd get around to drinking it."

"Let me know as soon as you can, okay?"

I nodded, but I was thinking about fifty thousand dollars and how I'd hidden the truth about my life from my husband. I was thinking about the daughter who hated me with all her heart. Justine's life looked utterly tranquil in comparison.

9

NADIA

I went into the kitchen, where Ruth was making dinner. It was obvious she did not like having me eat dinner with them every night. She hardly talked while she sat at the table, leaving Cheryl and me to make conversation with each other, mostly, and with Cameron. It was a little sad how cold she was to her mother. Sometimes she acted like she didn't even want her there. But Cheryl lived about twenty feet away from the back door of their glamorous house, so she must have wanted her there a little bit. It was confusing. When I hinted about it to Cheryl, she didn't give me a straight answer, but I would find out sooner or later.

There were three expensive-looking knives lying on the pale gray granite, and Ruth was using all of them to chop veggies for whatever she was making. I couldn't see why she needed three knives, but I guess if you have more than one of something, you find ways to use them. It was the same with their utensils and glasses—different glasses for red wine and white wine, different forks for salad and the main course and dessert, and special spoons for soup.

Cheryl asked if she needed help fixing dinner, and Ruth

said no thanks. Cheryl and I stood there like mannequins, watching her chop and scrape the results into bowls, wiping the wood cutting area after each item was turned into tiny bits or slivers.

"I heard Cameron turns forty next month," I said.

"I'm aware," Ruth said.

It was funny to me that she was so worried about keeping her secret, but she treated me like a disease-spreading rodent. Her mother and husband weren't going to believe her story for very long if she kept doing that. I wondered if I should give her some advice about how to keep her cool.

She worked her knife through an avocado, arranging the slices on a plate.

I finally put it together that she was making tacos, but without the meat, because they didn't eat meat. "I think he thinks you're planning a fab surprise party."

She laughed.

"If you need help, I could do some things—"

"I'm not planning a surprise party."

"Oh." I took a piece of avocado off the plate and ate it.

"Please don't do that."

"Why?"

"Because it's rude."

The avocado was amazing. I wondered if she went to a farmers' market to get her veggies. They all looked pretty enough to use in a photoshoot for a cookbook or a social media post. "I hope he won't be disappointed. I'm sure he thinks there's a party planned."

"I have no idea why he would think that. We've never thrown birthday parties for ourselves."

"What are you planning?" Cheryl asked.

"I have a few things in mind," Ruth said.

"Like what?" I asked.

She ignored me, turning away to open the refrigerator.

"I think he's expecting a party," I said.

"How would you know what he's expecting?" She took a half-empty bottle of white wine out of the fridge, pulled out the cork, and poured some into a wineglass. She took a sip, closing her eyes.

"He was hinting around," I said.

"Why would he be hinting around about a *surprise* party? And why would he be talking about it to you?"

I laughed. "Jealous?"

"No." She gripped the stem of the wineglass so hard, her fingertips turned white.

"A surprise party would be fun," Cheryl said. "He would love it. Cameron's a kid at heart. And forty's a big deal. You need to do more than a weekend away or a dinner out."

"What I think is that I can plan his birthday the way I know he'd like, since I'm the one who's married to him."

"You don't want him to be disappointed," I said.

She took another sip of wine. She glared at me for a few seconds, then put down her glass. "What did he say?"

"Oh, little things." I tried to think. Pretty much the only thing he'd said about his birthday was that it was April 17, when I asked the date.

"Such as?"

"He said he doesn't feel forty at all."

"That's not a hint."

I laughed.

"He mentioned it a few weeks ago," Cheryl said. "He was surprised he didn't feel anything coming like the midlife crisis that everyone told him to expect."

"Still not a hint." Ruth took another sip of her wine. I wondered if she was planning to offer any to her mom or me.

"He told me you two don't usually do much to celebrate birthdays," I said.

"We don't."

"That's a hint all by itself," I said.

"It's not," Ruth said.

"I think he wants something special. Why don't you do something wild? Exceed expectations," I said.

"You really should. He'd love it," Cheryl said.

"I don't think he would." Ruth opened the refrigerator, grabbed the wine, and refilled her glass. When she closed the door, she slammed it too hard, and the sound of bottles and jars rattling against each other filled the room.

"I really think he's expecting something."

"So you keep saying. Did you give *him* the idea there's going to be a party?"

"No. That would ruin the surprise." I laughed. "Why would I do that? You know, I'd love a glass of wine too."

"I think you should do it," Cheryl said.

As Ruth took out glasses and the wine bottle, Cheryl and I talked about the party and discussed ideas for a theme. It was obvious Ruth was pissed off. She said less and less as we kept going on about it. But by the time she was ready to start frying the taco shells in her avocado oil, she was starting to give in. By then, her cheeks were bright red from the wine she kept sipping.

I wasn't sure why I was so eager for her to throw a party for her husband. The minute I heard he was turning forty, it just seemed like the obvious thing to do. I love parties, and I hadn't been to one in a long time. Of course, the guests would all be people twice as old as me, but I knew the food and alcohol would be awesome, and the music probably wouldn't be awful. They could afford amazingly cool decorations, and it would be something to do.

Besides, the more things Ruth had to worry about, the better I felt. It was nothing like the pain that my mom went through, but it was something. Maybe it wasn't pain in her body, but she had a lot to worry about, and that made her look like she was in pain. Maybe she could know how it felt to be scared to death. Maybe she could know what it was like to be scared someone wasn't going to love you, and she would get a clue about how it felt to be me. Because she was obviously worried her husband wouldn't love her if he found out she had a child she never told him about.

After dinner, Ruth made a pot of tea. She and Cameron took a tray with the teapot and cups and went to their bedroom, probably to look out at their private little pond with a waterfall. I sort of wanted another glass of wine. I sure didn't want to sit alone in the guest room I was using, even though it was a very nice room.

I went outside and walked along the path to Cheryl's cottage. I knocked on the door, and she opened it right away. "Want some company?" I asked.

"Absolutely."

I went inside, and she moved a ridiculously long, red scarf she was knitting off the couch so there was room for me to sit down. "I'll make tea. Or would you rather have another glass of wine?"

"Wine sounds good."

She smiled and went to the kitchen. A minute later she was back with two glasses.

We talked about California and my impressions of it. Then we talked about the places she'd visited in Washington State when she was in her twenties. She told me about how she'd *loved* her job as a legal secretary. Working for a small law office didn't include a retirement plan, and she hadn't saved as much as she should have. She was so lucky to have her daughter helping out, which ended up allowing her to retire a few years early. Then, her husband had a heart attack and died when he was only forty-two. She said maybe this was why she felt so strongly that Ruth should make a big deal out of Cameron's fortieth birthday.

She asked about my family, and I told her about my one older brother and four sisters—two older, and two younger, the younger sisters also adopted. I think my mom would have kept on adopting kids if she hadn't started feeling sick, which was the start of the cancer, but no one knew that at the time.

I explained my job, which was just a job, nothing that I could say lit up my world. I told her I'd had a few boyfriends but no one right now.

"Do you wish you had grandkids?" I asked.

She picked up her wineglass and held it so I couldn't see her mouth. I wondered if she was doing that on purpose. She didn't try to drink any wine. Maybe she was just thinking, but it sure looked like she was trying to hide behind it. "I try not to wish for what I know I can't have."

"You can't help what you wish for," I said.

She sipped her wine but kept holding the glass in front of her face.

"It's so sad that Ruth can't get pregnant. They could always adopt, like my mom—"

"Oh, she can ... I mean ..." She took a sip of wine.

"What?"

"It's fine."

"What's fine?"

She laughed softly. "I'm content. I don't need grandchildren."

"So, it's not that she can't get pregnant?"

"Let's talk about something else," Cheryl said.

I leaned forward and gave her a tender smile. "I'm sorry if I brought up something painful. But you can tell me. I don't know anyone in the entire state of California. It might feel better if you talk about it. Whatever it is."

She sighed. She put her wineglass on the table and ran her fingers through her hair. She glanced at her long scarf.

"I'm good at keeping secrets," I said. "I promise you can

trust me. I think I can already guess anyway. Did she get pregnant when she was a teenager or something?"

Her eyes filled with tears. She looked away so that all I could see was her right ear and the side of her cheek where her skin was bright red.

"It's nothing to be embarrassed about," I said. "Lots of teenagers have sex. Lots of teenagers get pregnant. It's old-fashioned to think you should be embarrassed about it." Cheryl didn't say anything, and she still didn't look at me. "Did she have an abortion?"

"No! I'm Catholic. I don't ..."

The room was quiet for a long time. I took a few sips of wine. I thought about leaving. It seemed as if she was done talking.

Finally, when I thought she wasn't going to say another word, she half-whispered, "She gave the baby up for adoption."

"Did you stay connected to the baby?"

She shook her head. "It was complicated." There was another very long silence. "Sometimes ... sometimes, I wonder if it was a mistake. It would be nice to have a grandchild." She gave me a watery smile. Then she changed the subject like she was flipping a light switch. She started talking about the Wellness Center and asked how my back was doing and what I thought of the program.

It sure seemed easy for her to think that ignoring me for my entire life was a little tiny mistake that she could put out of her mind just by changing the subject.

10

RUTH

Nadia hadn't said another word about the fifty thousand dollars, but it was all I thought about. I didn't even get the sense it was on her mind when I caught her looking at me, which was all the time. When I was preparing dinner, I would look up and find her staring at me. When I was eating the meals I no longer took pleasure in, I felt her gaze on my face. Often, I walked out of my office at the Wellness Center to find her nearby, watching me. She was there constantly. If she wasn't working out or getting a massage or participating in a yoga class, she was sitting in the café, drinking smoothies or looking at her phone. I wondered when she found the time to do her job.

There was nothing in her continued staring that made me think the fifty thousand dollars was at the front of her thoughts, but I knew she hadn't forgotten about it. And I knew she would remain in my house until I figured out how to get it.

My brain felt like a snarl of loose threads, unable to find an answer to how I was going to come up with that kind of cash. She thought I had loose cash filling my wallet, that I could stick my ATM card in a machine and pull out more than I needed. We had a beautiful home and enough space to provide a nice home for my mother, but we didn't live lavishly. The enormous wrongful death settlement had all gone into establishing the Wellness Center in memory of Cameron's mother.

I'd never been attracted to designer purses or lavish jewelry, so there was nothing I could sell, hoping Cameron wouldn't notice. Clearly, I couldn't ask any of my friends. And my mother certainly didn't have that kind of money. Besides, I absolutely did not want my mother to know who Nadia was. It was too risky. Once she knew, it would no longer be a secret, and I wasn't entirely sure how she would react. Maybe after all these years she would be thrilled to welcome Nadia into her life.

I still could hardly believe it myself.

It was possible Nadia caught me staring at her as often as I'd noticed her watching me. And it's possible that's all it was. A mother and a daughter who had never laid eyes on each other trying to become familiar with this other being who was so much a part of them, yet an absolute stranger. The feelings that ran through me were unfamiliar and uncomfortable. Most of the time, I couldn't even describe to myself what I was feeling.

If Nadia hadn't come into my life with a belligerent attack and a demand for money, how would I have felt about her? I couldn't answer that question because I'd barely made sense of the fact she was the baby I'd never been given a chance to hold before she was threatening me.

I'd spent two decades putting the baby out of my mind, detaching. Moving on. From the very start, when I'd had the sonogram, my mother stayed by my side, telling me not to look at the screen for my own peace of mind. To not become emotionally involved. It was better that way. Now, I wondered, shouldn't some love have been shown to a human being developing in my womb? But what did I know?

I was so confused, I was mostly numb.

I needed money, and I wanted my life back to normal. I wasn't sleeping, and my appetite was weak. I was distracted and short-tempered. Nadia obviously didn't want love from me, so why was I even thinking about it?

When the numbers on the bedside clock drifted past midnight, I found myself considering illegal paths to extra cash. Maybe I could steal something and sell it. Maybe I could get some prescription drugs and sell them. My thoughts disturbed and upset me. Who was I? Had I always been so very close to the line that my morals dissolved in the space of a single week?

Everything seemed frozen. My relationship with Cameron. Time. My heart. When Cameron talked to me in the evenings, he often had to repeat what he'd said. Even then, I couldn't always give him a coherent answer. He'd asked if I was feeling okay. Maybe he had hinted for a party, and he thought I was busy planning it, another pressure I absolutely did not need.

So, while the number fifty thousand spun slowly around in my head like a mantra, I felt as if my entire being was slowly coming apart.

A FEW DAYS after Justine told me about her biopsy and asked me to be Kellyn's guardian, she appeared in my office the moment I arrived at work. She closed the door, then spun around, her loose top twirling like a dancer's costume as she flung her arms out. "It's benign."

I hugged her. She squeezed me so tightly I couldn't breathe for half a second. I felt tears blurring my eyes. "I'm so relieved," I whispered. She let go of me, and we faced each other, both of us teary.

"I don't think I really knew how scared I was until they told me it was nothing. I've looked at the test result about forty times since I got it. Just to be sure I heard them right."

"I think I would do the same thing."

She flopped onto my couch. I sat on the arm of the chair, facing her. Fifty thousand dollars flashed through my head, and I felt the tears start again.

She smiled. "Thank you for caring. It means a lot."

I nodded, feeling guilty about how self-absorbed I was.

"Even though everything is okay, I still want you to be Kellyn's guardian. She adores you. She trusts you, and so do I. And Cameron too, obviously. It's something I need to do even when it doesn't seem so urgent."

I gave her a watery smile.

"I need to figure out how to make it legal and all that."

"I haven't ... well, I haven't had a chance to talk to him yet."

Her smile disappeared. "But you ... why would he say no?"

"I just need to talk to him."

"Doesn't he like her?"

I sat beside her on the couch. "Of course he does. That's not it."

"Then what is it?"

"I just, it's a big thing, and I need to ask him, that's all. I can't just assume."

"Why haven't you?" She moved away from me. "God, Ruth. I thought you were scared for me. I thought I could die. I mean, obviously a lot of other things could happen before that—surgery, a mastectomy, chemo. A cancer diagnosis doesn't mean death, but of course that's the first thing you think about. You don't know how it is to hear that word applied to you. It's terrifying."

"I'm sure it was. I know I would be scared."

"Then why didn't you ask him right away? How could you forget something so ...?" Her voice caught, and she looked away from me.

"I'm sorry. I've been distracted. Nadia's staying with us for a while, and it's been hectic."

"Yeah." She stood and walked toward my desk. "I heard. What's that about?"

"She was commuting a few hours to get here ... and with her back problems, that's difficult. And we have so much extra space. It's almost embarrassing how much space we have."

"Yes."

I felt my skin grow hot.

"Why are you so involved with her? It's a little strange, don't you think?"

"She's hurting."

"Now that you say that, I've never once seen her look like she's in pain. And when I gave her a massage, I didn't feel anything that suggested—"

"It could be emotional trauma."

"Maybe." She looked away from me. "Asking a client to live with you seems risky. Doesn't that put you in some kind of weird liability situation?"

I shrugged. "I didn't think about it."

She picked up the emerald heart off my desk and cupped her hand around it. "I think your attachment to her is a little unhealthy."

"I'm not *attached* to her. Not at all."

She laughed. "Inviting her to dinner when you hardly know her. Trusting her to watch Kellyn without thinking

twice about it. Now you have her living in your house? That's
... weird."

"You're making it sound like something it's not."

"Then what is it?"

"It's hard to explain."

"Why?"

I felt like my jaw was locked in place. It ached when I
talked. There was nothing I could tell her that would make
sense. Of course it looked strange.

"Do you even want to be Kellyn's guardian?"

"Of course!"

"I'm not sure you do. It feels like you're not taking it seriously. Like maybe you're hoping I'll forget about it after the
scare from the biopsy fades."

"It's important to have a guardian for her. I'm taking it
very seriously."

She put the emerald heart on the center of my desk, far
away from its normal spot. "It doesn't seem like it to me. To
me, the only person you seem concerned about is Nadia."
She walked out of the office without looking at me again.

I stared at the closed door after she left. How had we gone
from her spinning dance of joy and our spontaneous hug to
this in a few brief minutes? There was a knot in my stomach
as tight as the ache in my jaw. And then I thought about the
fifty thousand dollars. Again.

That evening, when I turned off the light and moved
toward Cameron, he didn't take me into his arms as he
usually did. "How much longer is that girl going to be
here?"

"I ... I'm not sure."

"What do you mean, you're not sure? What did you tell
her?"

"I told her it wasn't good for her to be driving all that
distance with her back issues." The lie felt like a knife in my

stomach. "I told her it would undo all the good the therapy was doing."

"So, until she's better? Which could be weeks? Or months?"

"We didn't discuss it."

"You invited a stranger to stay in our home, and you didn't place an end date on it?"

"I did run the background check like you suggested." I wondered if he heard the tension in my voice as I recalled the terror I'd felt when I asked Nadia for her social security number. I'd said it was necessary in case there were any issues with her insurance company and she'd seemed to believe me.

"It wasn't a suggestion," Cameron said. "It was a requirement. Something I would think you'd have thought of yourself."

"I might have." And I truly might have, under normal circumstances. But most of the time, I couldn't think rationally when Nadia was around. I rubbed my temples gently.

"I don't understand why you're doing this," he said.

"I told you, we have so much space. I'm trying to be generous."

"Why her? We've had thousands of clients over the years."

"I guess she just touched me somehow."

"You're not making sense."

"She's not in the way. She's polite."

"Since she moved in, your mother is here for dinner every single night. We never get any time alone."

"We're alone now."

"You need to put a deadline on this. I think she should—"

"Speaking of deadlines, have you talked to Lacy about the lecture program yet?"

"We're talking about our *houseguest*."

"There's nothing to talk about. She's not bothering

anyone. But what is bothering me is that I was looking at our annual plan today, and it's almost the end of the first quarter. You said you were going to work with her on getting a structure in place so we could spin this up by summer."

"Don't change the subject."

"Did you talk to her? I've already mentioned it to seven or eight new clients, and they were excited about it, and we have nothing set up yet."

"It's on my list."

"We need time to promote it, Cameron. Not to mention lining up speakers. If we're going to get people with good credentials who will draw a decent crowd, we needed to start last month. Those people book out six months in advance, sometimes a year."

"I'm trying to talk about—"

"You said you were going to take care of it, and every week I see it in the plan with no action taken. It's going to fail before it starts if you don't get busy."

"Why are you talking about business when we're going to sleep?"

"Because I see it every single week, and it's been nagging at me."

"And you just brought it up now?"

"You said you would take care of it, and you haven't done anything." I felt awful, attacking him like that. Now we were lying as close to the edges of the bed on each side as we could manage. It flashed through my mind that we were also starting to raise our voices. I did not need Nadia out in the hallway listening to us fight. In a rough whisper, I hissed at him, "It stresses me out when you say you're going to handle a big project like that, and you don't do anything."

"Sorry for stressing you out. I'm going to sleep. I'll take care of it tomorrow."

I was surprised he didn't lash back at me with a demand

that I give Nadia a timeline for moving out, but I guess I'd upset him as much as I'd hoped. He never liked it when I suggested he'd dropped the ball on something. He didn't usually let things slip, and I knew I'd made him feel bad.

I turned on my side and let the tears start falling across my face. I thought about the fifty thousand dollars and felt a sob rise up that I had to hold my breath to suppress. Nadia was going to ruin my marriage even if she didn't tell Cameron the secret I'd kept from him for more than half my life.

Parties in the house where I'd grown up consisted of cake, ice cream, and a few balloons. We ran around the backyard with water balloons or chased soap bubbles. When we were older, we had music and danced in the living room. My dad was a tile layer, and my mom took care of all the kids. There wasn't enough money for more than that. Maybe this was also part of the reason why I wanted Ruth to have a surprise party for Cameron. Besides wanting to watch her fake excitement about a party when she was lying to her husband and trying to come up with fifty grand to keep him from finding out.

Ruth was in her home office with the door closed. I knocked.

"Come in."

I went in and closed the door behind me so Cameron wouldn't hear us.

"I'm busy," she said.

"I really want to help with the party. I was thinking a Mardi Gras theme would be cool. I could do all the planning if you want. I'd run every decision by you, obviously."

"I can handle it."

"Aren't you busy working out how you're going to get the fifty thou?"

She glared at me. "I need to finish this email."

"I'll just wait." I curled up in the oversized white armchair by the window. It was dark, but I still looked out because there were fairy lights all over the yard, and I loved seeing how they sparkled in the darkness. It was so magical. Also, they made me think of stars.

Thinking about stars made me remember the last few weeks of my mom's life. She loved having me take her outside. She would lie in the lounge chair on our patio with a fleece blanket wrapped around her and look up at the sky. None of my siblings were around much. They came to see her most days, of course, but they didn't stay very long. Even my sister who still lived at home was out with her friends a lot of the time. They got too upset seeing how thin my mom was— just bones with skin wrapped around them like plastic wrap that doesn't fit very well. It was hard to look at her. I seemed to be the only one who could deal with what she was going through. They were afraid watching her cry, seeing her get sick. They ran like cats that had fallen into a tub of water.

A lot of the time, lying on the lounge chair, she closed her eyes, but I still looked at the stars for her. When she did open her eyes, she said they made her feel peaceful, like the universe was so much bigger than the things going on inside her body or inside her head.

It was one of those nights, looking at the stars, feeling the warm air at the end of August on our skin, when she broke her vow. At least that was what she called it. "I should tell you something," she said.

I waited. Sometimes it took her a long time to say things. She was weak, and it made her feel more tired if I tried to make her talk faster than she could. But it turned out this wasn't about her body's slow collapse. It was about getting the courage.

"I made a vow, but I think I need to break it," she whispered. "It wasn't like when we adopted your sisters. Your father and I promised we would never tell you about her."

"I know." I hated it when they mentioned her. They hardly ever did, but sometimes she just slipped out—*her*. They'd told me a long time ago that she didn't want me to know her name. I hated her for that. Why couldn't I know? My sisters knew their birth mother's names. One sister even had a picture of her birth mom and a high school yearbook photo of her father. But not me. The woman who carried me in her womb was a shadow. I guess shadows can grow so large they block the light in every part of your life.

"But it's not fair to you," she said. "I've thought about it a lot. I can't leave you alone. I can't leave you not knowing for the rest of your life. Vows don't take the future into account. I never, ever imagined I'd get cancer. I never once thought I'd die while you were young."

"I'm all grown up. I'll be fine."

"You are." She closed her eyes, as if she'd done her job. "But a girl in her twenties still might want her mom once in a while." She tried to smile, but it was too much work. All she ended up doing was pulling her lips away from her teeth as if she were trying to suck air into her mouth, her teeth clamped together.

I felt like crying. I wanted to tell her I needed *her*, not some shadow. That woman who didn't want to be my mother.

But my mom told me her name. She told me my grandmother's name. She told me that Ruth was only fifteen when I was born. It wasn't very much, but a name changes everything. I thought about that name every day until the day my mom died. Two days after she was gone, I Googled Ruth Ellis. First, I found out about Cameron's horrible car accident that almost killed him and did kill his mother. From there, I found the announcement of Ruth's marriage to Cameron Monroe.

There are so many things you can learn on social media and the internet in general. Absolutely everything is out there, if you're patient, and you look deep enough and long enough. And I was patient. Besides, I had a job where I sat in front of a computer all day long. What could be easier?

Ruth had finished typing her email, finally.

She turned and looked at me, slightly shocked, as if she'd forgotten I was there. "I don't like being watched."

"I was waiting to find out what I can do to help plan the surprise party."

"I told you I don't need help."

"You only have three weeks. Of course you need help. And you should be busy getting the fifty—"

"You don't need to remind me." Her voice was loud, almost like the sound of a hand slapping my cheek.

"I have so many ideas, and it would be fun to work on it together."

"This isn't a cordial relationship, Nadia. You're *black-mailing* me."

"Only because you made it so easy. I guess you're really desperate not to have anyone know about me."

She stared at me, and I wondered what was fluttering around in her brain. What did she even think of me? Did she think I looked like her? It was hard to say. I couldn't see myself in Ruth or Cheryl. Although maybe a little because we were all about the same height, and our shoulders were similar. We all had brown eyes, but so do five billion other people. So that didn't mean anything.

"If I do most of the planning, it will be easier to surprise him because you won't have to hide anything from him," I said.

"I'm not sure he'll even like being surprised."

"Everyone likes a surprise party, even if they don't want to admit it. They like knowing people were thinking about them when they had no clue."

"Is that right? What made you an expert in human nature?"

"I just know. Please let me help. You know I'll do a great job."

"How do I know that?"

"Because I have your DNA." I grinned. "I must have inherited some of your brains and talent."

I could see a tiny bit of red in her cheeks and that she was trying to keep it from showing, but that is not something you can control, unless you're a sociopath. Maybe they can.

Finally, she agreed. She had to. She was too worried about the fifty thousand dollars she had to get without him finding out. Hiding a surprise party and a daughter and all that money is practically impossible. We talked about ideas. She gave me a notepad to write things in because she didn't feel *comfortable* giving me her personal email or her cell number.

"This will be fun," I said. "We can work on it together. It's a family effort to surprise Cameron."

"It is not a family effort. Think of yourself as an employee. After all, I'll be paying you quite a lot of money. You should do something useful while you're staying here."

In my room, I didn't feel as excited about the party. I thought I would help her and give her ideas, and she would be amazed by how clever I was. She was acting like I was just one of her minions.

I tried not to think about that. I forced myself to start looking at the catering websites she'd suggested. I'd never hired a caterer, and I wondered what it was like to not even think about making your own food, but to immediately default to getting a pro to whip up savory treats that left you free to enjoy your own party.

When I'd seen the amount of money Cameron got in the wrongful death settlement for his mother, I could hardly breathe. It made me wonder if Ruth had ever thought about me at all. Didn't she wonder what happened to me? Once she was all grown up and had all that money, didn't she ever once think about looking for me and trying to take care of me, even though it was a little late?

If she'd paid attention to what happened to me, if she'd asked about Lisa and Barry, she might have found out they adopted two more kids after me. She might have found out they could barely afford the kids they already had. She should have cared about what was going on in my life!

If she'd cared one little bit about her daughter, she would have wanted to make my life better with her twenty-two million dollars, not just make strangers' lives better. What about her own flesh and blood?

A small sliver of the twenty-two-mil could have saved my mom's life. But Ruth Monroe didn't even know where I was. She didn't know how my parents were doing. She didn't even know if I was dead or alive. She knew nothing because she rejected her own sweet little baby and never looked back. She might as well have tossed me in a dumpster.

Maybe that's not fair. She gave me to a family that loved me. But every so often, it's a little bit hard to feel that love when the one person who is supposed to love you first, sight unseen, and love you the most, no matter what you do, does not care *at all*.

After my mom died, my dad might as well have been dead. He hardly worked. He sat in his lounge chair and drank beer. He kept the TV on all the time with no sound. He stared at it and talked to himself. I'm not sure he even noticed when

I left. I kissed him and said goodbye and told him I'd call, and he just kept talking to the TV in the same monotone.

I cried a lot for my mom, and the only thing that got me to stop crying was having a plan. First the doctor who couldn't be bothered with people who didn't have boatloads of cash. Then Ruth. But Ruth caught me off guard. After all this time, I still wanted her to love me. The desire snuck up on me, and I hated her for that. I kind of hated myself too.

12

RUTH

I felt like my brain had been branded with a flaming iron, the numbers *fifty thousand* burned into my flesh, the wound raw and bloody. A ridiculous part of me fantasized that Nadia wasn't serious. She hadn't done anything to pressure me beyond the constant, almost teasing, references to the money. It seemed as if she wanted me to worry more than she actually wanted the money. Maybe that *was* all she wanted—to see me anxious and upset and scared out of my mind.

More than that, she seemed to want to be around me. She wanted to live in my house, eat dinner with me, get close to the people I cared about, and plan my husband's birthday party. I felt like I was living in a surreal stage play.

At least the party planning was buying me time. She seemed happy with the project. And I had to admit she was doing a good job with it. Even though it was the wrong season, I liked the Mardi Gras theme. It was fun and colorful, and Cameron would love the New Orleans–style food, so that was good.

For now, we had a truce.

Maybe she had truly wanted to find her birth mother. Maybe the demand for money was a protective wall she had built around herself until she decided how she felt about me. If that was the case, I wondered if I should be even more scared. At some point, I would need to figure out how to tell Cameron. But the thought of how he would react was so horrifying to me I couldn't even allow myself to imagine the conversation.

There was so much more to it than just getting pregnant when I'd already known him, then not telling him when we started dating a few years later, then staying silent because of his accident ... So much more to it than ... I couldn't think about it. For twenty-two years, I'd lived as if none of it had ever happened. When I was a teenager, I'd blindly followed my mother's guidance. For the first few years, I'd believed absolutely in her wisdom. After that, I wasn't so sure, but I continued to trust that maybe, probably, she was right.

A tiny voice inside sometimes whispered that wasn't the way to deal with what had happened, but it seemed to work out, and I couldn't change the way I was now. Not that quickly. I needed to think, and there didn't seem to be any time or space for that. I was busy at work—running the center consumed me, and I'd always loved that. At home, despite the size of our house, I now felt like there were always people around.

My mother had swept Nadia into her life. It almost seemed as if she knew, as if she sensed some kind of biological connection. But that couldn't be. She would have said something.

It was Saturday afternoon, and I was taking Kellyn bowling. I'd suggested it. I was eager to make up for hurting Justine. I wanted her to know I cared about her daughter and that our friendship was important to me. Justine had a date, and the minute she mentioned it, I offered to take Kellyn and her friend wherever they wanted to go.

I still hadn't talked to Cameron about becoming the guardian for Kellyn. I knew what he would have said even before Nadia had moved into our house. Now, I could only imagine how he'd react. He would tell me that we'd agreed not to have kids, and we weren't running a home for motherless teenagers and young adults, or something equally cold.

It wasn't that Cam was a cold person. He was the opposite. And it wasn't that he didn't like kids, he just liked us— him and me. And we'd agreed. He didn't like broken promises. I could see how the Nadia situation looked to him. I was almost shocked that he hadn't pushed harder to get her out of our house. I supposed that said a lot about our relationship after all. He figured there must be some good reason I wasn't doing an adequate job of explaining. Or maybe he was distracted by turning forty.

It wasn't likely we'd ever be called upon to raise Kellyn the rest of the way to adulthood, but we couldn't go into it thinking that. I had to ask him, but I couldn't find the words or the will.

Nadia was turning me into a world-class liar. I was lying to one of my closest friends, lying to my mother, and worst of all, lying to my husband. Worst of the worst, her physical presence in my life had shown me very clearly that I'd lied to him every single day we'd been together. It made me so sad, I could hardly breathe.

I drove to Justine's apartment and entered the patio area she shared with a guy in his forties. He lived with three cats that Kellyn took care of when he was traveling, which seemed to be nearly fifty percent of the time.

Justine swung open the door before I knocked. "Kellyn's still in the shower." She laughed. "I know, one in the afternoon. She's prepping to be a teenager, I guess."

I settled on the couch, and she handed me a bottle of sparkling water. She buzzed around the living room, dusting.

"Where are you going?" I asked.

"The Palo Alto Art and Wine festival. Then out to dinner at a Thai place."

"Sounds nice."

"Thanks so, so much for doing this."

"I love being with her, you know that."

"I mean Emmy too."

"I haven't been bowling in years. I hope I can manage."

"Did you talk to him?"

Because she was excited about her date, I hadn't expected her to be so sudden and so direct, but I should have. I'd planned my response in my head, but still, I wasn't ready. "It's been impossible to get time alone with him." It sounded awkward and very much like a lie. I'm sure she picked up on it.

"If you don't want to do it, just tell me," she said.

"Of course I want to do it, but I have to discuss it with Cameron. It affects both of us."

"It's a simple question."

"But it is a big responsibility. And I want ... I don't want to make it sound like a burden. It's not. I just have not had a single minute to talk to him. It's not a question I want to ask him at the dinner table in front of my mother and—"

"You're making excuses. You live in a huge house where you can go anywhere to get five minutes alone, and you work together all day long."

I put down my bottle of water and pressed my fingers against the bridge of my nose. There was no way to explain it to her. As close as we were, I didn't want to make a big deal out of not wanting children. Of course, she knew we didn't plan to have children, but that was nothing like being a guardian. The truth was, I couldn't deal with it right now.

And there was no rush. I didn't understand why it felt so urgent to her.

"I know it sounds like an excuse, but it isn't. Nadia is around all the time. And when she's not—"

"Why are you so obsessed with her?"

"I'm not obsessed." I heard the water stop running. Any minute Kellyn would be in the room, and I didn't want to leave for the day with Justine upset at me. Nadia was forcing me to lie, again. Everything I said sounded like a lie, even when it wasn't.

"Why is she still living in your house?"

"Because—"

"You have lots of room for her, and no problem with Cameron letting her stay there indefinitely, but you need lots of private time to ask the scary question about taking care of my daughter, someone you've known for three years, if she loses her only parent."

"Justine, please."

"I don't get it. Who invites a stranger, a client, to live in their house? It's messed up."

"She just lost her ... well, her mother died of cancer a few months ago."

"I know."

"She and my mother have bonded over it."

"Why?"

I shrugged. "Not over the cancer. I guess my mother feels ... I don't know, she's just taken her under her wing is the best way to put it."

Justine went into the kitchen. I heard the water running as she washed her hands. She returned, rubbing lotion into her skin. She pulled her rings out of the pocket of her jeans and slid them back onto her fingers. Before I could think of anything else to say, probably because there was no way to explain any of it without telling the truth, Kellyn was in the room.

After that, the afternoon moved forward with the momentum of Kellyn's excitement about bowling and the arrival of Emmy, and Justine's instructions for their behavior. I left with a sick feeling in my stomach.

13

NADIA

I t was Saturday afternoon, and Ruth had taken off to spend the day with Kellyn.

A vicious, jealous feeling wormed through my belly like some kind of disgusting green slime out of a horror movie from the 1950s. It burned in my veins and made me feel like my eyeballs were bleeding. I couldn't believe this was happening to me.

I already had a mom. I knew when I was a little kid that my birth mother was a secret. I knew I would never see her face and never speak to her. I knew she wouldn't tell me stories or take me shopping or bake me a birthday cake. If I got married, she wouldn't be there. If I had children, she wouldn't be their grandmother.

I knew this, and I put her out of my heart a long time ago.

Why was I feeling these things?

She liked this girl, Kellyn, and I had no idea why. She acted like Kellyn was practically her adopted daughter. She even had a picture of her on her desk! What was wrong with her? Or maybe it was me. Was there something she didn't like about me? Did I make her feel bad when she was pregnant?

Was there some terrible thing about me that I didn't even know? It made no sense. I knew it made no sense. How can you not like someone you've never met? But I felt what I felt, and what I felt was—there must be something awful about me. I didn't like thinking that way, so I made myself think that she was the awful person, treating me like I was an annoying little minion.

The burning inside me made me think about that huge green heart on her desk. A jealous heart. That's what they say. I don't know why a jealous heart is considered green, but that's what I've always heard. I should probably Google it to find out why. Instead, I wondered how much that heart cost. I was pretty sure it was a real emerald. And she just had it sitting out there like she wasn't worried about it at all.

Did it cost thousands of dollars? Or was it just glass and she called it emerald because of the color?

She said Cameron gave it to her. I wondered why. Maybe he was a jealous guy.

I'd put on a swimsuit and gone outside. I spread a towel on one of the lounge chairs beside the pool. That gave me a reason to put sunglasses on so that if Cheryl or Cameron saw me, they wouldn't notice that my eyes were red and wet with tears.

How could Ruth like that girl so much, and she didn't want anything to do with me? I didn't understand, and I didn't understand why I cared at all. She should have been dead to me.

Even when I thought things like that, I thought about how I kind of liked Ruth. She was calm. She never raised her voice. She was an amazing cook. Her house was beautiful, and she was really sweet to Cameron. And to Kellyn and Justine, obviously. I wondered if she could ever be nice to me like that.

The water glittered in the sunlight. The sun was out all

the time in California. I could see why people loved living here, always looking up at a blue sky, always kind of warm. You could practically live outdoors.

I got up and went inside. I washed my face and redid my makeup. I changed into leggings and a workout top. I drove to the Wellness Center. Inside, I walked around the place, watching people work out and do yoga. The place was packed on a Saturday.

Then I sat in the lobby and read some of the brochures that talked about what they had to offer and shared their success stories. When I was finished reading, I went to the café and bought a smoothie. While I sipped it, I thought about the emerald heart.

After I finished the smoothie, I walked slowly toward the offices in the back. I tried the handle on Ruth's door. It was locked, of course. I took my cell phone out of my purse. I knelt down and shoved it under the door, aiming it in the direction of where I thought the couch was. I went back to the lobby and walked over to the reception desk.

There was a guy sitting there who looked super busy. He was talking on the phone, and the lights on the console were blinking with two more calls waiting for him. He had a screen open on his computer that showed a schedule filled with different-colored blocks. There were four people waiting to talk to him.

I wandered back to the café and ordered a coffee drink. I had all afternoon to wait.

When my coffee was gone, I went back to the lobby again. The same guy was still at the desk, but the lobby was empty now. I walked up to the desk. "Hi. Sorry to bother you."

"No bother." He smiled. "How can I help you?"

"I don't know if you can. I was here yesterday. I was talking to Ms. Monroe and—"

"Oh, Ruth?"

I nodded. "Yeah. She was changing my program slightly, and while I was meeting with her, I think I dropped my phone in her office. My purse fell over while I was sitting there. I didn't think about it at the time, but I haven't been able to find my phone, and that's the last place I remember having it."

He called another staff person who walked with me to Ruth's office. He waited in the doorway while I stepped inside. I made a big show of lying on my stomach, my arm stretched underneath the couch. I told the guy I could feel it. He said, *yeah,* in that distracted voice people use when they're looking at their phones. He heard me, and he understood what I said enough to give an answer that made sense, but if I asked him two minutes later what I'd said, he would stare at me as if I had three eyes. I grabbed the phone, stood, and swiped the emerald heart off the desk and into my purse in one graceful movement. I felt like a ballet dancer as I floated to the door with an innocent smile on my face.

That night, I slept with the heart under my pillow.

I don't know when Ruth noticed the heart was missing. Probably the minute she sat down at her desk, but I wasn't there, so I can't say that for sure. When I showed up at the Wellness Center later on Monday afternoon, she didn't mention it to me. She never told me anything that was going on in her life, so I shouldn't have expected it. I think I only thought she might because it was the only thing I'd thought about all weekend.

When Kellyn's carpool dropped her off, I met her at the lobby doors. I asked her if she wanted a smoothie. While she tried to decide what fruits she wanted, I slipped the heart into her backpack, which I'd offered to hold for her.

The next part was trickier to pull off. I had to figure out a way to get someone else to find the heart inside her pack. If

Kellyn found it, she would immediately give it to Ruth, and it might not seem stolen. Finally, I thought of a perfect plan.

The same guy who had been there Saturday was covering the reception desk again. I asked him if Ruth had found her emerald heart.

He shook his head, looking worried. "It gives you such a bad vibe to think a client here is a thief," he said.

I nodded.

"It poisons the energy of the whole place. Knowing that someone you're trying to help stole from you."

"Or maybe someone who works here," I said.

"That would be even worse."

"Does anyone have any thoughts about who it might be?" I asked.

"Not that I've heard."

"Did anyone call the police?"

"Ruth did, but they didn't come to take a report. They just talked to her over the phone."

"I guess they can't do very much about it," I said. "Maybe they should search everyone's bags."

He laughed. "That would be very bad PR."

"I guess so." He and I talked about the café and our favorite smoothie flavors. I offered to treat him to a smoothie, and he accepted. I headed toward the café, knowing what I needed to know—the police were not coming, and no one planned to search. I was surprised Ruth wasn't going to do more about it. That heart was valuable, and it was obvious that someone she knew had taken it.

I asked Kellyn if I could leave my workout bag on the bench across from her, right beside her backpack. Of course, she agreed.

I ordered two smoothies and asked the person who placed them on the counter if she would do me a huge favor and carry them to the table where Kellyn was working. She did. Before she could walk away, I picked up my bag, knocked over Kellyn's backpack, and held my smile inside as the jealous emerald heart slid out onto the bench like a slick piece of carved ice. It sat sparkling, almost glowing, as it caught the bright overhead lights. The smoothie chef let out a little squeal of horror. Then things unfolded as if I'd written a script and directed the film.

Ruth came right away and picked up her heart, holding it in both hands. She pressed it against her chest. She looked at Kellyn as if Kellyn had reached inside her body, taken her real heart, and twisted it like a sponge. When Justine was finished giving a massage, she showed up.

Kellyn cried and said she hadn't taken it. As mothers do, Justine believed her. Ruth looked at her like she wanted to say that's the lamest lie I've ever heard.

I didn't hear what happened after that because Justine and Kellyn went with Ruth to her office for a private *talk*. I took the smoothie to the guy at the reception desk and told him I was sorry for taking so long. He said he wasn't going to complain about a free smoothie and thanked me three times.

At dinner that night, Ruth hardly talked. When she did, it sounded like she wanted to cry. She told Cameron about Kellyn stealing the heart. He said it was normal for kids that age to steal. Ruth said taking something precious from a person who cares about you isn't the same as shoplifting a lip gloss from a chain store.

That was the end of the conversation.

14

RUTH

It was incredible to me that I'd somehow lulled myself into a state of numbness. I thought constantly about the fifty thousand dollars Nadia wanted from me, but at the same time, the number seemed unreal to me. The impossibility of getting that amount of cash made it feel like a dream that was lingering into the daylight. I flipped back and forth between that numbness and panic.

Added to this sense of unreality was the fact that Nadia acted like we were close. She was bursting with smiles and ideas for Cameron's party. In the evenings, she offered to help me cook dinner and was eager to clear the table and load the dishwasher. When she wasn't hovering around me, she swam in our pool or sat outside, drinking cocktails in the dark and gazing up at the sky.

It sometimes led to an absurd hope that she'd forgotten. That she'd changed her mind. That she was simply waiting for me to find the right time to tell Cameron who she was, and then we would all become a family. But I couldn't tell him. I wasn't sure I would ever find the right words to tell him. I'd waited too long. I'd hidden too much, and it was all so complicated.

I took a sip of my own drink and tried to concentrate on the podcast I was listening to. I felt something change in the room. I looked up and saw Nadia had walked into my office that also doubled as a room where I went to relax and be alone. Not that I needed such a thing in a large home that I shared only with my husband, but most of our rooms were spacious, designed for entertaining, and I liked the coziness of my office and sitting room more than the soaring ceilings of the living room.

I pulled my earbuds out. "Please don't sneak up on me."

"I knocked, but I guess you didn't hear me."

"You should wait for a response."

"There are only eight people who haven't RSVP'd for the party."

I smiled, trying to make it warm and genuinely grateful, because I was. Even though I hadn't wanted the party. "Thank you for organizing it."

"I just hope that with all the party stuff, you haven't forgotten what you owe me. I wanted to check on when it's coming."

I felt the smile slide off my mouth, across my tongue, and down my throat, where it stuck like a rough piece of wood. I coughed.

Her eyes widened until I could see the whites around her irises. "You *did* forget. Or you thought I would."

"No."

"I don't understand why it's so hard."

"Maybe because you don't understand marriage."

"I think I do. You hid a very big secret from your husband. Fifty thousand dollars is a small thing compared to a baby that's grown into an adult human being."

I closed my eyes. My phone buzzed beside me. The sound

made me feel tired. I used to welcome text messages from my friends. Now I felt like I was running from everyone. Running and hiding.

"There's not a huge rush. I definitely want to be here for the party. Especially after doing all this work."

"I thought—"

"And I have the added bonus that I have to admit I did not see coming—I get to be with the grandma I never had. She's kind of sweet. And she treats me like a princess, so that's kind of great, making up for all that lost time."

"But she—"

"*And* ... I am loving this house. It's so beautiful. You have great taste. Those gardens. Wow. It's like a palace. Not as big as a real palace, obviously, but it feels like it's completely isolated from the world. I'm in a secluded place that's all my own. I absolutely love it." She smiled.

I would have expected a smile that showed pleasure in all the things she'd said about my house, but her smile was so cold I actually shivered.

When she was gone, I saw how stupid I'd been, as if someone had propped a mirror in front of me. This was part of her game. She wanted me to let down my guard and start to feel affectionate toward her, and then she would smack me again. Each thing she could do to make me miserable was another moment that made her happy. I'd been hopelessly naïve to believe even for a moment that she might have changed her mind. It made me laugh thinking I'd actually considered it. It was a bitter-sounding laugh in a room that no longer felt at all cozy.

That night, I hardly slept. I had to find a way to get the upper hand with her. I was irritated with myself for not having thought through a way to do that sooner. I'd drifted along, frozen by the enormity of the sum of money she was demanding. Frozen by my fear of seeing my marriage crack and splinter into a million pieces. Losing the man I adored.

Most days she was holed up in our guest room, using our internet and her own laptop to do her job as a customer support rep. When she wasn't working, she hung out at the Wellness Center. She hadn't mentioned her phantom back pain in more than a week. She walked like she'd never known pain in her life, and she dove into our pool without any suggestion of favoring her back.

While she was at the Center, she got massages, participated in yoga sessions, and worked out in the strength training room. When I saw her starting a ninety-minute hot yoga class, I slipped out the back door and drove home.

I ran down the hall as if she were chasing me and entered the guest room. I hadn't been in the room since she'd arrived. I had to give her credit for keeping it nice. The bathroom was in good condition too—all the counters wiped down, the sink sparkling, and the shower door had obviously had the squeegee applied that morning. It smelled fresh.

Starting with the dresser, I began searching the room.

It was surprising how few things she'd placed in the drawers—several pairs of leggings in one, a pair of denim shorts and two pairs of jeans in another. A third drawer contained a handful of T-shirts, the fourth, her underwear—nothing exotic. The other two were empty. In the nightstand, there was a small box with some rings, the leather bracelets that were always wrapped around her wrists, and two long silver chains. One had a turquoise stone and the other a silver bird. A cloth bag held a few pairs of earrings. In the drawer below was a nightshirt.

Two dresses, two skirts, and three nice tops hung in the closet. On the floor sat a pair of boots, tennis shoes, and flip-flops. She was wearing her only pair of sandals.

Her collection of makeup was equally conservative, and

all of it was still stored in the carry case she'd packed for travel. There were a few bottles of hair product and other personal care items, and that was it.

I stood in the bathroom doorway, holding the door frame, and looking at the bedroom. Nothing in it said there was a person living there. The room had the same look and vibe our guest room always had. She was like a ghost, resting lightly on the furniture, leaving only a faint impression of her feet on the carpet. I wondered if I would find even one strand of dyed red hair if I swept my hand across the comforter.

She had to have something more personal. Her large suitcase and backpack were in the back of the closet. It felt more intrusive and wrong, somehow, to search her bags. The moment the thought passed through my mind, I wanted to laugh. She'd blackmailed her way into my house! I opened the closet door again and pulled out the bags.

The suitcase, as I'd expected it might be, was completely empty.

The backpack was heavy. I carried it to the armchair in the corner, sat down, and opened the zipper. Inside was a hoodie jacket and a turquoise notebook with an elastic strap holding it closed. I desperately wanted to read it, but my stomach felt queasy at the thought, so I placed it on the floor on top of the hoodie. Next were two paperback books, a tablet with no battery charge left on it, and a dark blue cotton scarf. The bag still felt heavy. I reached to the bottom and felt something cold and metallic.

I gasped as my fingers ran across the metal, and I recognized what I was feeling. I pulled it out. A decent-sized handgun. I stared at it, terrified that I was holding it in my hands. I'd never touched a gun before. I was afraid to put it down, afraid to return it to the backpack. What if it went off? They were supposed to have safety locks, but I wasn't sure how that might work. I didn't want to turn it around and find out. I didn't want to even look at it. I wanted to unsee it.

Holding it carefully, I slid it back into the bag. I folded the scarf on top and gently placed the other things inside. I zipped it closed and returned the bag to the closet, lowering it to the floor as if I were holding a bomb that might detonate at any moment.

I slipped out of the room, my heart thudding so hard I didn't hear the door close behind me.

Part of me wanted to take the gun, but when she discovered it was missing, there was no telling what she would do. I was suddenly afraid to be in my own house. As I walked toward the kitchen, where I'd left my purse and keys, I wondered if I should tell Cameron. It felt like a terrible secret to keep. It made all of us unsafe. But telling him, or my mother, risked them finding out the much bigger and, for now, more dangerous secret.

Surely, she didn't plan to shoot us in our beds.

It was clear she took a lot of pleasure in seeing me anxious and worried, but if she wanted to kill me, wouldn't she have done that immediately? Besides, despite her obvious anger, she didn't seem like a killer. Although, I'd never known a killer, so I wasn't sure why I felt that way. Despite the blackmail, despite her animosity, there was a sweetness about her that contradicted those other things.

I was terrified of her and, at the same time, trying to give her the benefit of the doubt—a very uncomfortable balance that was impossible to keep.

The minute I returned to the Center, I stopped by Cameron's office. I suggested we go out to dinner, and he agreed eagerly. It calmed me, seeing how he'd forgiven me for attacking him simply to divert his attention from Nadia a few nights earlier. Of course, he'd since talked to Lacy, and they'd developed a fast-track plan for getting the lecture series underway. Still, I felt anxious and guilty seeing the pleased expression on his face. The list of things I was keeping from him seemed to grow every day. And now I couldn't tell him our houseguest was keeping a gun in her room. I hoped our evening out would distract me from all that.

The rest of the day passed in a blur.

At dinner, I realized I'd misread his delight.

"What's the occasion?" he asked as he lifted his glass, ready for a toast.

"I just wanted to be alone with you."

"We used to be alone every night," he said bitterly.

I gave him a weak smile. I tapped my glass against his. "To us."

"That's it?"

"Isn't that the most important thing?"

He took a sip of wine and put his glass down. "I thought you brought me here to tell me she's leaving."

"Nadia?"

"Well, obviously not your mother. Or is she going too?"

"No one is leaving. Yet."

"She's taking advantage of us. What if other clients find out? It could cause a real problem."

"How would they find out?"

"She's not the epitome of discretion, from what I've seen."

"It's fine."

"Is it? *Fine?* How much longer have you invited her to stay?"

"I'm not sure. I—"

The server interrupted us to take our order, which was good, or we might have erupted into an argument. When the server was gone, Cameron was quiet.

"It won't be much longer," I said. "And she's promised not to mention it."

"Has she?"

The sarcasm was thick and left me feeling like a child. I didn't know what else to say to him. I tried to talk about our plans for a trip to New York City in the fall. I tried to discuss the Wellness Center, but every topic I brought up dissolved into a trite conversation that sounded as if I was trying too hard. Finally, I lapsed into silence.

15

NADIA

Justine was not thrilled to see me when I walked into her massage room between clients.

"I'm expecting a client in five minutes," she said.

"No surprise. You're amazing."

She turned to the shelf behind her and began readjusting the infusion sticks in the bottle of scented oil.

"I won't stay. I just—"

"You can't, because—"

"I just wanted to say I believe what Kellyn said about the heart. I don't think she stole it."

"What does that have to do with you?"

"I don't think she's the kind of child who steals. And she's definitely not a liar."

"She doesn't need you to defend her. You don't even know her," Justine said.

"Not very well, you're right. But she's a sweet girl, and I know her well enough to know she wouldn't do that. I'm sorry Ruth doesn't trust her. That must be so hard for you."

She turned to face me. "Why are you talking to me about this?"

"I wanted you to know I believe her. Because I know how hard it is when people think you're lying."

"You're sticking yourself in where you don't belong."

"Not really. Everyone was talking about it."

"About Kellyn?"

She looked upset. I knew she and Ruth would probably drift apart over this. Mothers always take their child's side, even when they shouldn't. Almost always. It was obvious Justine didn't like knowing that the entire staff was talking about her daughter, wondering if she was a thief. Some of them would keep wondering for a long time. Even now that they'd found the heart, even though Kellyn said she hadn't taken it. Even if Ruth decided to believe her, after a while, which I figured she would. "They didn't say much about her. Just about the heart disappearing and reappearing."

"So it was about Kellyn."

I shrugged.

"You can leave now."

"Sure. I didn't mean to make you upset."

"Didn't you?"

"No. I honestly didn't." I wasn't sure if that was exactly the truth. I didn't want her and Ruth to be friends, or maybe I just didn't want Ruth to like Kellyn more than me. Or I just wanted Ruth to be worried about everything. I wanted her to know what it felt like to be worried and scared. At least I thought that was what I wanted. Sometimes it was hard to know. Since I'd walked into her world, my feelings were surprising me. They changed suddenly at the most unexpected times. "I believe your daughter, and I'm glad you do too. The way she reacted when it fell out of her pack, I knew she didn't take it."

She glared at me. She folded her arms across her ribs, tightening her shoulders in a way that made me think she was going to need an expert massage if she didn't relax. "You seem to know a lot about the circumstances."

"I was there when it fell out of her bag. You know that."

"Maybe you're the one who put it inside her bag."

"What are you talking about?"

"Maybe you took the heart and put it in Kellyn's bag to make it look like she stole it."

"Why would I do that?"

"Because you're a manipulator."

I took a step closer to her. She tightened her shoulders even more. I couldn't tell if it was from fear or something else. Still, she didn't back away from me.

"You'd better be careful," I said. "Ruth and I are really close, and I don't think she'd like you slandering me."

"I'm not *slandering* you. I'm curious why you know so much about how the heart went missing. I'm wondering how the heart got into Kellyn's bag and how you just happened to be there when it suddenly *fell out*." She made air quotes around the last part of what she said.

"I don't think you get how close Ruth and I are," I said. "If she found out you were accusing me of stealing something so precious to her, she would be really upset. And trying to make a child look like a thief ... that's a terrible thing to say."

Justine's lips curled into a tiny, overconfident smile. She was so sure she was right. But that didn't matter.

"I know you're upset that everyone thinks she's a thief when she's not, but that doesn't make it right to accuse me just because you don't like me. I'm not even sure why you don't like me. What did I do?"

"There's never been any issues with theft here until you showed up," she said.

I walked over and hopped onto the massage table. I crossed my legs.

"Get off the table. I just put a clean sheet on it."

I swung my leg and waited to see what she would do.

"What do you want from me? What are you doing here? There's nothing wrong with your back."

I pressed my palm against my lower back and scrunched up my face.

"Stop playing that game."

"You should be careful, Justine. I could really hurt you."

"Are you threatening me?"

She glanced at the clock on the wall behind her.

"I know you have a client coming. In five minutes. But that sounds like a lie because I've been here a lot longer than five minutes. I guess your client is late."

"This conversation is going nowhere. I want you to leave."

"I don't know why you don't like me. I told Ruth what a great therapist you are. The absolute best. I'm sad you won't give me any more massages. The one you gave me really helped."

"There's nothing wrong with your back. That's how I know you're a manipulator. Now please leave."

"You're very bold. And you're taking a huge risk. Have you thought about how I could hurt your career? Quite a lot?"

"Stop threatening me. I'm good at my job, and Ruth and Cameron value me." She walked to the doorway. "I need you to leave right now."

"Have you always taken risks like this? Ruth listens to me. I talk to her every day. We have private conversations over dinner. You know that, right? One word from me and you could lose your job. Then what would happen to Kellyn?"

"I'm not worried, so stop the ridiculous threats. You're not as tough as you sound."

I laughed. "Trust me, Ruth will believe anything I say over you. I have total confidence. You can test it if you don't believe me. I wouldn't be saying it if I didn't know. So I would be very careful."

She glared at me.

"If I were you, I would think about how hard it might be to get another great job like this, even if she gave you an okay reference. I came in here to be nice and to tell you I believe Kellyn, and all you want to do is attack me. For someone working in a place that's supposed to want to help heal and restore their well-being, you're not very nice." I smiled and slid off the massage table. I smoothed the sheet and gave the table a little pat. "I really wish you would think about giving me another massage. It doesn't seem right to turn away people who need relief from terrible pain. Even if that pain isn't obvious to you. It's not like you're a doctor and you know all the complexities of pain."

I took a few steps toward her. She backed away from me.

"I was going to give you a hug to show you all is forgiven, but I guess not." I moved closer and patted her arm. "Take good care of your daughter. She's a sweet girl."

I walked out of the room, and she didn't say anything. I thought she might want the last word and would say something to my back when she had the chance, but she didn't. So I guess she was a little worried after all.

16

RUTH

J ustine charged into my office, slamming the door closed behind her. The window shook, and the blinds clattered against the glass. I wondered if our accountant in the office beside mine heard the racket. Instead of lounging on the couch facing my desk like she usually did, she stood in front of the desk. She put her hands on the edge and leaned forward. Her eyes were glassy, her pupils tiny pinpricks of rage. Her dark hair that she kept in a tight, single braid when she was working had come loose, making it look like she'd been taking a walk on a windy afternoon.

"Your houseguest, or friend, or whatever she is, just threatened me."

I felt a sharp pain in my stomach, and my throat tightened so that I couldn't speak. My thoughts raced, tripping over each other, wondering what Nadia had said to her, terrified that she'd revealed something about my secret. I don't think my face showed any of that, because Justine's expression grew more upset.

"Aren't you going to say anything?"

"I'm not sure what ... how did she threaten you?"

"She told me you two are so close that if she asked, you would fire me."

I laughed. It was the wrong reaction, and I knew right away it was the worst thing I could have done. But it sounded so crazy and so far from anything that would ever happen, it struck me funny. I think my laughter also came from relief that Nadia hadn't said anything about being my daughter or blackmailing me.

Tears filled her eyes.

"I'm sorry." I stood and walked around the desk. "I don't know why I laughed. It sounds so ... I would never fire you." The moment I spoke, I wondered if it was true. How many things had I already done that a month ago I would have vowed I would never do? I went to the couch and sat down. "Tell me what happened."

Without joining me on the couch, she told me how Nadia had gushed about her belief that Kellyn was telling the truth, that she knew nothing about how the emerald heart had found its way to her backpack. I closed my eyes and pictured the heart now nestled among my T-shirts in my dresser drawer. It hurt that I no longer felt comfortable keeping it on my desk.

Only a handful of people knew it had gone missing. And once it had been recovered, most of them probably forgot all about it, brushing it off as a childish prank. What would an eleven-year-old girl do with an object like that? It wasn't as if she could sell it for cash. She could keep it for her own guilty pleasure, but that would fade quickly.

Thinking about it now, it was so obvious that Kellyn would never have taken it.

"She made it sound like you don't trust Kellyn," Justine said.

"You probably misunderstood, because that's not true."

"Why do you keep defending Nadia? What's so special about her? I don't get it."

I looked away from her steely gaze. Anything I said sounded like a lie because it was. Justine and I were close enough that I was certain she picked up on the weakness in my voice. "I—"

"This has gone beyond kindness to a girl who lost her mother and needs some comfort or encouragement or whatever it is you think she needs. And there's nothing wrong with her back. You know that, don't you? She went out of her way to make my daughter look like a thief. Who does something like that? It's malicious."

There were no words to calm her down or to convince her to give Nadia another chance. She wouldn't. I wasn't even sure why Nadia wanted to make Kellyn look like a thief. It made no sense. Maybe she just liked to make trouble for everyone. Maybe it was simply another way to hurt me and the people I loved.

The memory of the fire alarm flashed through my mind. Of course Nadia had been the one to pull it. Why hadn't I seen that at the time? I felt utterly defeated. She was going to disrupt my life in every way she could until I paid her the money she'd demanded. And then what? The thought sent a chill through my body. I felt my shoulders tremble.

"What's wrong?" Justine asked.

"I'm sorry I doubted Kellyn. Even for a second. I know she would never take something that wasn't hers. I don't know what I was thinking. I'm ... I just want to forget it even happened."

"Well, I can't forget it happened. Kellyn is devastated. She adores you, and she would never steal anything. From anyone. Knowing you don't trust her has hurt her more than you can imagine."

"I'm so sorry."

"You don't sound very sorry. If you were truly sorry, you would get rid of Nadia. There's something wrong with a person who does something like that. Especially to a child."

She was right, but I had to be careful about agreeing. I had to be careful about every word I spoke. If it got back to Nadia, the situation would get worse. She was unpredictable.

"You know nothing about her," Justine said.

"I know she's hurting, and when people are hurting, they—"

"Don't give me that. I lost my parents when I was young, and I never did anything like this. The father of my child walked out on us, and I didn't try to hurt other people."

"Everyone reacts differently."

"No one I've ever known has tried to hurt people they don't even know."

"Some people do. They—"

"Stop it, Ruth. Stop defending her. It's like she can't do anything wrong in your eyes. What do you even know about her? How do you know her mother died of cancer? How do you know her mother died at all? I've given hundreds of massages to people with back injuries, and she's lying about her back pain."

"It could be—"

"Stop arguing with me. She walked in here with a lie, and she's done nothing but lie since. And you invited her to live in your house. Do you see how that looks to every single person but you? And Cameron? I have no idea why he's on board with this, but whatever. That's between you two. I don't trust her."

"She's troubled. I'll admit that."

"She could be conning you. Have you thought about that?"

I laughed again.

"It's not funny. Haven't you thought about how she was so, *so* friendly so fast?"

"She's a people person. Cameron was worried too. So I did a background check, and she has no criminal record, no credit issues."

"That doesn't mean anything. A good con artist doesn't have a criminal record. She could destroy everything you've worked for."

"I don't see how."

"How naïve are you? She's already gained your trust. You believe everything she says. You trust her more than you trust me."

"That's not true."

"Isn't it?"

It wasn't true. I didn't trust Nadia at all, but there was nothing I could say to defend myself. I couldn't tell her that Nadia had the power to destroy my marriage and everything that mattered to me.

"You know I'm right. I can see it in your eyes."

"You can't see anything in my eyes," I said.

"Inviting a stranger to live in your house is not smart, someone who has already proven she's a liar. You're trusting someone who your close friend is telling you is going to cause trouble. You're ignoring obvious warning signs. That is the very definition of a con. You're acting like a classic mark."

"Please don't dramatize this."

"I'm not." She walked to the door. She touched the handle and looked at the floor for a moment, then directly at me. "By the way, I guess you just aren't interested in being Kellyn's guardian?"

"No. Of course I ... it's just that—"

"Yes. You have to discuss it with Cameron. I know. Maybe when Kellyn is sixteen?"

I stood and took a few steps toward her. "I want to. But it's a serious commitment and—"

She held up her hand, palm facing me. I wasn't sure if it was to stop me talking or to keep me from coming closer. "I get it. You haven't been alone with him for one single *minute* now that Nadia is there. Because she needs so much care and attention. Her excruciating pain. And her grief." She gave me a scornful smile.

Everything about the way she was standing, her hand on the door, the expression on her face, told me to back off. I moved closer and put my arms around her, pulling her into a hug. "I adore Kellyn. Both of you mean everything to me. I want to be her guardian. Not just to give you some peace of mind, but because I love her. I'd be happy to care for her if something unimaginable happened."

A ragged sob came out of her; then she sucked in her breath and held if for a moment before pulling away. Her eyes were moist, but she recovered quickly. "I'm really not sure you mean it. Cameron ..." She turned her face away from me.

"First of all, nothing is going to happen. But more importantly, Cameron thinks the world of both of you. You know, I don't even have to ask him. I know he'll say yes." I felt a wave of panic move through my chest as I said this. But I also knew I'd find a way to persuade him. Part of me believed what I was saying. And part of me knew it would be a while before I needed to deal with this. One thing at a time. I'd learned to live that way when Cameron was lying in a hospital bed, and I wasn't sure if he'd ever open his eyes and look at me again.

She gave me another hug, much warmer this time. She said nothing else about Nadia, which was what I'd hoped for when I said yes. It made me feel I'd done the lowest thing ever.

When I sat at my desk after she'd gone, there was a

calendar alert reminding me about the date of Cameron's surprise party. Throwing a birthday party was the last thing I wanted to be doing right now. But maybe the party would be a surprise he loved. Could I dare to hope it would bring us closer?

I closed the calendar reminder. I opened a search window and typed in Nadia Fairchild. The background check had come up clear—no criminal record and a pristine credit history. But Justine clearly had more street-smarts than I had. Of course, a good con woman wouldn't necessarily have a prison record or any arrests.

Justine had made the comment in total innocence. But I now realized I should have thought through the situation more carefully. How did I know Nadia was even my daughter? Although that probably didn't matter because she knew my secret. Besides, studying her face, my gut told me she was telling the truth. Still ...

The first hits were an Instagram account in her name that hadn't been updated for over a year, a TikTok profile with the same username, so I assumed it was her, and that was all. I discovered some photos from her high school yearbook and a list of the members of her graduating class. For someone her age, I'd expected more. Didn't everyone in their twenties exist almost exclusively online? Maybe that was an urban legend, more hype than reality. Or maybe she was good at hiding her footprint.

I knew from the form she'd filled out for her background check that she'd lived in Bellingham, Washington. I Googled her parents' names and found nothing but the generic pointers to multiple people with those names and a variety of ages and cities, although two were Bellingham, so I was close, but there was nothing else, so the information was useless. Then I found Lisa's obituary. It was short—the names of her husband and children, a brief line about how deeply she would be missed, and some religious sentiments.

I clicked on the *Bellingham Washington news* button, followed by the link for the *Bellingham Herald*. I skimmed the headlines—everything from sports to the closing of a national retail chain outlet to the opening of a bubble tea shop. Just as I was about to close the window, I saw a headline that caused my fingers to freeze on the keyboard.

Still No Leads in Execution-style Shooting Death of Bellingham Physician

Something about Nadia's gun and her outrage toward the doctor who, in her mind, had abandoned her mother and caused her death gave me a chill that reverberated through my bones. But Nadia was practically a child. She was not a cold-blooded killer.

I closed the window.

There were a lot of people in Washington State who owned guns as a matter of course. All over the country, for that matter. She might be an angry, hurting young woman, but she wasn't a criminal. Not really. It was clear she hadn't approached me with a plan in mind, that even her blackmail attempt had been something she thought of on the spot. I wasn't going to start taking huge leaps into more fantastical fears. I needed to deal with the actual problems facing me, not the ones my imagination might create.

17

NADIA

I was impressed with myself for the party I was pulling together with very little help from my biological mother. I'd never planned a catered party or, actually, an event of any kind, and I thought I'd done an amazing job. It seemed like she appreciated my work, but I didn't think she realized how impressive it really was that I'd figured out how to figure out a delicious menu and order the right kind of wine and choose the best kind of alcohol and mixers for cocktails to fit the Mardi Gras theme.

The budget she'd given me seemed like enough for a small wedding, but what did I know. I'd even had enough money to hire a live jazz trio and rent glasses to make authentic hurricane cocktails.

The guest list meant nothing to me because Ruth had kept me locked out of every part of her life. It was just a bunch of random names. I'd picked up some bits and pieces of information about their friends by listening to them talk during dinner every night, but when I asked questions to try to learn more about their friends, she was vague with her answers.

One glaring hole in the guest list was their relatives. Ruth's father was dead, and she had no brothers or sisters. So that part was a no-brainer. Cameron had a brother who lived in France, so obviously he wouldn't be invited. His mother was gone, but his father was still alive. He and his wife lived in Southern California. I'd asked about him when Ruth first handed me the list, and she'd flat out ignored me.

It was only a seven-hour drive from Southern California. A one-hour plane flight. It seemed strange to me that she didn't want to invite them to her husband's fortieth birthday party. She treated her own mother like she was slightly annoying, and she didn't want anything to do with her daughter. Her father-in-law wasn't even being told about his son's birthday party. What was wrong with her? Did she hate her entire family? Maybe she didn't even really love her husband. But if she didn't love him, why did she care fifty thousand dollars' worth about not letting him find out her *terrible* secret?

I didn't understand her at all.

I wondered how Cameron would feel about not having his father at his surprise party. I couldn't imagine he would be happy about it. Even if he mostly wanted his friends around, wouldn't he at least feel a little guilty about it? If it wasn't a surprise, I would have asked him myself.

I'd spent almost a week trying to figure out how I might get his father's cell phone number or email address without Ruth finding out. I'd wondered if maybe there was a way to get it from Cameron without him finding out about the party. But no matter how many ideas I tossed around inside my head, none of them seemed like they would work without spoiling the surprise. Finally, I decided to ask the one person who seemed to like having me around the house, even though she had no idea who I was. My granny.

While Cameron was cleaning up the kitchen after dinner

and Ruth was watching the news on the huge TV in the living room, I went outside and walked along the path to the guest cottage. Cheryl hadn't eaten dinner with us that night for some reason that I couldn't figure out. The first few nights I was there, she was at the table across from me for every meal, and then she suddenly disappeared, only showing up at random times.

I supposed it made sense that Ruth and Cameron didn't want her mom there every night for dinner, but I couldn't figure out their arrangement. When she was there, the conversation seemed formal, as if she were a guest they didn't know very well. Or something. I couldn't really explain it.

I knocked on the guest cottage door. She didn't answer right away. The second time, I knocked harder. She opened the door wearing her bathrobe. Her blondish-gray hair was pulled back into a stubby ponytail.

"How sweet of you to visit," she said. "Would you like a glass of wine?"

"Sure."

I went inside and settled on her couch, putting my phone beside me, hoping I was going to leave with an email address for Mr. Monroe. I didn't even know his first name.

Cheryl went into the kitchen. I heard her getting out glasses, and then I heard the fridge door open and close. A few minutes later she came back carrying two wineglasses. She handed one to me and sat in the chair across from me.

"How is the party planning going?" she asked. "Almost done?"

I took a sip of wine and put the glass on the coffee table beside a small wood bowl filled with polished stones. I wanted to pick one up and hold it in my hand. They looked so smooth and solid. There was something about them that made them look comforting to hold. As they continued to hold my attention, the colors reminded me of candy I wanted to put in my mouth, closing my eyes as they dissolved on my tongue.

I looked away from the stones. "Everything is done. It's going to be really good."

She smiled and sipped her wine.

"I love arranging all the pieces of it."

"Maybe you should become an event planner."

"I don't even know how you do that."

She shrugged. "Neither do I, but I think you have a lot more talent than whatever it is you do on your computer all day."

I laughed. "It is a little boring. And everyone I chat with is in a bad mood, so it gets tiring."

"That's too bad."

"The whole reason they contact me is because they're mad that something went wrong. So ..." I took a sip of wine.

She nodded.

"Anyway, if you can find out how someone gets paid to plan parties, let me know."

"Ruth might know."

I laughed. "Sure." I took another sip of wine. "The only thing is, she didn't give me Cameron's dad's email address."

She was still looking at me, but it felt like she was staring past me, or doing that trick where you look at someone's forehead so they think you're looking at them, but you're really not. I waited for her to say something. Instead, she kept staring at me.

"It seems like Cameron would want his dad at his party," I said. "I asked about it, and Ruth just ignored me."

She sipped her wine. Her gaze flicked away from me, toward the corner of the room where there was nothing but a chair and a table with a plant on it. Obviously, she wanted to ignore me too. *What the hell?* "Do you have it? His email or his cell number?"

"You should ask Ruth."

"You don't have it?"

"It's her party."

"But she just ignored me. It's not cool that the party is only two weeks away."

She took another sip of wine.

"So, you don't have it?"

She sighed and put down her glass.

"I told you, it's Ruth's party, and she gave you the guest list. It's her decision."

"Doesn't Cameron get along with his dad?"

"He does."

"Do you not like him?"

"It has nothing to do with me."

"So you don't like him?"

"He's an old family friend. Of course, I have fond memories of him. But this is *Ruth's* party, and you need to discuss the guest list with her, not me. I'm not sure why you thought it was a good idea to go behind her back."

I picked up my glass and finished the wine in one gulp. Obviously, I was going behind her back. I was trying to think about Cameron. Not whatever drama was going on with Ruth. But Cheryl was more worried about Ruth's drama, and maybe even her own, because she was also acting awfully weird about it. "Is he crazy or something? Is his wife a bitch?"

"Don't start making up stories out of thin air. You need to talk to Ruth. You should do whatever she wants to do."

"I already told you—she ignored me."

"Then that's your answer."

"Won't Cameron be upset? This is supposed to make him happy. How can it make him happy to not invite his father?"

She sighed so loudly it sounded as if she were picking up a twenty-pound box. "You need to talk to Ruth. Please. I'd offer you more wine, but I'm really tired." She scooted forward in her chair and smoothed her robe over her knees. "I was just getting ready for bed, and I'm really tired, so ..."

It was only seven thirty when I knocked on her door. I couldn't believe she went to bed so early. It wasn't as if she was old. Probably less than sixty-five. She was acting like she was ancient. I got up and carried my wineglass to her kitchen and left it on the counter. When I returned, she was standing near the front door.

"I had a tiring day. We can get together another time, okay?"

"Sure," I said.

As I walked back to the house, I decided I was going to get that email address from Ruth or find out what the issue was no matter what. They were acting like the guy was an ax murderer. It was crazy. This was Cameron's biggest birthday. It was his last birthday when he was still sort of youngish, and I couldn't believe he wouldn't want his dad there.

18

RUTH

The world news was making me anxious, so I turned off the TV and picked up my tablet to play a game. I was close to winning the next level when I was suddenly aware of Nadia's blue-painted toenails a few inches from my feet. I hadn't heard her enter the room, and I wondered how she'd walked so quietly in her flip-flops. It terrified me that she was able to get so close to me without me sensing her presence.

My finger slipped across the screen and the game in a loss. The tablet started to slide off my lap, but I caught it before it fell to the floor.

"We rushed to pull everything for Cameron's party together so fast, I realized we forgot something important," she said.

"Please stop sneaking up on me."

"I didn't sneak up on you."

I put my tablet on the side table and edged away from her. I stood and picked up my empty tea mug.

"Cameron's father and stepmother."

She'd asked me about them before, and I'd ignored her. I hadn't wanted the party to begin with. I'd given in because she pushed relentlessly, and my mother had piled on. They'd insisted Cameron seemed to be expecting something more than our usual style of celebration, which I still had my doubts about. But the thought of inviting his father and Deanne was too much. It wasn't that kind of party. We didn't have a close extended family that gathered for every holiday and birthday. Throwing a party with our local friends would be surprise enough.

"Why didn't you add them to the list?"

"We have quite a few friends who aren't in the area who weren't included."

"That's not the same as family."

"You're making too big a deal out of this. It's just a birthday party."

"His *fortieth*."

"So?"

"His father should be there. And his stepmother."

"She's not really his stepmother. He was an adult when they were married."

"Is that the problem? You don't like her? Or he doesn't?"

"Please drop it." I started toward the kitchen. My fingers were clenched so tightly around the handle of my mug that it shook slightly as I walked.

"Are you okay?"

"I'm fine."

"You're shaking."

"I'm not." I loosened my grip and walked faster, supporting the mug with my other hand.

She came up beside me. "Do you need me to carry that for you? I don't want you to drop it."

I stepped around her and went into the kitchen. I rinsed the mug and put it into the dishwasher.

Cameron would probably feel his father's absence. At the same time, Micah had never been in our home. We always visited him, and those visits were somewhat rare. We saw him for Christmas or Thanksgiving every year, but never both. We'd stopped by his San Diego home on our way to visit friends a few times over the years, spending only a single night.

If Micah was there, Cameron would be pleased. It might smooth things over between the two of us. In fact, if I told him how hard Nadia had pushed to invite his father, maybe Cameron would warm to her extended and inexplicable stay in our home. At this point, I was starting to feel as if she was going to be living with us forever. My whole life felt like it was going to continue in a state of suspended indecision and anxiety forever.

And Nadia was not going to stop pushing. It was clear, if it hadn't been the moment I first spoke to her, that she was a person who pushed hard until she got what she wanted, until she received answers to her questions. I could imagine her finding a way to hack into my phone or Cameron's to get the information herself if I didn't give it to her.

I went to the small utility desk in the kitchen and took a sticky note out of the drawer. I wrote down Micah's email address and handed it to her.

"Should I explain why we're inviting him at the last minute?" Nadia asked.

"It's not necessary."

"He won't be hurt?"

I sighed. She never let up. "No. He'll be pleased to be invited."

She took the note and left.

I went to my office and closed the door. I left the overhead light off and turned on the table lamp. I collapsed on the small couch and curled into a fetal position. I pulled the soft quilt over me, tucking a throw pillow under my head. I closed my eyes and let my mind fall back in time to Cameron's car accident.

I'd been so young. The same age as Nadia was now. Had I been that eager and determined? It was hard to remember because I became a different person after his accident. We both did.

His mother was dead, killed instantly in the accident. As a twenty-two-year-old woman, I didn't have the emotional skills to comfort a man who had been behind the wheel when he looked over and saw his mother dead in the seat beside him. Nothing about the accident had been his fault when a drunk driver ran a red light at fifty miles an hour and plowed into the passenger side of his car, but he was filled with irrational guilt on top of his grief. On top of that, he was in excruciating pain and unable to think rationally due to the drugs pumped into his veins to help him cope with his fractured pelvis and other injuries.

And then there was Micah. What a piece of work. That was the cynical view I had toward him now. But at the time, I was flooded with so much rage I felt like my mind was a red-hot coal, incapable of anything but hatred.

Micah visited Cameron once after the accident.

I could still see him now as he walked into the hospital room, with his dark brown hair, gray sideburns, and a few beautifully placed gray streaks across the sides of his hair as if they'd been professionally dyed. His posture was as perfect as always. He was the kind of man people watched for as long as he was in their range of sight. It felt as if he purposefully kept his posture even straighter to call attention to his son's broken body.

He stood beside the bed, the railing a barrier between him and his son, and stared down at Cameron.

I stood and offered him my chair, but he ignored me.

"When do they expect you to be out of here?" he asked.

I watched as Cameron's eyelids eased closed.

"It's too soon to know," I said. "The doctor will be by at eleven, and you can—"

"Eleven? I can't hang around here for an hour and a half."

"But Cameron needs you to—"

"I hate hospitals."

I didn't know what to say to that. No one *liked* hospitals, but I didn't have the inner strength to talk back to him. I stared, hoping the fire in my brain burned through my eyes, screaming my feelings at him, shaming him into seeing how Cameron was suffering, into recognizing what I too was feeling. Of course, my eyes said nothing at all. Even if they had, Micah was blind to the humanity of others. He only saw how he felt. He always only cared how he was feeling. But I hadn't yet realized that about him.

Cameron drifted in and out of consciousness. His father took a step away from the bed. He refused to let his gaze connect with mine for more than a second or two. Maybe that was partially due to my own reaction. I was staring hard at the linoleum floor, wondering how it could look so absolutely clean but also dirty in a way that I couldn't describe. It showed years of wear from shoes and the wheels of beds and carts scuffing over it, the stripping of harsh chemicals used to keep it antiseptically clean. I had no doubt it was clean, but it felt unclean to me. Just as taking a hundred showers after a woman is raped can leave her still feeling damaged and filthy and not clean for weeks, for months, for years.

I wanted Micah to leave, and I wanted him to show some affection for his son. Some concern for his life. At that point in time, although the doctors had assured me otherwise, I was terrified Cameron might die. Maybe my terror came from the despair in his eyes. His inability to control the tears that oozed out when the morphine wore off before the next dose was allowed. Maybe my terror came from the catheter and the tubes putting fluids into his body and the fact he couldn't move and the doctor's explanation of how a fractured pelvis would heal, and the physical therapy required.

Maybe it was my selfish thoughts about the wedding I'd dreamed of, the terrified vision of our first dance that now appeared in my dreams as an image of me holding up a broken man who could barely shuffle his feet.

Worst of all was Cameron's refusal to talk about our future, his long silences, his guilt and sadness and lack of will to think about anything but getting relief from the pain.

Cameron wasn't able to attend his mother's funeral, so I went alone, leaving immediately after the service.

His father never returned to the hospital. He sent periodic text messages to ask if Cameron was walking yet. Then nothing. Cameron was released from the hospital and finally showing glimpses of optimism about his physical therapy. He was well into his three-times-a-week sessions before we bothered to tell his father.

Four months after his mother had died, Micah and Deanne were married.

How Cameron managed any kind of relationship at all with his father after that was a mystery to me, but he did. I knew he still had a complicated, disappointed love for his father, and I knew it still mattered to him that his father was part of his life. I was mostly numb.

That night in bed, just as I thought I could escape into sleep, Cameron smashed his pillows against the headboard, leaned against them, and folded his arms across his chest. "Having one of our clients living in our house is not appropriate. I'm getting really concerned about it. What is the timeline for her leaving?"

"I honestly don't think it's a problem. She hasn't told any other clients. None of the staff, except for Justine, know about it. She keeps mostly to herself when she's at the Center. I've kept a close eye on her."

"So you don't trust her?"

"I didn't say that. I'm just … I knew you were concerned, and I wanted to be able to reassure you."

"Reassuring me shouldn't be your focus. I just don't get it. I think it's risky, and it's a liability."

"Sometimes you have to trust people and not always be worried about liability and rules and regulations, don't you think?"

"That's a nice belief, but not realistic. And it doesn't sound like you." He laughed, with a sharp edge to his tone. "It feels like you're almost … obsessed with her. I feel like keeping her happy is more important to you than our relationship is."

"That's not true." I slid down and rested my head on his lap. I wrapped my hand around his thigh and massaged it gently. "Not ever. No one is more important to me than you."

"Then what is it with her?"

"It just feels really good to be helping someone who's hurting. She took her mom's death so hard. It completely knocked her off balance. Not that anyone wouldn't, especially at her age. She's just trying to figure out her place in the world. I think she's a little lost. And it's such a simple, easy thing for us to do."

He rubbed the back of my head, pressing his fingers into the muscles at the base of my skull, relieving tension I hadn't known was there, thinking the tightness had all been inside my mind. I sighed, then moaned softly.

He laughed. "I didn't know a scalp massage would have *that* effect."

"Can you just let me do this for her? I'm sure it will work out. If I hear anything at all about her talking to other clients,

I'll tell her right away she has to go, but for now, it seems fine." I ran my hand up his leg and felt him react to my touch.

A moment later, he was sliding down beside me, wrapping his arms around me, and pulling me on top of him.

19

NADIA

U sually when Ruth and Cameron left home for the Wellness Center before sunrise each day, I was online solving customer problems for people on the East Coast. But on Wednesday morning, I was still upset with Ruth. It seemed like she hardly appreciated all the effort I'd put into planning Cameron's surprise party. I understood that she was afraid of me telling everyone who I was, but wasn't she even a little interested in getting to know me? Instead, she ignored me whenever she could. And at the same time, she didn't seem that worried, because she hadn't said anything about when she was getting the money I'd asked for.

I hadn't looked her up online and searched for details about her and walked into her life thinking about getting money. But now that I'd had all this time to imagine what I could do with fifty thousand dollars, I honestly wanted it. And knowing how much she didn't want Cameron, or even her mother, to know about me made me want it more. I felt like I deserved it. She had so much, and she'd never done anything for me. Couldn't she see that? I was her child, and it seemed like she didn't care about me at all. She didn't even seem to feel sad that the person who took care of me and who actually acted like my mother and did all the things she should have done had died.

Even though she was doing everything she could to keep me from being part of her life, to keep me from finding out more about her, she underestimated me. I don't know if she thought I was as dumb as a teenager, or she just thought I wasn't very smart because I hadn't gone to college. Maybe she just thought she was better than everyone, but I was a good listener, and I was good at making friends.

Justine didn't want me around Kellyn, but Justine was very busy not paying attention to Kellyn while she worked. And Kellyn liked to talk. She liked telling me about school and her friends. She liked talking about the books she read, and the TV shows she watched. And Kellyn told me that Ruth was going to be her guardian if her mom died, which made her worried and scared and sad. Hearing that made me so upset I had a long, complicated dream about it. When I woke up, my face was wet from crying, so it was almost like it wasn't a dream at all. And maybe it was real, because I think I was still crying.

Did that mean Ruth loved Kellyn instead of her own daughter? It sure seemed that way.

Ruth had lots of time to think about promising to take care of a girl who wasn't even related to her, but no time at all to think about giving a tiny fraction of her money to her own child ... the child she'd ignored her entire life. She pretended I didn't even *exist*. Sometimes, I wondered if she'd forgotten I was alive until I showed up that day.

I messaged my supervisor that I had a headache and was going to take a painkiller, but I hoped to be back online in two hours. After she gave me permission for time away, I logged off. I wove my hair into a French braid and put on lip gloss. Cameron and Ruth were in the kitchen. As luck would have it, Cheryl was there too. She'd come into the house to borrow their kettle because hers had stopped working.

I loved that I had an audience of all three. I couldn't wait to see what Ruth was going to do because I was absolutely sure that no one knew she'd broken her vow to not have kids in her life and promised to take care of a kid who was only half grown and had a mother who had just dodged a cancer scare. It's not as if people always die from cancer, but in my experience, it was hard not to think that way.

At first, no one noticed me standing in the doorway. Cheryl was holding their kettle with the cord wrapped around her hand. Ruth was packing yogurt into a cooler bag, and Cameron was filling travel cups with coffee.

"That is so sweet," I said. "Maybe that's not the right word … so generous and loving of you to say you'll be Kellyn's guardian if Justine dies."

In a single blink of my eyes, they were all staring at me, and the room was silent. I could hear my heart beating. I wondered if the other sound I could hear was Ruth's heart. I definitely could not hear anyone's breath because they were all holding the air inside their lungs.

"What?" Cameron asked.

"Ruth is Kellyn's guardian. I guess that means you both are. You might become parents when you least expect it. In fact, I guess not just from cancer. She could die in a car accident. Or even get murdered. Being a single parent is risky, isn't it?"

A choking sound came out of Ruth. I couldn't tell if it was a scared sound or an angry sound. Or if she wanted to cry. Maybe she wanted to kill me. Maybe she was afraid I was going to kill Justine so she would have to take care of Kellyn. That sound she made could have been anything, really. I didn't mean any of the things I said, I just wanted to find out what *she* would say. I wanted her to *feel* something. Anything at all. Even if she hated me with all her heart, at least she would have feelings for me.

Cameron carefully placed the travel cup on the counter. "You agreed to be her legal guardian?"

Ruth swallowed so hard I could see her throat contract as if she were a boa constrictor swallowing a rat. "I—"

"When were you going to tell me?"

"I was—"

"You didn't think to discuss it with me? Have you signed any documents?"

"I ... we can. She's eleven. Nothing is going to happen. Justine's biopsy was benign. And—"

"Ruth!" Cameron said.

"Oh." Cheryl placed the kettle on the counter. The cord fell over the edge and dangled down the side.

"It's just a safeguard," Ruth said. "Nothing will happen. In seven years, she'll be eighteen."

"I can do the math," Cameron said.

Ruth zipped the cooler bag closed. "We should get going, or we'll be late. We can talk about it in the car."

Cameron picked up the travel cups and followed her out of the room.

Cheryl picked up the kettle. "Well, that was ... something."

She looked at me. I could see she was hoping for an explanation. She knew I said what I had just to create chaos, and I think she was curious why I would do that. It was obvious that I liked staying with Ruth and Cameron, and now I'd made Ruth so upset she might tell me to leave. Cheryl was probably confused about why I would try to cause an argument right before the surprise party. She was probably confused about everything.

"That wasn't the best timing," she said after a few minutes.

I went to the cabinet for a mug and poured coffee for myself. I turned to face her. "It's a big deal to raise another person's child. I was so surprised when Kellyn told me."

She nodded and picked up the kettle.

"Don't you think?"

"Yes."

"I'm adopted, you know."

She stared at me as if I'd smacked her face, as I'd expected she would. I was dying to know what she was thinking. Sometimes I really wanted to ask people what they were thinking, but then they could lie. It's better if they tell you, but that can also be a lie. What I really wished was that I could read her mind.

I wondered if Ruth had told her about me. Probably not or she would have treated me differently. Obviously, she knew Ruth had a baby when she was fifteen. Obviously, she helped Ruth get rid of me. Since I'd come to stay there, since I'd gotten to know her a tiny bit, I'd wondered if she ever thought about that baby. Had she ever tried to find out where I was or how I was doing? Probably she'd even been the one to arrange for my adoption. She must have been. Ruth was practically a child.

Now I felt her staring at me as if she wanted to read my mind as much as I wanted to read hers. Even as I looked at her eyes, I could feel that she wasn't really looking back into mine, she was looking at my entire face. She was wondering. Wouldn't she have looked at every twenty-two-year old girl she saw and wonder? Wouldn't Ruth? If they hadn't, shouldn't they have?

I thought normal people would.

She must be thinking—what are the chances? She must also be thinking—*Does she look like Ruth? Does she look like me?*

With my hair dyed red, she couldn't know anything about my hair. With all the eye makeup I liked to wear, she probably couldn't say much about my eyes either. And I'd always noticed that most people fixed their attention on the little ring in my nostril instead of noticing my smile.

Right that minute, she was probably trying to ignore the thin gold ring and figure out the shape of my nose and my lips. And then she was telling herself—*It's impossible. It can't be her. Could it be her?* She would be thinking—*If this is her daughter, Ruth would have told me.*

I smiled and put the mug to my mouth and slurped the coffee.

She was still staring at me, and she kept opening her mouth like she wanted to say something, but couldn't figure out what the right thing to say might be. She obviously didn't know. At first, I'd thought maybe Ruth would ask her for help with getting the money I asked for, finding a way to sneak it past Cameron, although I wasn't really sure how that would work. But obviously Ruth and Cameron were helping her since she lived in their guest cottage, and maybe she didn't even pay rent.

I put my mug on the counter.

It had been quiet for so long the chirping and singing of the birds outside sounded like they were moving into the kitchen. Cheryl had cleared her throat quite a few times, and now she was clicking her fingernails on the ceramic kettle.

"That's good to see how much you loved your mother, even though you were adopted," she said.

I smiled. "Why wouldn't I? She was the only mother I had. And she loved me so much."

She coughed again and edged closer to the doorway. "Well, it's not long until Cameron's party, right?"

"Yes," I said.

"When is your birthday, Nadia?"

I wanted to laugh, her question was so obvious, even though she thought she was making it a casual question about birthdays. "February third."

I was sure she was absolutely dying to ask what year, but she didn't. The month and day were enough.

She gave me a smile that looked like something for a toothpaste advertisement. "Well, have a wonderful day." Then she scurried out of the room with the cord for the kettle dragging on the tiles.

20

RUTH

The moment we were seated in the car, Cameron assaulted me with a barrage of accusations. "What's going on with you? First that girl moving into our house, now this? You agreed to be her guardian without asking me, without even mentioning it? That's a huge responsibility. I can't believe how disrespectful that is to me, to our relationship, to everything we've ever talked about and agreed upon for how we want to live our lives. Are you trying to blow up our marriage? Do you want a divorce, but you're too much of a coward to ask me? Are you trying to force me to be the bad guy? What the hell is going on?"

"No!" I put my hand on his leg. I leaned toward him, but he raised his arm to block me from getting too close as he started the car.

He put the car in reverse and backed it somewhat violently out of the garage. He drove too fast down our street and barely paused at the stop sign before rounding the corner.

"Slow down."

"You owe me an explanation," he said.

"I'm sorry. I—"

"An explanation. Not a limp apology. Those are just words."

"Justine was so upset about the biopsy. I ... Nothing is going to happen to her. I said yes without thinking about it because she—"

"You can't know that. Anything could happen. And that's beside the point. It's not a decision you make lightly. This isn't a promise to take care of someone's cat when they're out of town for a week. Come on, Ruth. You need to tell me what's going on with you."

"She was desperate."

"She's not desperate. You said the biopsy was clear. She's not lying in a hospital with stage four cancer. She has options. You're not her only friend. She has relatives."

"I—"

"Why would you do that without talking to me? Why does Nadia know, and I'm completely in the dark?"

"Kellyn must have told her."

"So Kellyn knows? This is a done deal?"

"I'm sure we'll never have to honor it."

"You're sure? You have a crystal ball? What if we do? And that's not the point. I thought we always said we would tell each other everything. We make decisions together. We treat each other with respect. You've invited a stranger to live in our home and agreed to raise a teenager, both without talking to me."

"I'm sorry. I thought you would ..." A sob rose from my chest and broke out in a loud, tearing sound that scared me.

"Don't start crying like a child."

I hadn't meant to, but I couldn't control it, after everything that had happened since the day Nadia told me she was my daughter. And I couldn't give him an explanation. All I could do was apologize over and over. I knew he would never accept it because that wasn't the kind of relationship we had.

Justine wasn't desperate. I was. I couldn't figure out how to fix things with Cameron, and I was afraid I was careening toward the loss of the man I loved. I wasn't one of those women who could sob into her pillow, wailing that I didn't know how I'd ended up here. I knew exactly how I'd come to this point.

Quietly, I took a deep breath to stop the panicked tears that were filling my chest. I decided to be as honest as I could and hoped it would work, for now.

"I don't know why. Like I told you before, I felt sorry for Nadia. It was an impulsive move that I can't explain." For the most part, that was the truth, and I almost wanted to laugh as the words formed themselves and flowed out of my mouth. "Maybe I'm having an early midlife crisis. Maybe I'm just feeling some sort of need to take care of hurting women. I can't really explain it. I know I betrayed you by not talking to you about either situation. I'll tell Justine it's not going to work." My voice became soft and weak as I spoke. It was very unlike me, and I felt him glance toward me quickly before returning his attention to the road.

"You're right that the odds are against it ever being necessary," he said carefully. "I'm sorry I blew up. I just felt blindsided."

"I know. And this is the opposite of how I wanted to day to go, because I wanted to tell you what I have planned for your birthday."

He laughed. "I was starting to think nothing."

Feeling sick with guilt at my obvious manipulation, I leaned over and kissed his cheek. I felt better at the sensation of his freshly shaved skin against my lips. "I booked a couples massage. And dinner at Selby's. After, we'll spend the night at Rosewood."

"Very nice."

"You like it?"

"I do."

I kissed his cheek again and felt the most pleasurable sense of relief and contentment I'd enjoyed in weeks. I knew it wouldn't last, but I let it flow through me for a few seconds, hoping that he and I would be okay for now. Maybe it meant I would find a way through the mess I'd created. Maybe the love we had for each other was enough to overcome whatever Nadia wanted to do to hurt me, to tear my life to pieces.

The sense of hope was short-lived. By the time I'd eaten my yogurt and fruit and finished the coffee in my travel cup, my stomach was twisted with anxiety over the threat Nadia was holding at my throat like a virtual knife. I'd felt it moving closer every day until I imagined I felt the cut of its sharp edge each time I swallowed.

When she'd pushed me for Micah and Deanne's address, insisting that Cameron's father had to be invited to the party, I'd realized I did have one option for getting fifty thousand dollars without Cameron finding out about it—the man I hated more than any person on the face of the earth.

Micah.

I hadn't always known him as Micah.

When I was a child, he was Mr. Monroe.

He and his wife, Sylvia, and their two sons—Cameron and Josh—were family friends. We vacationed with them and enjoyed family barbecues and hiking together. I'd known them as long as I could remember, and I'd developed a crush on Cameron when I was fourteen.

Already close childhood friends, I felt Cameron returned my feelings, but he was a senior in high school when I was a freshman, and except for a quick brush of our lips two days before he left for college when I was fifteen, nothing much had happened between us. He did promise to text me and send me pictures of college life, and he had.

A few months after he was gone, Sylvia had gone to Florida to visit her sister. My mother invited Micah to dinner, but after they shared a bottle of champagne, my mother went to bed with a headache.

Instead of going home, Mr. Monroe opened another bottle of champagne. He filled his own glass, then poured some into a flute and handed it to me. I stared at the bubbles racing toward the thin layer of foam. "I'm only allowed champagne on New Year's," I said.

"Because the New Year is a special occasion." He smiled and held the glass out to me. "This is a special occasion."

"Why?"

"Because you're looking especially beautiful."

My face felt instantly hot, but it wasn't the heat of being embarrassed that I sometimes felt around other kids. Mr. Monroe was a good-looking man. He didn't seem so old like some of my mom's other friends. He'd helped her a lot after my dad died. He sent her flowers on her birthday, and he and Sylvia took her out for dinner every month and helped her not feel lonely.

"That isn't a special occasion," I said, embarrassed as I heard my voice tremble.

"It is. You're grown up."

I giggled. "I'm in high school."

"That's almost grown up." He took a sip from his glass. "It's very good champagne."

"My mom will be mad."

"She won't know. It will be our secret." He took another sip from his glass. "I won't tell her. I promise."

I liked knowing I could trust him. I liked feeling special enough to have a secret with my mother's friend that she didn't know about. And I loved knowing that he thought I was beautiful. No one had ever told me I was beautiful. It was almost hard to believe it was true. I wanted to run to the bathroom and look in the mirror to see if he really was telling the truth, but the way he was looking at me, I felt that it was absolutely the truth.

I took the glass and took a sip. The bubbles fizzed inside my mouth. The cold sharp taste and the fizz felt exciting on my tongue. I drank some more.

"Not too fast," he said. "It's to be savored."

He asked me about school. He asked about my favorite classes and what my dreams were. When I answered, he didn't try to interrupt. He didn't tell me to be serious like my mom did. He listened to every word and asked more questions. Before I knew it, the glass was empty. He refilled my glass. He pulled a glass tube out of his pocket and shook a tablet out. He dropped it into my glass.

"What's that?" I asked.

"It will help you relax."

"I'm relaxed."

"You don't seem relaxed."

"I am." I giggled although I wasn't sure why. It wasn't funny.

"Take a sip."

I shook my head.

"I can tell you like talking to me. The greatest feeling in the world is knowing you can say anything you want to another person. Is there anyone you can tell all your thoughts to? Everything? Even your darkest secrets?"

I felt my skin get hot. How did he know I had dark secrets? Did he have dark secrets? I knew from books I read that other people did, but those were in books. I wasn't sure if my friends did. And I was very sure my mother and other adults I knew did not.

"I know you want to. Try it. You'll feel better than you ever have."

I took a few sips, and we continued talking, although I didn't tell him any secrets. I did slowly feel more relaxed, and before I knew it, the glass was empty. He refilled it halfway, but I left it on the table.

Soon, I heard myself talking more, hardly knowing what I was saying, but loving the sound of my voice and the feeling of his eyes staring at me, studying every part of me as if I were a piece of chocolate cake. It seemed as if the only thing in the whole world that mattered to him right then was me and what I thought and felt.

My head felt strange, and I wasn't sure if I was tired or something else. I felt warm and tingly. I noticed his mouth and his eyes and thought he seemed like the nicest person I'd ever known. My body felt like it was melting into the couch. "I feel funny," I said. My thoughts were slippery, and it was hard to move my arms. I knew if I picked up the champagne glass again, I would drop it.

Mr. Monroe was sitting very close to me. His breath was warm on my neck, and after a few minutes where my mind drifted like a leaf on the water, I felt his lips on my skin. Then I felt something wet on my face. I tasted salt and thought it was champagne, but champagne wasn't salty. Tears were seeping down my cheeks and into my mouth.

After a few minutes or maybe less, or more, I was cold. I shivered. My top was off and so was my bra. He was biting and sucking on my breast. It felt funny—warm, but awful. I was still crying without any sound. I thought I was whispering for him to stop, or maybe I was asking him what he was doing, but I wasn't sure if he could hear me because he wasn't saying anything back to me.

He pushed up my skirt, and then he stood, unbuckled his

belt, and unzipped his pants. I closed my eyes, or they were already closed, and then I don't know if I passed out, or I didn't want to be there and I pretended I was somewhere else. I don't know what I did. I was embarrassed. I was afraid my mom would be so angry with me. I wondered if Mr. Monroe was going to tell her, and I was crying because what would Cameron say?

And then I woke up. Mr. Monroe was gone. It was one thirty in the morning. My clothes were on, but my underwear was wet, and I wondered if I'd slept so deeply that I peed in my pants.

The champagne glasses were gone. I was curled on the couch in a ball. And my face was still wet.

I sat up slowly, then stood. The room was spinning around me. I felt sore, like I might be bleeding, and when I took a few steps, it hurt worse. Then I felt my dinner and all the champagne rushing up from my stomach. I ran to the bathroom and threw up. When I was finished, I rinsed my mouth. I washed myself and walked down the hall to my bedroom.

It was seventeen days before I broke my promise to Mr. Monroe. When I told her, I wanted my mother to hug me. I wanted her to hold my head close to her and tell me I was okay and that she would tell him how bad he was.

"Champagne is a special treat," she said. "You had no business drinking alcohol when I wasn't there!"

"But he ..." I started crying.

Her eyes filled with tears. She wiped them away angrily. "Are you trying to tell me you had *sex* with him? You seduced him?!"

"No! I didn't. I didn't." I was crying so hard I felt like someone was punching me in the chest. I couldn't breathe. "I didn't do anything. He put something in my drink. He said it would help me relax. But then I could hardly move, and I couldn't even think. He started doing stuff to me, and he took off my top, and he was—"

"Stop. Mr. Monroe is a lovely, decent man. How dare you say things like that about him."

"That's what he did. I'm telling the truth."

"You're lying. You're twisting it around to keep yourself out of trouble. I told you I didn't like that skirt. It's too short. All your skirts are too short. And your shirts are too tight. Men are built to desire women, and it's our responsibility not to flaunt our bodies and tempt them."

"I didn't, Mommy. I didn't do anything. He said—"

She stood and walked to my bedroom door. "I don't want to discuss this again. I want you to stop telling yourself these ugly, untrue stories about him. I want you to behave yourself and treat him with respect. He's been a wonderful, incredible friend to me, and I won't allow you to destroy that."

———

WHEN I TOLD her I hadn't had my period for three months, she never said anything about Mr. Monroe. She told me that God would not allow me to kill the baby growing inside me. I would stay home from school and have a tutor for my junior year of high school. If people found out about me being pregnant, it would ruin my life. Mr. and Mrs. Monroe and Cameron and Josh would not visit our home; she would visit them. She would tell everyone I had a particularly difficult case of mononucleosis.

She talked to her friends at St. Michael's Catholic Church and found out about Lisa and Barry Fairchild, who would not only help deliver the baby, but would also adopt it. We would promise to never have any contact so the child would feel it was part of their family without any confusion about who its parents were.

This was for the best. Having a child in my life, having contact with that child would ruin my life. I was too young to care for a child, and all I would do was ruin the child's life and my own. I should forget it ever happened.

So that's what I tried to do. And I succeeded.

When Cameron asked me out the summer after I graduated from high school, the baby and the man who made me pregnant had become something that happened in a bad dream. A nightmare that I never talked about and mostly never thought about. Of course, I never said anything to Cameron about it.

How would he feel now if I told him? I had absolutely no idea. I'd wondered about it endlessly since Nadia told me she was my daughter. I'd lain awake at night imagining a hundred different conversations. I'd had dreams. I'd had nightmares. I'd relived that night with Mr. Monroe, and I'd relived my baby's birth. I'd relived every moment of the fifteenth year of my life.

I'd had fresh waves of loathing for my mother, fresh waves and pain and feelings of being abandoned.

How could I ever tell Cameron? Would he understand how it had been for me? Would he be like my mother and blame me? Would he hate me for lying to him all these years? Or would he understand? I had absolutely no idea, and the not knowing terrified me. I was frozen. I felt like I'd become that vulnerable, hurting, confused fifteen-year-old girl all over again, and I wondered if I'd ever matured past that moment at all.

21

RUTH

Knowing Micah was in town with Deanne sent chills down my spine. Over the years, when Cameron and I had visited him in their home, I felt like the power was in my hands. I decided when we arrived and how long we stayed. I decided how much I would talk to him. I never felt compelled to make eye contact, ask a favor, or even remain in the room with him. I certainly never discussed the past.

The thought of him driving streets that were so familiar they felt as if they belonged to me was an invasion of my space. Thinking ahead to the party, imagining him walking into our home and touching our things was almost more than I could bear, even after all these years—twenty-three, to be precise.

At the same time, I knew that he was the one person who had as much reason as I did to hand Nadia a large amount of money to prevent Cameron from finding out who she was. Despite Micah's coolness and his unwillingness to give Cameron what he needed at the worst moment of his life, Micah loved his son. He wanted a relationship with

Cameron, even if it was only on his terms. He would not want Cameron to know what he'd done to me when I was fifteen.

Deanne had messaged me that they didn't plan to arrive in town until the day before the party. I'd sent Micah a text and told him we needed to meet that afternoon. I chose a coffee place that featured private booths. The privacy made my skin crawl and my fingers tremble when I thought about being in that close space, but it was essential to the conversation I'd planned almost word for word in my mind.

I hoped I would be able to recall my mental script. Since an imagined conversation and the reality of talking to another person are never the same, I hoped that I would have the inner strength to remain calm when I was sitting across from him, his eyes gazing at me, the memories crawling through my mind like snakes slithering down to my gut.

I arrived early and ordered a cup of tea. My heart was racing. I felt as if my blood vessels were fluttering inside me. It truly felt like caffeine might stimulate a heart attack.

He arrived a few minutes after the hour, placed a large cup of cappuccino on the table, and slid in across from me. "To what do I owe this pleasure?"

"I'll get right to the point," I said, immediately proud of myself for not reacting to his comment designed to make me squirm. "Because I was a child, my mother made my decisions for me. So you were never told that your rape resulted in me becoming pregnant."

He pulled back against the bench as if I'd punched him. "Slow down. That's uncalled for."

"It's the truth. I had a baby, and that child has—"

"I did not *rape* you. I resent you using that word or anything like it. We had a completely consensual—"

"We did not. But I don't want to discuss it. As I said, I had a child."

"You wanted me."

"I had no idea what was happening. *And* you drugged me. I was a child. You were an adult. End of discussion."

"I didn't—"

"I had a child, and now, she's contacted me. She's blackmailing me for fifty thousand dollars, or she'll tell Cameron who she is. Obviously, I never told him what you did."

He stared at me, finally at a loss for words. He picked up his mug and swallowed some coffee. Foam clung to his upper lip, but he didn't lick it away. "What's her proof? What's your proof that she's mine?"

"Her birthday is the same day I gave birth."

He laughed. It was a loud, rough sound that made the guy working at his laptop two tables away turn to stare. Micah took another large gulp of the cappuccino. "That's not proof. Did she provide a DNA test? She could be anyone. She could have—"

"Does that matter? She knows who I am. You can believe it or not. I believe it, and if she goes to Cameron, it doesn't matter if she has proof."

"Yes, it does."

"Really?"

"I would deny it. I do deny it."

"The people who adopted her are people who knew my mother."

"So?"

"She looks like me. And she has your smile. Mirror image."

"A mirror image is reverse."

"You know what I mean." I sipped my cooling tea. "It would be simple enough for her to get a DNA test."

He looked away, staring at the coffee bar as if he was suddenly fascinated by the menu of exotic caffeinated drinks. "Are you asking me for fifty grand for some opportunist who claims to be a kid from a one-night stand twenty-five years ago?"

It took every shred of courage I had not to react to him reframing his rape of me as a one-night stand. It took everything I had inside me not to punch his smug face for calling me a liar.

I needed the money, and I needed to stop Nadia before she told Cameron she was my daughter. And I needed all of that right now. Today. I wanted him to give me the money the next day. I knew he had it.

He was a real estate developer. He was a man who could lay his hands on hundreds of thousands of dollars in cash whenever he pleased. He'd bragged about it often enough. I'd sat through several insufferable evenings listening to him brag about what an important, cash-flush guy he was, and how people didn't realize how easy it was for him to buy whatever he wanted, whenever he wanted. He boasted about how much power he had and how he could solve any problem. One of his favorite clichés was the belief that there were no problems because he could *throw money at it to make it go away.*

"I'm not asking," I said. "I'm telling you that if you don't want Cameron to know what you did, if you don't want him to know we have a child, you need to give me fifty thousand dollars tomorrow. Because I can't access that kind of cash without him finding out."

He pushed the coffee cup away from him. He stared at me, and I realized he was shocked that I was facing him toe-to-toe, unafraid, no longer meek and cowed. It bothered me that it was absolute fear of something worse that had given me this strength. I wished I could have felt this power over him on my own, without being pushed into it by an even greater fear, but it felt good, nevertheless.

I felt a smile pushing its way to my lips as I saw a look of respect in his eyes.

"Blackmail is a bottomless pit," he said.

"I can't think about that right now."

"You should. What's your plan when she asks for more?"

"She's a kid. She doesn't have much. Fifty thousand dollars is a fortune to her, so I don't think she'll want more."

"That's naïve. Of course she will once she sees how easy it is. So, what's your plan?"

"I'll think about that later. I've spent all my time trying to figure out how to deal with the immediate problem."

He was quiet, continuing to study me. I held his gaze, feeling calm for the first time since Nadia had told me who she was. I was so close to getting my life back. I couldn't wait to tell her to move out of our house.

"Deanne and I have a few friends in the area. I think we'll stick around for a week or so."

"Why?"

"Blackmailers always want more. Always."

He sounded as if he had experience. Maybe not. I'd been so filled with panic I hadn't thought past the impossible task of getting the money. Of course she would want more. It was so easy. And she knew we had a lot more. She was always commenting on how beautiful our home was, on how nice our furniture and garden were. They were unsubtle references to how the settlement from Cameron's accident had given us more than the seed money for the Wellness Center.

"When she asks again, I'll have to find a better solution," he said.

The obvious threat made me so cold I couldn't move my fingers to pick up my cup of tea. I didn't want to ask what a better solution might be. Fortunately, the remainder of my thoughts froze along with my muscles and bones. All I knew was that he was going to give me what I'd asked for, what I'd demanded.

"You need to bring the money to Cameron's party," I said. "I don't want to meet with you again. You clearly can't give it to me in public, and I'm not coming to your hotel."

He smirked. "Sure. No problem."

I looped my purse strap over my shoulder and slid out of the booth. I half expected him to suggest I thank him, but he didn't. I walked as quickly as I could out of the coffee shop, trying not to look like I was trying to escape, but feeling as if I was doing exactly that.

NADIA HAD DONE a beautiful job with the party decorations. When I'd thanked her, the glow of pleasure on her face created a tiny ache in my heart. But more than that, it confused me. How could she *blackmail* me and threaten to destroy my marriage and at the same time long so desperately to please me? It was impossible to understand what she wanted from me.

There were metallic green and gold streamers, dishes of confetti, and clusters of balloons in the living and dining rooms. Our patio glittered with fairy lights—aside from the ones that usually lined the patio covering and circled a few trees, she'd added more. She'd also hung paper lanterns. The jazz trio set up at the far corner of the patio.

Our guests were given an exotic mask upon arrival—emerald green with feathers for the women, and gold and black for the men.

When Cameron and I arrived after our massage, ostensibly to dress for dinner, our friends greeted him with loud shouts of *surprise* and *happy birthday*.

The expression on his face was impossible to describe.

The look of shock was like that of a child on Christmas morning—delight and a sense of magic. I was equally shocked. I'd thought Nadia and my mother were wrong to believe he would be pleased with a surprise party. I'd worried he would be disappointed in our change of plans. I'd worried he would think it was childish and too much fuss.

He looked absolutely thrilled.

When his father removed his mask, not that he needed to do that to reveal his identity, the look of joy on Cameron's face brought tears to my eyes.

He turned to me. He kissed my cheek, then drew his lips along my cheekbone and whispered, "Thank you."

I wasn't sure if it was for everything, but I had the sense that mostly he was thanking me for inviting his father. Had he forgiven Micah for abandoning him in the hospital, for rejecting him when he was so damaged? Maybe, along with the physical effects of the accident and the trauma of his mother's death, the memory of Micah's behavior had faded.

When we had a few moments alone after changing into our party clothes, he clicked his champagne flute against my wineglass. "I know my dad isn't your favorite person, but I really appreciate you inviting him."

I smiled and took a sip of wine.

"Should I be worried?" He laughed nervously. "With all the other weird things you've been doing, I'm not sure if your including him is a good thing or not."

I smiled. "It's a milestone birthday. I knew you would want him here."

"I need to give him a tour of the house. He's never seen it."

I smiled again and said nothing. I also needed to give Micah a tour. Directly to the safe in Cameron's study.

Right from the minute she arrived at the party, Ruth treated me like I was part of the catering staff. She thanked me for everything and commented on how amazing the decorations were and how it was nice that she didn't have to think about any of the details, but it didn't feel like we were giving the party together. It felt like I was her assistant, or not even that—the butler.

She didn't introduce me to their friends or ask me if I wanted a glass of champagne.

I was watching when Cameron hugged his father. I knew the minute I saw Micah that he was Cameron's father. First, because he was the only older guy there, but also because they looked a lot alike. Micah's wife was only about five years older than Cameron and really beautiful. She was tall, with long blond hair. She was wearing white pants and white stilettos and a silky white top with most of the back cut out.

Since Ruth obviously was not going to introduce me, I decided to do it myself. I found them by the bar in the dining room. Micah was holding two glasses of champagne, and his wife was laughing, trying to take one out of his hand. He kissed her with a very long, deep kiss before he would let her have it.

"Hi," I said. "I'm Nadia." He handed the glass to her and looked at me, staring at my nose ring first, as all older people do. Then he looked at my hair, which was in a messy bun. The roots were getting dark and long because I hadn't dyed it since I'd come to California.

"Pleased to meet you, Nadia." He stared at me like he wasn't sure what else to say. He took a sip of champagne and said, "Are you a friend of Cameron's?"

"Actually, I'm a client at the Wellness Center."

I could feel Deanne looking at me, annoyed and very unfriendly. I glanced at her. She didn't smile. Micah turned to the bar and picked up a glass of champagne and handed it to me. "Cheers."

"Cheers," I said. "I guessed you were Cameron's dad, so I wanted to meet you."

He was staring at me, looking over every inch of my face, his eyes moving up and down my body. I couldn't tell if he thought I was hot, or it was something else. It didn't seem like the kind of staring that says you're hot, but that was definitely how his wife was interpreting it.

"And you're Cameron's stepmother?" I asked.

She glared at me.

"What's your name?" I asked.

"Deanne."

I held out my hand. "Nice to meet you."

She dipped her head a little but didn't answer, and she didn't take my hand. She turned her attention to her husband, giving him a nasty look that he didn't notice because he was still letting his eyes crawl all over me.

It was getting a little weird, and I wanted to tell him that he should take a picture. Did he stare at every woman like this? What was wrong with him? At the same time, I wanted to laugh. He wasn't wanting me, I could tell the difference in that kind of staring, and I thought Deanne was a little stupid for thinking that's what it was. But she was a lot older than me. Maybe she was right. She knew him; I'd just met him. Maybe she'd seen him staring at a hundred girls like he was staring at me right now.

Finally, Micah got control over his eyeballs. He asked me how I liked the Wellness Center and bragged about how smart his son was to start something so unique and how successful it was. I asked how long he and his wife were staying after the party, and he said probably for a week, which got him staring at me all over again. I asked if they liked their exclusive luxury motel, and finally Deanne opened her mouth to complain that it was okay, but they didn't have a masseuse on staff, and she didn't think they needed to stay quite so close to Cameron's house. They could have stayed in San Francisco since there weren't a lot of choices where we were.

Micah started going on about his other son and then quickly switched to bragging about their next trip to Europe.

After a few minutes, Deanne interrupted him and said they should get something to eat. I smiled and said it was nice to meet them. He said the same. She ignored me.

I wandered around the party, sipping champagne and listening to conversations, most of them not very interesting. The whole time, I kept my eye on Ruth. After she and Cameron had walked in to the shouts of surprise and he hugged his father, they had disappeared for a while to change into fancy clothes for the party.

When they returned, she was wearing a black dress with an uneven hem that had specks of red sparkly stuff. It had thin straps and a low-cut front and back that showed off how much she kept in shape. All that yoga and working out and healthy eating paid off for her. For a minute, I almost forgot she was my birth mother. She just looked like a beautiful woman, and I saw her in a new way. But only for a few seconds.

Even though she looked really nice, with her hair pulled back off her face and more makeup than she usually wore, including shiny stuff below her eyebrows, she looked nervous and worried. She kept looking around the room like she was checking to see where everyone was standing and who they were talking to. She wasn't really acting like a hostess, making sure people had their drinks and food. She left all that to the catering staff. She seemed to want to know where Cameron was, or maybe she wanted to see where I was.

After a while, I realized what she was doing. She was watching Cameron's father almost like she was stalking him. It was really weird. Every time he came into the room where she was, she started drifting toward the doorway. She wouldn't leave the room; it wasn't like she was running away from him. It seemed like she wanted to know where he was, but she didn't want to be around him.

She hardly seemed to pay attention to the people she was talking to. Every few minutes, her head jerked around, checking to see where he was, then moving to adjust her position farther away from him. She never talked to him; she just kept moving like she was playing a board game.

I wanted to go outside and listen to the jazz group, but I really wanted to keep my eye on Ruth, and she was staying inside the house. Cameron seemed to be the only one having a good time. I guess that was a good thing, since it was his party. He was talking to everyone, laughing and drinking and eating like it was the time of his life.

Ruth, and Cheryl too, looked like mice running from a huge, hungry cat. Cheryl ate one egg roll and a bit of creamy cheese on a cracker. Ruth, as far as I could see, didn't take a single bite from all that delicious food. She sipped from her wineglass a few times, but mostly drank water. She smiled and nodded but did not seem like she was at a party at all. It made me tired watching her.

Just before eleven o'clock, she pulled her phone out of the tiny gold purse that had been hanging from her shoulder all night. She looked at the screen and tapped a short message. I thought all their friends were at the party, so I couldn't imagine who she would be sending messages to in the middle of a party late at night. A few minutes later, she walked out of the living room. I took a few sips of champagne to make sure nothing would slosh out of the glass when I walked, then followed her.

I stood at the end of the hallway and watched her. She was just outside the door of Cameron's study, looking at her phone. A few minutes later, Micah showed up, coming from the hallway that led from the entryway. They stood there whispering. At first, I thought maybe they were talking about a birthday present for Cameron. Then I decided it wasn't that at all. Ruth was almost shivering, like she was cold, but the sides of her hair were damp like she was sweating a little.

Then they went into the study and closed the door.

I put my champagne glass on a table and hurried back down the hall. I went through the living room and out onto the patio. I ran around the side of the house to the study window that looked out on one of the little garden areas that opened off several of the rooms of the house.

I crept along the side of the house until I was close to the window and looked in. The window was closed, but the desk light was on, so even though I couldn't hear them, I could see them clearly. They were standing next to the couch that was nestled between bookcases across from the desk.

They stood a few feet from each other. They were talking. Mostly Micah was talking, and Ruth was glaring at him. After a while, Micah took a few steps closer to the desk and patted

something I couldn't quite see. I moved closer and put my
face as close to the window as I could without pressing it
against the glass. He was patting a box wrapped with silver
paper with a red bow on it. So it was a birthday present after
all. Why were they being so secretive about it? Maybe
because the invitation said no gifts? But that didn't make
sense because he was Cameron's father. Of course he would
bring a present. And why were they hiding in Cameron's
study talking about it?

A minute later, Micah left the room. Ruth went to the
door and locked it. Then she walked to the bookcase and
pulled a bunch of books off the shelf. When the shelf was
empty, I saw there was a safe behind where the books had
been. She turned the dial and opened the door of the safe.
She picked up the gift, ripped off the paper and bow, and
opened the box. She started taking things out of the box and
putting them in the safe. Because her back was to me, I
couldn't see what it was, but all I could think was maybe
Micah had given her money. What else would she put in a
safe? She closed the door, turned the dial, and put the books
back in place. Crumpling the paper and bow in her hands,
and folding the box, she looked around the room. I ducked
away from the window and almost fell back into the little
pond behind me. Luckily, I grabbed the trunk of a small tree
and kept my balance. When I looked again, she was gone.

THE NEXT MORNING at five o'clock, there was a knock on my
bedroom door. The sound of it scared me because it snuck
into my dream like someone coming for me. Once I was
awake, I couldn't remember the dream, or what about it that
made me scared.

There was another knock, telling me it wasn't a dream,

but someone wanting me even though it was still dark outside, and I deserved to sleep in after the party. I got out of bed and went to the door.

Ruth was standing there dressed in jeans and a T-shirt, her hair washed and dried, and her face cleaned from all the glittery makeup of the night before. It was as if the party had never happened. This made me feel like all the balloons and confetti and champagne and seeing her and Micah whispering, then watching her rip open a fake gift and stuff something that must have been money into a safe had been the dream.

She was holding a dark blue zippered tote bag by the strap. It hung from her outstretched fingers as if a terrible smell were coming out of it and she didn't want it coming too close to her body. She moved her hand toward mine. "Here's your money."

I stared at the bag.

"It's the fifty thousand dollars you wanted. Take it."

I felt like I was still half asleep, back inside a dream.

"Will you take it? It's heavy."

She hung the strap over my wrist like it was a hook on the wall. My arm started to collapse from the weight, and it hurt as the bag pulled on my elbow.

She stepped back, turned, and walked down the hallway. I let the bag slide off my arm to the floor. I dragged it into the bedroom and closed the door. I put the bag on the bed, unzipped it, and took out twenty-five stacks of one-hundred-dollar bills held together with rubber bands. I stared at it for a few minutes, then started counting the bills in each stack. Sure enough, there was fifty thousand dollars. I couldn't believe there was so much. At the same time, it didn't look like such a huge amount, sitting in small piles on the bed.

I shoved it all under the blankets and crawled back into bed, feeling it touch my legs. I closed my eyes and thought about the money. I wondered what I would do with it. The idea of asking for it had come to me so fast, I hadn't thought about why I picked that number. I could buy a new car, but the car I had was good enough, and it seemed like a waste to spend so much on something I didn't really need. It wasn't enough to make a down payment on a house or even a condo. At least not in California.

For now, I would put it in my savings account. But the minute I had that thought, I wondered how it would work. I couldn't just walk into the bank with piles of cash and fill out a deposit slip. They would probably ask questions about it. I decided I'd have to worry about that later.

Turning onto my back and pushing the money away from my legs where it was tickling my skin, I closed my eyes. I thought about the night before. I thought about Ruth and Micah's whispering in the hallway and how Ruth looked like she really wanted to be yelling. I thought about the money.

Why did he give her the money to pay me? Did he already know about me all those years ago? Did she ask him for the money because he was the only person she knew who had enough or who would give her that much cash? Maybe he was the only one who would give her all that money without asking why.

But it seemed like she didn't really like him. It almost seemed like she hated him. She didn't want to invite him to Cameron's party until I made her. She tried to stay as far away from him all night until she had a secret meeting with him and got the money.

Then I remembered the very first night I had dinner with Ruth and Cameron and Cheryl. She went on and on about how she fell in love with Cameron when she was a teenager. She'd known him and his family a long time ago. Was it possible that Micah was my *father*? Why else would he hand over all that money? I remembered how Cheryl seemed so embarrassed that her daughter got pregnant, how she said it was *complicated*. She wasn't upset about her daughter getting pregnant when she was a teenager! It was *complicated* because my father was a friend of their family. Her boyfriend's dad!

My eyelids popped open, and I sat up as if a jolt of electricity had shot through my body. I remembered how he couldn't stop staring at me. It didn't feel like he was looking at my body because he wanted me. Not one bit. I knew that and I felt that, even if his wife didn't get it. He wanted to know if I looked like him.

I could not believe it. I could not believe the thoughts racing around in my head. Ruth had sex with her boyfriend's father! Before he was her boyfriend, I guess. But still. It was so icky. But she was a teenager. So maybe she didn't want to. No wonder she was so scared of anyone finding out. No wonder she didn't really like me. No wonder she didn't blink when I asked her to pay me so much money to not have Cameron find out.

It had to be true.

Micah was my father.

23

RUTH

Handing the cash to Nadia had made me feel oddly light. I knew it shouldn't have. It should have made me fear that she would immediately ask for more. It should have made me recognize that he'd been right, and I'd been utterly naïve in that it was just the beginning of her demands on me. It should have made me feel bound to Micah after having tried to sever any psychological connection to him throughout my life.

A voice in the back of my mind whispered these things to me, but I still felt ridiculously free in spite of that menacing sound clawing just beyond my conscious thoughts. Nadia had floated into my life, threatened me, then tried to play at being my daughter or my friend or something I couldn't define. She'd damaged my relationship with one of my closest friends, inserted herself into my mother's life, and treated my marriage like it was a carnival game. Now I could be rid of her. I so desperately wanted to believe that.

If she expected me to love her, she'd done everything she possibly could to prevent me from uncovering and nurturing those feelings.

The morning after his party, I doubted Cameron would go for his usual Sunday morning run, so I'd gotten up very early to get the money out of the safe before he discovered it. The chances of him opening the safe any time in the next few days were so slim they were nearly impossible, but I wasn't risking it. I handed her the money and walked away feeling calm and with a great sense of finality.

Tomorrow, I would tell her to leave our home and stop attending classes at the Wellness Center.

On Monday morning, I told Cameron I was taking the day off to finish putting the house back in order from the party. He gave me a strange look because the caterers had polished the kitchen as if they'd never been there. To her credit, Nadia had cleaned the dining room and removed all the decorations from the patio and inside the house. She'd vacuumed and dusted. There was no order to be restored, but he kissed me goodbye and thanked me again for the party.

The moment I heard the garage door close, I went to Nadia's room.

She opened the door and immediately glanced back at her laptop sitting on a pillow on the bed. "I'm working."

"I need to talk to you."

"My time on the keyboard is tracked. I can't be away from my screen."

"Tell your supervisor you need a break."

She heaved a dramatic sigh and went to the bed. She flopped down and tapped out a message. She waited, then began typing again. After several more minutes of this, she closed the laptop. "What's the fire drill?"

"Now that you have your money, it's time to move out."

She stared at me, her expression neutral. I waited for her to say something, but she continued staring as if she hadn't heard me.

"You can finish your work today," I said. "But you need to

pack this evening and be out of the house tomorrow morning."

Still, she maintained that steady, unconcerned gaze. It was making me nervous. I thought about the gun in the bottom of her backpack, and I felt a chill at the roots of my hair. It ran across my scalp like a hundred spiders, then raced down my spine. Was I the most incredibly blind, foolish, and naïve woman in the world? Her request for money was only the beginning. Her pretense at being my daughter and acting as if she wanted my love or affection were all part of some elaborate game.

A gentle frown spread slowly across her lips. "What kind of mother treats her daughter like this? I don't understand you at all."

"I could say the same."

"Could you?" She sighed. "You're living the dream. This fab house, running your own business ... a company with such an incredible brand you get interviewed on podcasts, and you have almost twenty thousand social media followers? You have a good-looking husband and *so* many friends. And, I should add, a mom who adores you." Her frown instantly changed to a wicked smile. "I'm staying right where I am."

"I gave you what you wanted."

"Did you?"

I had no idea what she wanted. It had become increasingly clear to me. How could I know? She refused to tell me, and it seemed to change on a daily basis. "What is your purpose in staying here?"

"Are you serious? Look at this house. It's amazing. I could never afford a house like this. Would fifty thousand dollars get me a house like this? I couldn't afford a one-bedroom condo with fifty thousand dollars."

Micah was right. The thought filled me with so much

shame I wanted to melt through the floorboards. It made me feel as if he had more power over me than ever. I felt as if both of them owned me, and I would never again have the life I'd always thought I had. Maybe it had all been an illusion. A long, elaborate lie I'd told myself.

There would be no end to her demands. And now that his birthday had passed, I had no way to distract Cameron from her inexplicable presence in our house. I felt like I was being crushed by concrete walls slowly moving closer together, pinning me inside. "I gave you what you asked for." My voice was shrill, and my panic was clear. "What more do you want from me?" The moment the words were out, I hated myself for asking. I'd offered her the world, and she knew it. The victory shimmered in her eyes.

She smirked. "I haven't decided."

"Why do you want to stay where you're not wanted?" That question too was a mistake. I was making this worse by the minute. If she did want my love, it was the worst possible thing I could have said. Her expression didn't register any hurt, but her expression was often disconnected from her behavior and her words, so it was impossible to know how she was feeling.

"I love this house. I like the Wellness Center. And it's so cool having a grandma. Even if my birth mother isn't much of a fan, my gramma seems to really like me. So I'm staying right where I am."

"I gave you the money you wanted. You said you would leave when I gave you fifty thousand dollars." I was repeating myself. I was losing. And I knew she had that gun. It was entirely possible I was putting myself and Cameron in danger, but I couldn't seem to stop.

"I could destroy your life. That's all you need to know." She smiled. "Now, I need to get back to work." She took a step back and closed the door in my face.

I stood there looking at the closed door. Tears began pouring down my cheeks. I couldn't stop them. I was terrified. I hadn't felt so alone since that day when my mother walked out of my bedroom after telling me it was my fault Micah had raped me, even though I hadn't known to use that word at the time.

Now the day stretched before me with nothing to do but entertain my fear of the unknown. Micah and Deanne were still at the hotel, as he'd promised. I wondered if he planned to get in touch with me to find out whether Nadia had made another demand for money. I wondered what he was planning in general. The way he'd spoken about needing to find a *solution* made me fear he would consider killing her if she didn't stop demanding money. Knowing about her gun, I wondered if even he was a match for her. Without ever knowing each other or having a moment's contact, perhaps father and daughter were cut from the same cloth.

I tried all morning to keep myself busy with an audiobook about nutrition. Only a few weeks earlier, I'd found the book gripping, but hadn't listened for a while for obvious reasons. Now my mind drifted every few minutes, and I was constantly pressing the circular arrow to go back a few paragraphs or a page. I finally gave up, my mind muddled and tired, feeling as if it were filled with rot.

Even though the weather was cool and cloudy, I changed into my swimsuit and dove into the pool. I swam thirty laps. While I swam, my mind was peacefully blank. I climbed out of the pool, immediately cold and instantly flooded with a fresh wave of fears. Rather, the same fears, recycled and amplified.

By evening, I couldn't have said what I'd done for the rest of the day. When Cameron asked, I lied.

I made dinner and invited my mother to join us, for the sole purpose of not having to engage in conversation. It worked. She and Nadia chattered like magpies. They behaved as if they were the best of friends, rehashing the success of the party for the second evening in a row.

Cameron was another story. His attention was focused on Nadia, as I expected it would be. The shock and excitement of the party had faded, and he'd now returned to wondering what she was doing in our home. Her presence defied explanation, and I could feel the question growing in his mind. The moment we were alone, he was going to pressure me into not only explaining my strange behavior, but into getting rid of her. I was a little surprised he hadn't ordered her out of the house himself. Only his inbred politeness and the natural concern he had for our clients kept him from packing her bags himself. I was so fearful of what was coming, I could hardly lift my fork to my mouth.

While I was loading the dinner plates into the dishwasher as slowly as was humanly possible, Cameron came up beside me. He touched my shoulder. "Let your mother take care of this. We need to talk."

"I—"

"Cheryl?" He raised his voice, walking toward the entrance to the dining room. "Will you finish with the kitchen? Ruth and I are going to have a glass of wine on our patio." It wasn't a request. His tone was clear and firm. He refilled our wineglasses, picked them up, and left the room. I followed like a chastised child.

We passed through our bedroom and out to the secluded patio surrounded by sheltering ferns and large leafy plants. Adding to the seclusion was a small pond with a waterfall that tumbled over an artfully placed pile of rocks. Several potted orchids stood at one corner, and two wicker chairs were side by side with a table between. When we were settled, he said, "When is Nadia leaving?"

I picked up my glass and took a long, unhealthy swallow

of wine. I wanted to down the entire glass, if for no other reason than to turn his attention to my dangerous consumption of alcohol. Anything but the question he'd asked.

"I haven't thought about it," I said. "I'm honestly still a little tired from the party." I was ashamed of the self-pitying tone in my voice, but it was the best I could come up with. And I was feeling decidedly full of self-pity, overwhelmed by a sense of failure, and utterly alone in the world.

Cameron sighed. He reached across the table and circled his hand around my wrist. "It was a great party. I appreciate everything you did for me. Especially inviting Dad. That shocked me almost as much as the party." He laughed as if he wasn't sure what to make of it. "After all these years of not wanting him in our house, what changed?" He let go of my wrist and picked up his wineglass, perhaps not sure he was ready to hear the answer. "It meant a lot to me. I really appreciate that you included him. But ..." He laughed again.

I saw my chance. It felt like an opening in the clouds after a week of torrential rain. "It was Nadia."

"What?"

"I hadn't planned such a large party. I was thinking of just a few friends," I lied. "She kept pushing for something grander. Then, because it was a milestone, she insisted your father should be here."

He didn't say anything. He put his wineglass on the table with a soft click of glass upon glass. We sat in silence for several minutes. When he spoke again, it was to ask a question about the Wellness Center.

I still felt the chasm growing wider between us, but for a while, I could put aside my fear that he would shove Nadia out onto the sidewalk himself. I wondered how much longer I had.

24

I was never leaving Ruth's house. Why should I? In my new home, I had a beautiful bedroom, a swimming pool, a good amount of money to spend however I wanted—even enough to quit my annoying job that chained me to my computer so that I couldn't even pee without asking permission. I hadn't decided if I wanted to quit, but I might.

First, I had other things on my mind. Like finding out everything I could about Micah Monroe, who I was ninety-nine percent sure was my father. Tiny explosions kept going off in my head that made it hard to pay attention to my job. The minute I finished for the day, I closed the windows I needed for work and opened a brand-new search window.

His name was weird enough that it was easy to find things about him. I found his Facebook page first. It didn't have a lot —just vacation photos and stupid jokes and a few funny videos. At least I knew he had a sense of humor. And I knew he had a lot of money, which I already knew since he'd pulled fifty thousand dollars out of his pocket and handed it to Ruth the same day he arrived for his son's birthday party.

He was a real estate developer. I wasn't really sure what that meant, but he did like to flash it around on Facebook that he took expensive vacations in five-star hotels and had a huge boat and two houses, one of which was in Hawaii.

I found out he lived in San Diego. His other son lived in France, which I already knew, and he and Deanne spent a month there every spring. He didn't have any grandkids, so maybe he should have been happy to find out about me, but it didn't seem like it. I guess considering the circumstances, I was as inconvenient and embarrassing to him as I was to Ruth.

It felt weird to know that the two people who should have loved me had made me by mistake and wished I never existed, but I tried not to obsess over that all the time. And I still wanted to know about him. I couldn't help myself. I did obsess over that. It was exactly the same as when I found out about Ruth. I had to find every crumb of information I could.

I found publicity pictures of him from his company PR department and a headshot on his company website. I even found pictures of him when he was in college and graduate school. I found a picture of him at a pub in Scotland when he was twenty-six. Each thing I found made me want more, but none of it really told me very much at all.

Finally, I got tired of looking.

The next day, I went to his luxury motel, which thanks to Deanne's complaining at the party, I knew the name of. I had no idea what room they were in, and I didn't want to ask since I was sure the motel would let them know. I sat in my car parked across from the parking area and waited. I also didn't know what kind of car they had rented, so I had to pay close attention to every single car going into the parking lot and also watch everyone coming out of the motel. It was very intense and tiring, but I had two cans of Red Bull, and I sipped them and ate spicy Doritos and waited.

Finally, I saw Micah and Deanne get out of a white sports car and walk toward the motel. I put on a huge sun hat and big white sunglasses. I was already wearing a skimpy bikini I'd bought in an expensive store with some of my money, and an exotic see-through cover-up, although it wasn't really a cover-up since you could see everything. I figured in that, no one would ask—*Are you staying at this upscale motel?* I looked like I had plenty of money to stay there.

I hurried across the street and slipped into the garden area. I saw them just as they stopped at the little patio outside their room. I walked along the path to the pool like I owned the place. I found a lounge chair and stretched out and spent the rest of the day looking at the door to their room.

They didn't come out until dinnertime. I had to get up off the chair really fast, but I managed to get to my car in time to follow them to an Italian restaurant. I was starving and would have liked a nice pasta dinner myself, but my outfit obviously wouldn't work in a restaurant. While they were safely inside eating dinner, I shimmied out of my cover-up, pulled on a sundress, and brushed my hair. I walked to a small market and bought a pre-made ham sandwich. I went back to my car and ate it. They stayed at dinner for almost two hours, which was boring, but also weirdly gripping because I could see them through the large window facing the street. I couldn't tear myself away, even though all I saw was a blurry view of them eating and drinking and probably talking, although I couldn't see clearly enough to be sure they actually spoke. What did Deanne have to say to an old guy like Micah? Maybe she just complained. Age doesn't matter when you're a complainer—anyone with a pulse will do.

At the motel, I wriggled around and pulled on yoga pants and a hoodie. I waited in my car until after midnight. I couldn't sleep because of the Red Bull, of which I'd slammed two more cans. I was all stirred up inside, and it wasn't just the Red Bull. It was these two people—Ruth and Micah—who threw me away like an empty can, not even bothering to recycle, just tossing me into the landfill.

They had so much money it was like a thick shell that nothing could get inside. Maybe more like an underground bunker, the kind of shelter rich people build so if there's some global disaster, they will be safe with food and water and luxury at a remote, well-protected location, while the rest of the human race suffers horrifying disease and starvation and pain.

I wanted them to feel something, and they felt nothing.

Micah had stood there at that party and stared at me for more than ten minutes, and not even a single tear came into his eyes. He didn't smile or look like he had a moment of feeling or sadness. He didn't look like he wanted to give me a hug or ask me how I was doing. He didn't want to know anything about me. He just wanted to tell me how successful his sons were and let his wife complain about all her first world problems that were even more precious than the usual first world problems.

If seeing me didn't make him feel something about me, the only thing left to do was the same treatment as for Ruth. Maybe I could make him feel a tiny bit afraid.

I drove to a discount store and bought a kitchen knife, some antiseptic, bandages, and a dish towel. Then I drove to a liquor store and bought a pint of vodka.

With my new purchases in my bag, I returned to the motel and walked to the garden area. Most of the rooms were dark, including Micah's, but the path was lined with dim lights that showed my feet as I walked. I found a bench nestled by a small flowering tree and sat down.

I drank a few shots of vodka and waited. It hit me after a few minutes, even though combining it with all that Red Bull made me wired and boozy at the same time, which was a very weird feeling. I swallowed a few more shots and waited some more. When I was feeling good and relaxed and a little numb, I used the towel to wipe the top of the bottle where my mouth had touched it and put on the cap. I wiped the whole bottle, just in case, and dropped it into my bag.

Using my phone for light, I walked to Micah's room. Without stopping to think long enough to be afraid, I dragged the knife across my lower arm just below my elbow until blood bubbled out. I let it drip all over the ground in front of the door. I smeared some on the towel and rubbed it on their doorknob and on the door. I let more drip on the ground. I used the towel to take the bottle out of my bag and dropped it on the ground. It broke, as I'd hoped it would. The sound wasn't too loud.

It felt as if the breeze shifted slightly. I turned, wondering if someone was out walking around in the dark. Maybe the crash was louder than I'd realized. I peered through the shadows, but saw no one. I took a slow, steady breath. When I let it out, everything around me was silent.

I wrapped the towel around my arm and ran along the path and out of the garden toward the street, imagining Micah's fear, even if it was just a tiny flame, when he saw that blood. I walked two blocks to a little park, where I sat down and cleaned my arm and bandaged it. After I caught my breath and made sure I wasn't feeling dizzy, I walked slowly back to my car.

I sat for a while in my car, feeling my heart beat so hard I could feel it in my fingertips. Finally, I drifted to sleep. It was almost three in the morning when I woke and drove back to Ruth's house. They had a security camera, so I went around the side of the house and spent the rest of the night on one of their lounge chairs beside the pool. I'd been staying with them long enough that I knew the parts of the backyard where the camera couldn't see. If it still caught me, and if they noticed, I could always tell them I went out for a late-night swim but fell asleep before I got in the water.

25

RUTH

I worked from home for the second day in a row. I felt
the need to keep an eye on Nadia even though while I
was there, she was sequestered in our guest room, and I
couldn't actually see what she was up to. When I'd been out
of the house, our security cameras told us when she was
coming and going, but not what she was doing when she was
alone in our house.

During most of her days, she'd been hanging out at the
Wellness Center after her early morning work schedule, so I
hadn't been concerned about it, but now I was suddenly overcome with worry about what she was doing when she had
unrestricted access to our home. It wasn't as if she could rob
us, so I wasn't sure why this fear had just now surfaced.
Maybe it had been suppressed by greater fears while I was
trying to find a source for the money. Maybe it had emerged
because giving her the money had shown me I had absolutely no idea what she wanted or how long she planned to
torment me. I was beginning to think she planned to stay
until she could claim some kind of legal right to avoiding

eviction. Maybe she thought she could make a life inside our house for the rest of my life.

It was possible my mother's presence in the guest cottage had given me a false sense of security.

After doing some work on the computer, catching up on email and writing performance reviews for some of our employees, I went to the kitchen to make a cup of tea. I stood waiting for the kettle to boil, looking out the back window.

As I gazed at the garden, my thoughts nearly frozen, I saw my mother step out through her front door. She looked across the yard, and our eyes met. We stood like that for a long time, looking directly at each other. The kettle reached a boil and shut off, but I didn't lift it off the heating disk as I watched my mother begin walking toward the house.

She opened the door to the kitchen and stepped inside. "I've been wanting to talk to you," she said.

Instinct told me what was coming next as she looked into my eyes, her gaze unwavering. "Is Nadia your daughter?"

I laughed. I didn't even have to fake my reaction that suggested her question was ridiculous. All the stress, the constant fear erupted in the hysterical laugh that burst from the pit of my belly. "What kind of question is that?"

"It's a yes or no question. And I think you just answered it."

"I have no idea why you would think that." I turned to the kettle and picked it up. I poured water over the strainer holding my tea leaves, moving it gently to soak each section equally.

"You can't hide from me by turning your back. I know you. Her birthday is February third."

"So? Hundreds of thousands of people were born that day."

"Ruth, don't play games. The odds are astronomical. I admit, I don't know the year, but she's the right age. She showed up here out of nowhere, and you gave no explanation for inviting a total stranger to live with you. All this nonsense about back pain is laughable. And she told me she's adopted."

The kettle felt unbearably heavy in my hand as I tried to place it carefully back on the stand. My wrist felt so weak, it seemed the weight of the kettle would cause my bones to fracture. There didn't seem to be any point in trying to misdirect her attention any further. She knew. I was prolonging the inevitable. "The woman who adopted her told her my name before she died."

"Maybe it's not such a bad thing ... after all this time."

I whirled to face her. "Not such a bad thing? Are you insane? She's trying to destroy my life! She demanded fifty thousand dollars not to tell Cameron who she is. Can you imagine how he'd feel? And how am I supposed to get that kind of money without Cameron finding out? Have you forgotten everything? You never understood what happened. You never *acknowledged* what happened. And now, I gave her the money. Micah paid it, but she won't leave!"

She took a step back as if she thought I might slap her. She stared at me for a few seconds. "Calm down."

"Don't tell me to calm down."

"Okay. I understand why you're upset. And it's awful that asking for money is the path she chose—"

"She didn't *ask for money*. She demanded it. She threatened to tell Cameron who she was!"

"Maybe it's time for him to know."

"That his father raped me?!"

"If you wouldn't be so ... it was a long time ago. And he never ... he didn't. Why do you have to use that word? It's so ugly."

"What he did was ugly. You should have helped me report it. You should have told him then I was pregnant."

"I was trying to protect you from more pain." She moved toward me, coming around the kitchen island as if she planned to hug me.

I shoved my hips into the corner formed by two lengths of the counter. "You were trying to protect yourself."

The words stopped her from coming closer.

"That's not true, sweetie. I love you so much. You have no idea. I wanted you to have the best life possible. And a baby would have ruined that. I did my very best under the circumstances. Why can't you see that? Why can't you forgive me?"

"Because you refuse to say what's true. Micah raped me."

My mother's eyes grew teary. "I know you have bad memories, but it's not fair to use that word against such an old family friend. You drank champagne with him. That gave him the impression you were an adult. Men interpret situations like that in a certain way and—"

"I was fifteen! And he drugged me. How is that *interpretation*?"

"Yes. I'm aware, Ruth. And legally that makes it what you say. But Micah loved you. He loved our family. He was a friend. Yes, what he did was very wrong. But you should have spoken up. He didn't really hurt you."

We'd had this conversation before. Not often, but often enough that my hatred for her bloomed again each time, and it took months for it to wither and finally fade into a simmering resentment that mostly remained in the background. Sometimes, I wondered why I allowed her in my life at all, why I felt the obligation I did to support her with housing and the occasional gift of extra cash. Most of all, I wondered whether we even had a genuine relationship at all. How could we?

Many women, most women with self-respect, would have cut all ties with a mother who refused to acknowledge their rape. I wasn't sure if part of the problem was that it had taken me well into adulthood to acknowledge it myself, or if I should have been proud of myself for being a person with enough generosity to find other facets to love in my mother. It was possible I had been still living in a state of confusion that prevented me from seeing anything clearly, so I simply put it all in a virtual closet that I never used, locked it, and dropped the key where I couldn't reach it.

After Micah assaulted me, after the baby was born and spirited away by my mother and that woman, I gradually began to recover, without help from anyone but my own inner resources. I realized I still had a powerful attraction to Cameron, and I wasn't going to let Micah destroy that, too.

He and his father were separate entities. I didn't see the faintest glimmer of that monster in his son. Cameron had been my friend since childhood, while Micah lived in my parents' world. After my father died, Micah was a friend to my mother. He meant almost nothing to me.

Cameron and I were engaged before I gave much thought to the implications of having Micah as my father-in-law. Only then did I consider the horror of having to encounter the man who drugged me and forced himself upon me at holiday dinners and family celebrations for the rest of my life. Maybe it was the agreement that Cameron and I made not to have children that allowed me to find a way to distance myself. But I wasn't really sure I could sort out all my reasoning for the things I'd felt and the decisions I'd made, even now.

All I was clear about was what I wanted more than life itself—I wanted to share every year that would be given to me with Cameron Monroe.

I spoke with the strength inside me finally matching the strength of my voice. "Micah hurt me in ways you can't imagine because you refuse to open your eyes and see reality. And you hurt me by always, every day of your life, believing his distorted perception over mine. It's as if my feelings aren't real and my experience never happened. You owe me."

"So you've said." She started toward the back door. "And you never let me forget. Not for a single day."

"Nadia has the fifty thousand dollars she demanded, but she still won't move out. Apparently, she likes thinking of you as her granny. I want you to tell her she needs to find another place to live. Now."

"That's not fair."

"Nothing is. You need to do this for me. Got it?"

"Sure. Whatever you say." She opened the door and went out. I didn't watch her cross the yard.

26

NADIA

I had just finished swimming ten laps in the silky warm water of the pool. I pulled myself up on the edge and was sitting there, staring up at the night sky. It seemed slightly dim because I was surrounded by pale blue, lit by an underwater light that made it glow almost neon. The stars were nothing but tiny flecks that hardly seemed to sparkle with all that neon blue filling my eyeballs.

"Did you have a good swim?"

Cheryl's voice was soft because she was standing very close to me. It scared me a little that she'd snuck up on me like that.

"Aren't you cold, sitting there all wet?"

"Not really."

"I'll get your towel."

"I'm fine."

A minute later, I felt the towel on my back and shoulders. She patted it along my shoulder blades. "There, isn't that better?"

I nodded. It did feel nice. No one had ever done something like that for me. It made me feel like I was a little girl and that someone was taking care of me. I really couldn't remember my mom doing things like that. She always seemed so busy and a little distracted. Obviously, she had, but I was too small to remember. Because there were so many of us, we started at a young age having to take care of ourselves—packing our own lunches for school and folding our own clothes when they came out of the dryer. We helped clean the house on Saturday mornings, and there were chores after dinner every night.

I heard the sound of metal scraping on the concrete as Cheryl dragged a chair to the edge of the pool. She sat down. She was behind me since I was still sitting with my lower legs in the water. I couldn't see anything but her feet, wearing brown leather sandals with a lot of crisscrossing straps, her toenails painted a dark color that I couldn't make out, even with the neon blue light.

"When you told me you were adopted and the date of your birth," she said, "I had a pretty good idea who you are."

I didn't say anything. I wasn't sure if she was trying to trick me into telling her or if she really knew.

"You don't have to pretend anymore. I'm really not sure why you felt you couldn't tell us right away. Or rather ... why you ... well, anyway. Now I know."

She didn't say anything else for a few minutes. Maybe she wanted me to talk, but I'm not sure what she thought I was going to say. I needed to know what she knew. And I had no idea where she was going with all this. Did she want to try to get the money back? Was she going to tell me Ruth really loved me all along? Was she going to tell me who my father was? There were so many things.

"I guess you're not going to tell me why, and I suppose that's your business. Maybe you were scared, and that's understandable."

That made me want to laugh. She knew nothing about me, and now she was going to assume that because we had some genetic thread connecting us, she could imagine she knew all the things in my head? It was really funny to me, but I kept myself from laughing out loud.

"The thing is, it might be better if you move out. Since Cameron doesn't know about you. And he can't, obviously, which I'm sure you understand." She laughed. It was a really nervous giggle, like she was a little kid, but also kind of hysterical. "Of course, you understand since you asked for ... well. It would be better if you found your own place. And you can certainly afford it now."

"You still don't want me? Wow. That's so harsh."

"No. Oh, no, sweetheart. That's not it." She leaned forward and put her hand on my shoulder.

"Then why are you kicking me out?"

"I'm not. I—"

"*She* is. She told you to kick me out because she never wanted me, and she still doesn't. I get it." I fluttered my feet gently, watching the water move, then lifted my toes out and stared at them.

A moment later, she was sitting beside me with her arm around my shoulders. "It's difficult to explain. It's confusing because Cameron doesn't understand why you're here, and we can't tell him. But I don't want you to feel unwanted. I love knowing I get a chance to have a granddaughter when I thought that was something I would never have. I feel so blessed to have you in my life." She squeezed my shoulders. "And that wouldn't change if you got a little apartment nearby."

I let my feet dip below the surface.

"Please tell me you understand," she said.

"Not really."

"Oh, Nadia. I'm so sorry. I made some mistakes in the

past. We all made mistakes. We're flawed human beings, every single one of us. You know that, don't you?"

"Absolutely."

"And I definitely made mistakes. But I'm so grateful for the chance to correct them. It's almost like a do-over."

"Is it?"

"Well, maybe not that. But a chance to fix things, to do better, to make life better for you. And for Ruth. I wasn't always the mother I should have been. I—"

Her voice was very weak and so quiet it was almost hard to hear her over the rumble of the pool filter. The motor suddenly sounded obnoxiously loud. It was a mechanical sound that destroyed the soft color of the water and the silence of the night sky above us. Just that rumble and growl. It sounded so much louder at night when there were no other neighborhood sounds. Or maybe because that's all I was paying attention to.

"Please tell me you forgive me. I want to do better. Maybe Ruth has let you down because I let you down. No one meant to hurt you. We did the best we could with the situation we were faced with. Ruth's daddy was gone; it was just the two of us. And she was so young. She had no idea what to do with a baby. And I couldn't ... I just couldn't ..." She heaved a loud sigh as if I was supposed to understand how difficult her life was or something. I don't know.

I waited to hear what other interesting things she would say. Nothing. I guess that was all she had.

"It's a lot to think about," she said. "I'm thankful you gave me a chance to tell you how I feel, and to ask for your forgiveness. For myself and for Ruth. You have to know we did our best. Our very best that we could at the time. And now, we can start fresh from here. Right?" She squeezed me again.

I thought she might leave, but she stayed right there with her arm gripping my shoulders.

More than anything, I wanted to fling myself into the pool, dragging her under the water with me.

"When did she say she'll be leaving?" I was so certain my mother had succeeded where I'd failed with Nadia, I blurted out the words the moment she opened her door.

I'd rushed out of the house as soon as I was dressed, before the sun was fully up. I wanted to talk to her without the curious eyes of my husband or the young woman I couldn't call my daughter, even in my own thoughts.

My mother was a force to be reckoned with. She'd always had her way in my life, and I had no doubt she'd found a way to convince Nadia to move out of our house, to get out of my life and give me some breathing space.

"She was deeply hurt."

I stared at her, unseeing, hardly able to think. "Hurt?"

"She feels very rejected that you didn't want her as a child and that you can't find love in—"

"You told her you know who she is? Why would you do that? She's a time bomb, and she's going to tell Cameron if I can't get her out of my life! Don't you get that?"

"What's the big secret? I know about her, so I don't see why—"

"Because it gives her power! The more she knows, the more she can find ways to destroy my life."

"Don't be so dramatic."

"I'm not. You should not have told her. You've made things ten times worse."

"I can't do anything right."

"This isn't about you. I asked you to help fix this situation, and you turned it into something emotional. She doesn't want a relationship with me. Or with you. She wants money. She wants to destroy my life."

"She's a young woman in pain who just lost the only mother she knew."

"Just stop. Stop feeling sorry for her."

"I'm her grandmother."

"*Now* you want to be her grandmother? Where was that feeling twenty years ago?"

She stepped back from the doorway. "You need to calm down. I'm doing the best I can. I've always tried to do the best for you, and no matter what I do, you're angry. I know I made mistakes. I did what I thought was best at the time. Why can't you let it go? You're making everything worse by hanging onto the past."

Tears welled up in my eyes. I couldn't see her face, couldn't read her expression. I wasn't sure if I was angry or scared out of my mind. I did know that I was getting absolutely no help from her. It felt like she was sabotaging my pathetic attempt to get control of my life out of Nadia's hands.

"Please don't get yourself so worked up."

The tears spilled over. I felt an inexplicable sense of shame for crying in front of my mother. I hated myself for it, hated that she saw me weak and vulnerable. Since that day she'd walked out of my bedroom after telling me not to speak about what Micah had done, after telling me to treat him with respect as if it hadn't happened, as if it had all been a huge misunderstanding.

After that day, I'd closed myself off from her. She was a person in my life to whom I owed attention and respect because she'd raised me. She was my mother. But once again, she'd failed completely to do the simplest thing to help me. She'd made it worse.

I could imagine what Nadia would do now that she was aware that my mother knew who she was. I couldn't think of what the specifics might be, but I knew her mind was far craftier than mine. She would come up with something. She would find a way to turn it back on me, to frighten me more, to threaten me until she broke me.

My mother put her hands on her hips. The disapproval in her gaze made me feel like I was ten years old. In a single beat of my heart, I was looking up at her, knowing I'd done a terrible thing, stealing a candy bar while she was doing the grocery shopping. She was going to make me return it to the store and tell the manager what I'd done. It didn't matter at all that she'd promised me a candy bar and changed her mind. I was to stop blaming her for things I did that were wrong.

"I think you need to do some soul-searching, Ruth. You need to realize that I'm not the whole problem here. Maybe if you stop blaming me for everything bad in your life, you'll be able to heal. I admit, I made some mistakes. Some big mistakes. But you won't ever acknowledge that you did a single thing that wasn't absolutely perfect. You need to stop blaming me. He was the one who upset you, not me. I tried to pick up the pieces as best I could, but what happened to you, what he did, is not my fault." She put her hand on the door and closed it slowly until the latch clicked softly into place.

I walked back to my house. I wasn't sure if I hated her or

just felt utterly defeated. I was tired of trying to explain. Tired of fighting. Just tired.

NADIA

After Cheryl had her "grandmama talk" with me, it was really clear things were getting ready to change. Now that Ruth had given me all that cash, she was going to find a way to get me out of the house, even if she had to get her mom to do it. I wondered if she would go so far as to call the police. I didn't think so because she still had to be worried that I would tell her secret to Cameron. No matter how much money she gave me, I would always have her secret. Unless she finally got so sick of me, she decided to tell him the truth. So far, it didn't seem like she was thinking in that direction.

The thing that was bothering me the most was that it had been four days since Cameron's surprise party and Micah and Deanne were still staying at their exclusive motel. I knew because I'd driven past it every day, several times a day, and looked for their car. I'd sat by the pool a few more times and watched their room. Twice I'd seen them go out, but I hadn't followed them. I'd just waited to see what time they came home.

I wasn't sure why I was doing that. I just felt like I should know what they were up to. I hoped I would notice they were acting afraid after finding the blood, but of course, they weren't. I couldn't figure out why they were hanging around town instead of going back to their home in San Diego. Cameron had been home for dinner every night, and when I went to the Wellness Center, he was always there, so as far as I could tell, he hadn't spent a single minute with his dad.

Did he and Ruth think I was going to ask for more money right away? So maybe, instead of me watching him, he was here keeping an eye on me!

Then I started worrying. Ruth hadn't gone to work at the Wellness Center for two days after the party, *working from home*. But what was she really doing? Maybe they were planning something. Maybe she already knew I wouldn't move out just because Cheryl asked me to. Maybe that was a game to give me a false sense of security.

I could totally believe that Ruth and Micah had some idea of how to get rid of me. Maybe they were working on a way to make it look like I stole the money. But no matter what they came up with, I still knew their secret. I could still tell Cameron. So there wasn't anything they could really do to me.

Were they planning to *kill* me? Would they actually go that far? They didn't seem like killers. But how else could they make sure Cameron didn't find out what happened? I thought about Micah's icy-cold wife. All she cared about was the motel living up to her five-star standard and her sumptuous hair and expensive clothes. She seemed like she would be up for killing someone. Absolutely.

The sun was going down when I drove to their motel. It was hard to think of Micah as my father. He didn't even seem like Cameron's father. He didn't seem like a father at all. He seemed like a character in a movie who wore a gold ring on his pinkie and unbuttoned his shirt too far to show his chest hair even though a lot of it was gray. He didn't do either of those things, but that's what he made me think about.

When I entered the garden area, I saw Micah and Deanne lying on lounge chairs by the pool. Two glasses of red wine stood on the table between them. Finally, some luck. Watching them was much better than staring at their door, wondering if they would come out, then seeing them only for the few seconds it took them to walk through the garden to their car.

I sat on a bench near a small flowering tree and tried to make myself look inconspicuous. I watched them sip wine. I watched Micah get up and dive into the pool, swim one lap, then climb out and walk back to his lounge chair. I listened to Deanne squeal when he shook his hair and let drops of water fall on her skin.

After about forty-five minutes, they picked up their things and went to their room. Seeing how she walked, how she acted as if the gardens were her personal space, I could imagine her doing whatever Micah wanted, including getting rid of the inconvenient daughter that had come crashing into his life. Maybe I was going to have to change my plans. Not that I had a solid plan anymore. Everything had gotten all messed up in my head. But I would keep watching them, and I would start watching my back.

I went to my car and rested my forehead on the steering wheel.

The first day I walked into the Second Chance Wellness Center, and even before that, when I was driving down Interstate 5 from Washington to California, I thought I had a plan. I knew what I wanted. But somewhere along the way, it had gotten messed up.

One minute, I still wanted to punish Ruth for not trying to find me, and the next minute, I had all these feelings coming up out of the ground where I thought they were buried. I still wanted to make her see what a bad mother she was and make her feel scared that her life might not turn out so great either. But I also wanted her to cry and say she was sorry she hadn't kept me.

Why couldn't my life be simple? Like Kellyn's. She was lucky to be an only child, with a mom who was completely devoted to her. I thought about Kellyn doing her homework in the café. I thought about how pissed her mom got just because I took her for ice cream. Maybe her life wasn't perfect either.

Justine acted like she was some magical fairy-godmother type of mom. The mom of your dreams. A TV mom. She was such a perfect mom she guarded her daughter from scum like me. But she wasn't all that great. Kellyn couldn't have her own life; she had to practically live at the Wellness Center, where there was no one her age.

I started my car and entered Justine's address into my map. Kellyn had given it to me when I told her I wanted to add her to my Christmas card list. And that was the truth. I did. I drove to their apartment and found a spot right next to Justine's car.

Leaving my headlights on, I stared at the picture window into a room that looked like a combination living and dining room. The blinds were down, but they hadn't twisted them closed, so I could see them moving around. Every so often, one of them walked to the table and put something down. They were obviously getting ready to eat dinner.

After a few minutes, both of them sat at the table. I turned on my high beams, and I saw Justine wince. She put her hand across her brow like she was trying to block the glare. She stood and walked to the window, looking out at my car. She reached for the wand to close the blinds.

I flashed my lights from bright to regular three times.

She let go of the wand and stepped away from the

window. For a moment, I saw nothing; then the front door opened. She came outside.

After watching her squint at me, trying to figure out if she knew who was in the car, I turned off my lights.

I saw the recognition flash across her face as she looked angry, then scared. She quickly turned angry again and hurried up to the car, so close I could see the stitching on her jeans. She pounded her fist on the glass. "Open the window."

I poked the button and lowered the window a few inches.

"You need to leave right now, or I'm calling the police."

I laughed. "Chill a little, will you? I just pulled off the street to make a call." I held up my phone.

"It doesn't look like you're talking to anyone, and you—"

"They didn't answer." I smiled.

"Then you can leave."

"What are you so *upset* about? It's a public lot, and I'm being safe ... not using my phone while driving."

"It's not a public lot, just so you know. And you were flashing your lights at me." She pulled her own phone out of her pocket. "Leave. Now."

"Did anyone ever tell you that you're a little paranoid? I turned my lights to bright when I meant to turn them off. Sorry if they bothered you."

She unlocked her phone. "I'm calling the police now."

"Why don't you go back to your apartment and eat dinner before it gets cold? And keep your little girl company. She shouldn't be left alone."

"Don't talk to me about—"

I started the car and put it into reverse. I stepped on the gas, not too hard, but it forced her to jump away from the window, and she almost lost her balance.

I felt pretty excellent driving out of the parking lot and heading toward Ruth's house. But by the time I turned into Ruth and Cameron's driveway, I didn't feel better at all.

Justine approached me in the parking lot as I got out of my car. I hadn't even pulled my bag out of the backseat when she was standing beside me as if she'd materialized like a prophetic angel from the cloudy sky.

"Hey," I said. "Is everything okay? You look—"

"No, I'm not okay. Your little friend sat outside my apartment last night, flashing her lights at me, scaring me half to death."

"Are you sure it was her?" I reached into the backseat and grabbed my bag.

"Yes. I wouldn't make an accusation like that without being sure. I confronted her, and she laughed at me like she was deranged. Which was even more terrifying."

I slammed the car door closed. Justine was standing so close, I felt myself pressing my back against the side of the car. "She's not deranged. She ..." As I spoke the words, I wondered. Was I lying to myself as well as to Justine? Nadia certainly wasn't behaving like a normal person. She'd been unstable from the start. My mother thought it was simply from experiencing grief so recently, and at a relatively young age. Was that all? I couldn't be sure.

"She sat in her car, watching us, then flashed her lights like it was a warning. That's creepy and you know it. She meant to scare us. She might have sat there all night if I hadn't gone out there. Poor Kellyn—"

"Was she upset?"

"The point is, she's got some kind of hold over you that I don't get. She wants something. If nothing else, she's taking advantage of you, and you're letting her."

"You're misinterpreting everything."

"I don't think I am. As long as she's around, I can't trust you. I hate saying that, and I'm sorry, maybe I'm wrong, but I have to go with my gut. So I'm going to ask my cousin to be Kellyn's guardian. I know it's just names on a paper and probably nothing will happen anyway, but I don't feel comfortable. I wanted to let you know." She turned and began walking away from me, her running shoes allowing her to move much more quickly than I could in my gladiator sandals.

I called after her—"Wait!"

She kept walking, moving faster as if she wanted to escape from me.

"Justine, please wait. Let me talk to you."

I thought she slowed, but I couldn't be sure. I started jogging, my bag thumping against my hip, making me feel off-balance. I caught up to her, so she must have allowed it, which gave me hope that her decision wasn't final.

The fact was I felt honored to be Kellyn's guardian. The thought of Justine not trusting me, of thinking I couldn't provide a good home for Kellyn, hurt more than I would have imagined it could.

It was so strange that Nadia had sat outside Justine's apartment, watching them. Justine had a right to be scared.

And when I thought about the gun, I was even more scared. I could imagine what Justine would say if she knew about that. I felt slightly guilty for not telling her, which made me doubly scared.

Part of me thought Nadia only had the gun to make herself feel safe, but another part of me thought she'd already proven who she was. If I continued to close my eyes instead of considering that she might use it on someone I loved, I could be writing their death sentence myself. I shivered.

Justine looked at me. "You know I'm right."

I shook my head. "It's really strange that she sat in her car, I know. But I don't think ... she would never hurt Kellyn. I know you don't trust her, and I can understand why, because you don't know her."

She started walking again. "I don't want to hear your denial."

"Please." Again, I was scrambling to catch up. "I'm the same person I've always been. Your friend. I adore Kellyn. Look, since it's spring break, let me take her to the Boardwalk tomorrow. She loves the arcade games, and we can get veggie burritos or something and eat lunch on the beach after she's done with the amusement park stuff."

"I don't—"

"I won't tell Nadia anything about it. It will just be Kellyn and me."

"It wouldn't change anything. I still can't trust her in your home. I can't trust that you'll—"

"I know. I respect your feelings even if I think ... it's okay. But let me do this."

"Sure. Okay. She would love it." She gave me a thin smile even though she was taking small steps away from me. "You absolutely cannot tell Nadia. Don't even tell her you're spending time with Kellyn. And make sure she doesn't follow you."

I laughed.

She glared at me. "I'm serious."

"Okay. I'm sorry I laughed."

We walked to the lobby doors together. I told her I would pick Kellyn up at ten the next morning. She nodded but didn't turn to say anything more. I felt like her straight shoulders and firm posture told me that I shouldn't expect her to think any differently after my outing with Kellyn. I was not going to prove how much Kellyn enjoyed my company and how connected she felt to me. To Justine, I'd become nothing but a backup childcare provider, helping out during one day of spring break. At least it would give me a chance to finally apologize properly to Kellyn for having that moment of doubt when she said she hadn't taken my emerald heart.

I settled at my desk, feeling utterly defeated.

Was there something deeply broken in me that I cared so desperately about winning the affection of a girl who was the daughter of my employee, but I'd spent twenty-two years pretending the child who actually belonged to me didn't even exist? I hadn't mentioned that child to a single person. Ever.

Despite the blackmail and her obvious desire to see me suffer, despite the way her eyes gleamed with pleasure when I was upset, Nadia had another side to her. She had been clearly longing for my approval when she was planning the surprise party. She seemed to want to be around me all the time, lurking around my office at the Wellness Center and hanging out in the kitchen whenever I was making dinner.

She didn't feel like part of my family. She felt like a stranger, like someone who told a story that I recalled from a long-forgotten dream. But still I felt guilty for caring so much about Kellyn, for wanting so badly to spend time with her to strengthen our connection, while entertaining an ongoing fantasy of watching Nadia walk out the front door and dissolving into nothing, never seeing her again.

But for those twenty-two years, I hadn't even known if she was a girl or a boy. All I knew was that I'd given birth.

Maybe the circumstances of her conception, especially, but also her birth, set me up to feel alienated from her. It was possible that my mother and the woman who helped with her birth, who I now guessed was probably Nadia's adoptive mother, had conditioned me to reject her by doing everything they could to break any natural attachment.

Still, the fact remained, despite her moments of vulnerability, Nadia didn't really want me any more than I had wanted her. I might feel guilty about my feelings, but they were the same as hers. She preferred to get money out of me. She preferred to play games with my life.

She didn't show up at the Wellness Center, lying with the very first word out of her mouth, because she wanted to bond with her birth mother.

And then a whispering thought passed through my mind, the headline I'd seen when I was trying to find out more about her

Execution-style Shooting Death of Bellingham Physician

Could it have been her? With equal parts of my terrified heart, I believed she had absolutely nothing to do with that headline and that it very well could have been her.

30

R uth was being very cagey on Thursday morning. She acted like she was going to work, but something didn't feel right. Her clothes were more casual than usual. It wasn't as if she wore heels and skirts to the Wellness Center. Most of the time she dressed in yoga pants and sandals, with silky tops and lots of bracelets and necklaces. Today she was wearing jeans and flip-flops.

She made the same breakfast and filled the travel mugs with coffee as always. She and Cameron headed out in the car together, which they didn't always do; sometimes she drove their compact SUV. But even with that, she seemed—relaxed? She didn't have that look on her face that said her mind was going a million miles an hour thinking of things that had to do with running the Center.

I told my supervisor I was swapping shifts with someone on the seven p.m. to midnight segment. It was strange how having a decent amount of money was making me feel like I didn't have to follow all the rules right down to the smallest detail in my job—like too many shift swaps. And it was also strange that so far, it hadn't affected me at all.

I drove to the Wellness Center, going faster than I should have on the expressway, and I managed to get there just as Cameron was getting out of the car—on the passenger side. He closed the door, and as he walked away, Ruth backed up and started toward the parking lot exit.

I followed her.

I tried not to let my car get too close to hers. At the same time, I wasn't too worried because my car was white, and there are a hundred white cars on the street at any time. I pulled down the sun visor so it was hard to see much of my face. At the first traffic light, I twisted my hair into a knot so none of it could be seen from the front.

With me always a car or two behind her, she drove directly to Justine's apartment. She climbed the stairs, and ten minutes later, she came out with Kellyn, who followed her down the stairs and got into the car. Then they headed toward the freeway, and within fifteen minutes, I realized we were on our way to the coast.

Once we hit Santa Cruz, Ruth turned toward the Boardwalk, driving through town, then slowing as she drove past the towering Big Dipper roller coaster. Now that I knew where they were going, I didn't have to follow too closely. It would be easy enough to wander around the different rides and food stands and games and watch what they were doing. Besides, on the twisting, turning drive through the foothills, an idea had come to me.

Once they'd parked and disappeared from my sight, I set my phone timer to thirty minutes. I figured that would give them time to buy their ticket package and go on at least one ride. Based on the number of cars in the lot, the amusement park wasn't very crowded yet, partly because the sun was still completely buried behind a thick layer of fog.

When the timer rang, I sent Ruth a text message. Two days before the party, I'd convinced Cheryl to give me Ruth's cell number. The first time I'd texted her, she was pissed. But she'd more or less gotten used to it by now, even though she constantly told me not to.

Nadia: Where did you go? I'm at the Center, and I can't find you.

She didn't respond right away. After four minutes, I started to worry she wasn't going to reply. Maybe my plan wasn't going to work. Maybe she wasn't paying attention to her messages. Or maybe she'd decided I wasn't worthy of her attention when she was with Kellyn. It was almost ten minutes before she texted back.

Ruth: I'm busy.

Nadia: What's going on?!

Ruth: Stop texting me.

Nadia: Why didn't you tell me this was happening?!!!

It was eight minutes before she replied.

Ruth: What are you talking about?

Nadia: Cameron showed up and threw all my clothes in the front yard!!! He just threw them on the driveway and dumped things on the lawn and in the dirt!!!

I sent another message that was all crying and upset emojis.

She didn't reply.

Nadia: You have to help me. I don't understand. You can't just throw me out. He wrecked one of my shirts because it caught on a thorn and tore!!!!!! But that's not even the THING!!!!

There was no response.

Nadia: You can't do this. It's probably illegal. I'll tell him … you have to make him stop.

Ruth: I'm busy.

Nadia: Doing what???

She didn't answer for six minutes. I almost texted again, but I told myself to be patient. Patient. I had to wait. Then I decided, no, I didn't have to wait. She needed to think I was freaking out and I was going to do something scary dangerous to her at any minute.

I sent a whole string of upset emojis.

Ruth: Stop with the drama. Pick up your things and ask him to explain.

Nadia: He changed the lock on the front door! I can't even get in, so how am I supposed to pick up my things?

Another four minutes passed. While I waited, I began walking toward the entrance. You didn't have to pay to get into the amusement area. You only paid if you wanted tickets for the rides. I entered the park and walked toward the iconic Big Dipper roller coaster.

Ruth: You'll have to wait until I get home.

Nadia: I can't! My stuff is all over the yard. And now I have to pee, and I can't get in the house.

Ruth: Stop bothering me! Go in the back and ask my mother.

Nadia: I'm not stupid. Do you think I didn't already think of that? She's not there. You need to come home. You need to tell him to come home and tell me what's going on!!! I don't understand. I didn't do anything.

She didn't reply, so I texted her again after five minutes.

Nadia: Do you want me to text him and tell him who I am?????????

I kept walking, looking into buildings I passed to check the games for a glimpse of Ruth or Kellyn. Finally, I saw them. They were standing in front of a wall of balloons where people could throw darts to pop balloons to try winning a giant stuffed toy.

Ruth: Calm down.

Nadia: I can't! Didn't you see what I said? My stuff is all over the yard.

There was no response.

Nadia: This is where I live. You can't treat me like this!!!!

I waited four minutes, and she didn't respond.

Nadia: You need to tell him to let me in. To give me a key. To pick up my stuff.

Ruth: Stop texting me!

Nadia: I'm going to have to tell him. You're forcing me into it.

Ruth: I'm not forcing you into anything. Get a grip and wait until I get there.

Nadia: I need you to fix this right NOW or I'm telling him who I am.

Ruth: Hold on. I'm going to call you.

I smiled and slid my phone into my pocket. I had no doubt she would leave Kellyn alone at a game or eating a treat in order to call me. She wouldn't want to be overheard negotiating her way out of another blackmail threat.

31

RUTH

I was furious with Cameron for acting without telling me. I was also confused by his sudden decision to force Nadia out of the house. Going to the trouble of getting a ride home just to take a sudden and somewhat irrational stand against having her in our house seemed extreme and unlike him. I thought about texting him first to ask what he was thinking, but there wasn't time. I needed to get her calmed down before she told him who she was.

"Kellyn, should we get some cotton candy now?"

"I thought you said after lunch?"

I laughed. "This is a day for playing. We don't need to follow rules about snacks, right?"

She smacked her lips dramatically and made a goofy face. She began walking toward the stand featuring blue cotton candy. The blue-tinted stuff disgusted me, but I bought her a spun cocoon of it and maneuvered her toward a bench. "Will you wait here for a few minutes? I need to make a quick phone call."

"You can make it here."

"It's too noisy."

She pulled the plastic bag off her cotton candy, pinched off a bit of fluff, and stuffed it in her mouth. She nodded.

"Don't move."

"I won't."

"Promise? I'm really serious. You can't—"

"God. How to suck the life out of cotton candy. I'm not going anywhere." She pulled off a long thread of cottony sugar and let it drift into her open mouth.

"Sorry. It will just be five minutes. Not even that."

"Yep."

Tapping a message to Nadia that I was calling her now, I walked as quickly as I could back toward the cotton candy booth. I could step behind it and be out of the stream of people on the main pathway, but able to peek around the corner to keep an eye on Kellyn.

The call was already on the second ring. I'd expected Nadia to answer immediately. A moment later I heard her voicemail recording telling me to leave a message. I said, "Call me," hung up, and redialed. Again, the call rang several times and went to voicemail. I was so angry I wanted to throw my phone on the pavement. How could such a useful device be so completely unhelpful? Was it possible I had a weak signal and that was causing it to go to voicemail?

I stepped out from behind the cotton candy stand and glanced toward the bench. Kellyn was more than half-finished with her cotton candy. I felt terrible seeing her eating her treat all alone. She looked slightly lost and kind of sad. This was not what I'd planned for the day.

I started walking toward the bench, furiously tapping out another text, telling Nadia I was trying to call and to pick up the phone. The call went immediately to voicemail. I checked the signal and turned away from Kellyn, hoping for a stronger connection as I called again. When it went to voice-mail, I cut left, looking at the signal bars as I dialed a third time. After repeatedly getting her voicemail, I stabbed the icon to end the final call before it reached voicemail, and typed a text message in all caps.

Ruth: I CAN'T REACH YOU. CALL ME RIGHT NOW.

I shoved the phone into my pocket and started back toward the bench where I'd left Kellyn, knowing the cotton candy stick would be bare, and she would look lonelier than ever, angry at myself for leaving her for so long. I wanted to cry. As I came around the line for the Ferris wheel, I saw the bench. It was empty.

That wasn't right. I must have gotten turned around. I'd walked farther than I'd realized, and this was a different bench. I jogged toward the bench, looking for the cotton candy stand. There it was. This was the right bench. It felt as if a huge wind tunnel had opened up inside my body and all the life was being sucked out of me.

I tried to pull my phone out of my pocket, but my fingers were stiff and couldn't seem to grab the edges. It vibrated, and I clawed inside the tight space, desperate to answer the call before it went to voicemail. The vibrating stopped, and I realized it was a text. I began walking quickly toward the balloon darts, calling Kellyn's name. At the same time, I glanced at my phone. A message from Justine.

Had Kellyn slipped away and called her? I wanted to cry, thinking about how upset she'd be. I tapped to read her message.

Hey. Hope you're having fun.

I stared at my phone, then shoved it into my pocket and continued walking, looking frantically in every direction. Every few steps I called Kellyn's name. I doubted she would hear me over the din of voices, the screams from the rides, and the shouts of the game operators trying to lure people into their booths.

It was getting harder to make out individuals in the crowd as my eyes filled with tears and my heart grew tighter inside my chest. I had no idea where to start looking. It felt as if she'd vanished off the face of the earth. Was she even at the Boardwalk anymore? How long had I been gone? How long had she been gone? How many minutes had I been looking for her now? I had absolutely no idea.

Another text buzzed. Justine again.

Hi. How's it going?

Alongside her message was a grinning emoji. I ignored that one too. I started toward the entrance. They must have security people who would be able to help. And it wasn't as if Kellyn was a small child who could be easily lured away. Of course, her very age was against me. I could imagine a security guard giving me a smug look and suggesting she'd run off with friends. What eleven-year-old wants to spend spring break at the Boardwalk with a middle-aged friend of her mother's?

My phone rang. Justine. If I didn't answer, she would panic. If I did, and I told her, she would never trust me again. I stopped walking and bent over slightly, holding my stomach as if I might be sick. I knew I wouldn't, but I still felt a sensation like waves of thick syrup passing through my stomach.

I answered the phone.

"Hi. I sent you a few messages. How are things going? I want to make sure my baby is having an awesome day."

"She—"

"Send me a selfie of you two, okay?"

"I can't right now. She—"

"What's wrong? You sound funny."

"I can't—"

"Is everything okay?"

The panic in her voice made me feel like I'd been punched in the stomach. "I'm on the way to the security office. She ... I asked Kellyn to wait for me while she ate her cotton candy, and she ..." I knew I shouldn't blame her. "I had to make a phone call, and she ... disappeared." It was the wrong word. Why had I used that word?

"Disappeared?" Instead of the shriek I expected, her voice was so quiet I could barely hear her. And so calm she sounded like someone I didn't know. "Where is she, Ruth?"

"That's what I'm trying to find out."

"Oh my God. If you ..."

"I'll find her. She's a smart girl. She probably went to the restroom or ..." Of course! The restrooms!

"Or what?"

"I'll find her."

"Why did you ...?" Justine's voice caught and broke. Now she was crying.

I began crying too, even as a voice in the back of my head whispered that she couldn't have gone far. I was definitely right. She'd gone to the restroom. How obvious. I turned back in the direction I'd come, walking quickly toward the bench, then looking around for the nearest restroom.

I squinted at the glare now that I was facing into the sun. I removed my sunglasses and closed my eyes for a moment, trying to calm my breathing. When I put them on, I saw Kellyn walking toward me.

I rushed toward her. I grabbed her and pulled her close to me. A sob burst out of me as I pressed my face against the side of her head. "Where were you?"

"Re-lax. I ran into Nadia, and she bought me an ice cream. What are you so worked up about?"

I pulled away from her. "You *ran into* Nadia?"

"Weird, right? Anyway ..."

"You shouldn't have left without telling me." I pulled out my phone and sent a text to Justine. "It's all good. I found her."

She texted back a row of question marks. I knew that once I explained, my friendship with Justine would not be the same, if it existed at all. And there would be no more days spent with Kellyn. But I was too numb to cry.

The minute Ruth found me at the Wellness Center, her mask of sweetness slipped away. "I need to speak to you in my office," she said.

Now she suddenly had time to talk to me. I knew what she wanted to talk about, but I thought it was funny she was going to get all angry and tell me what a bad girl I was. It was too late. I already did what I wanted, and it worked, and I didn't see why she was going to waste energy getting upset and telling me how wrong I was after it was over.

I followed her into her office. She waited for me to move away from the door, and she closed it. Hard.

"Sit down."

I giggled.

"What's so funny?"

I went to the couch and sat down. "You sound like my mom."

She didn't smile. She went to her desk and sat in her chair. Now she looked more like a boss getting ready to fire me. Although I've never had a boss who sat behind a desk and looked at me. The people I worked for were online, and I saw them on video calls.

"Why did you lie about Cameron?"

I shrugged. I put my purse on the floor, and it slumped down a bit like it was about to fall over. I crossed my leg and swung my foot. I didn't think she liked that.

"Don't play games with me."

"It's not a game."

"Tell me why you lied and why you followed me and Kellyn and tried to make me think she was missing."

"Maybe I wanted to see if you were more worried about her or me. And I guess I know the answer. You sure weren't crying when you thought Cameron locked me out of the house and trashed my things. But you couldn't find Kellyn for five minutes, and you completely lost your shit."

"It was an entirely different situation. I'm really angry that you lied to me. You have no idea what you've done. Justine is—"

"Is that all you wanted to talk about?" I stood.

"What you did was childish and cruel."

I sat down again. "You were more worried that I would tell Cameron who I am than about him throwing me out on the street. Literally."

"It wasn't a crisis. I would have dealt with it when I got home. But it wasn't even true."

"You need to pay me another fifty thousand dollars if you don't want me to tell him."

"No."

I laughed. "*No?*"

"There's no more money."

"I doubt that."

"Not without Cameron finding out."

"You got fifty thousand from someone. I figure that

anyone who has that much cash lying around probably has a whole lot more. Right?" I smiled.

She looked so angry I was a little worried she might have a heart attack or something. "You need to back off," she said in a very quiet voice. "I paid you a lot of money, and that's the end of it."

I leaned forward and put my elbows on my knees. I rested my chin on my hands and stared straight into her eyes. "I know who your sugar daddy is. And I think he has a lot more money."

"You don't—"

"If he won't help you, maybe he'll have a terrible accident; then all his money would come to Cameron and you."

She looked really scared, and I wondered if I had gone too far. But it was so easy to mess with her head. I could just say things, and she believed them. I didn't even know if I believed them myself. They were just words. I wanted to see what she would say, what she would do.

"I don't know what you're saying ..." Her voice was a whisper. "But you should know that's not how an inheritance works. His wife would likely inherit everything."

I smiled. "Calm down. I'm not going to murder your sugar daddy."

"Stop calling him that."

"I still need another fifty thousand dollars to keep your secret. I think that's fair."

She stood. "It doesn't matter what you think is fair. You have all the money you're going to get. And it's time to end this pretense that there's any mother-daughter relationship here. You need to move out and—"

There was a knock on the door. Ruth turned toward the sound, then jerked her head back to look at me. "You—"

A second knock came, and the door opened. Kellyn stood

there. "Hi, sorry to just open the door, but my mom wants to talk to you."

Ruth stared at her. Kellyn looked like she was going to cry, and I never felt so strange in my whole life. Part of me hated her because it was so absolutely clear that she wanted to cry because she knew Justine wasn't going to let her be around Kellyn anymore. She never, ever looked that way about me. But part of me felt so sad for her, I wanted to rush over and hug her.

She didn't even look at me as she went to the door, stepped around Kellyn, and went out.

"Is your mom pissed that Ruth lost you for a while?"

"I think so." Kellyn stood in the doorway as if she wasn't sure where she was supposed to go. It was obvious she felt a little bad that agreeing to ice cream was getting her mom's friend in trouble.

"You didn't do anything," I said.

"Ruth told me not to leave the bench. I shouldn't have."

"Don't worry about it. She shouldn't have been so sneaky about her phone call. What was she talking about that she has to hide it from you?"

"Everyone has private calls," Kellyn said.

"Do they?" I sat up straight and uncrossed my legs, kicking my purse. The side collapsed even more, and the opening sagged closer to the floor.

Kellyn glanced at my purse. "Oh!" She jumped slightly, and her voice came out like a squeak. "Is that a ... is that a gun?" She moved closer to the door, jamming her back against the edge. "Ow." She rubbed her back. "Why do you have a gun? That's scary."

"It's not scary."

"Yes, it is. I don't think you should have it here, at the Wellness Center."

"It's not scary if you know how to use it."

She stared at me. Then she backed out of the doorway, turned, and hurried away.

33

RUTH

I had listened silently to Justine while the fear she'd felt during that awful fifteen minutes surged out of her. *Those fifteen minutes felt like fifteen hours*, she'd cried.

I took it all, as if I were sitting in a chair, my arms tied to the sides, and she was slapping my face, one cheek, then the other, with fierce, stinging blows. She repeated her opinions of Nadia, her belief that I was obsessed, her concern over how I'd changed. She was convinced I'd been lying to her. She wasn't wrong.

I'd decided not to speak unless it was required. There was nothing I could say that wasn't another lie, so it was best to keep my excuses to myself. Maybe, eventually, once Nadia was gone, which I still was wildly, foolishly hopeful could happen, we would forget about this and rebuild our friendship. Eventually.

The door opened, and Kellyn stepped into the massage room where Justine and I were sitting. Her eyes were almost bulging. It looked as if whatever she wanted to tell her mother was physically filling her brain, taking up so much space, it pressed against the backs of her eyeballs.

"Nadia has a gun," she said.

I didn't think my body could absorb any more jolts of terror. Each time, I thought it was the worst, the last. And then came another.

"Where?" Justine asked.

"In her purse."

"How do you know?" Justine asked.

"I saw it. After Ruth left, I was standing there, and she accidentally kicked her purse, and I saw it."

Justine glared at me. "You need to deal with this right now."

"Absolutely." I stood, glad for something to do, even though I knew it was a charade.

She looked at Kellyn. "Will you go outside for a minute?"

Kellyn looked mildly frightened, but left.

Justine whirled to face me. "You need to stay away from Kellyn until you deal with Nadia. Don't even talk to her. And if that girl comes to the Wellness Center anymore, I'm calling the police to report the weapon. What's the policy here, anyway?"

"I know," I said. "I'll take care of it. I'm sorry. I'm really—"

"You're *sorry*?" Justine pushed me toward the door. "No *sorry*. Fix it."

When I returned to my office, Nadia was gone. I got my purse, locked the office, and told Cameron I was taking the car again. He said it was no problem for him to take an Uber home.

As I drove, I felt as if my heart was shattering like a piece of glass. I'd lost one of my best friends and my relationship with her intelligent, clever daughter. Even if Nadia didn't completely destroy my marriage, it felt broken now. Cameron and I were not connected as I'd always told myself we were. I'd lied to myself, and I'd lied to him about absolutely everything. He hardly even knew who I was.

The pain cut through me, but I'd moved to a place beyond tears. My eyes were so dry that when I blinked, I felt a fine layer of grit.

Nadia would keep asking for money. And it sounded as if she knew that Micah had paid her blackmail. I had no idea how she knew, but she did. If I went back to him, he would find another *solution*. He was still staying in the motel, just waiting for his opportunity.

Thinking about what she'd said earlier, it was beginning to seem as if father and daughter were cut from the same cloth—they both had thoughts of murder.

I was losing everything. I'd paid Nadia to keep my secret, and I was still losing everything. I'd made a terrible mistake. I shouldn't have hesitated in that first moment when she asked for money. It had been the shock of finding out who she was. Looking her in the eye and not knowing how I felt—because I hadn't ever taken the time to consider how I might feel if she did somehow find me—had caused me to panic. I hadn't been prepared, and I'd run like a hunted rabbit.

The physical reality of my child was too much for me, and when she'd said those words, my brain froze. My life froze. I almost didn't know where I was. It didn't seem real. Then I thought of Cameron and how everything that was real to me had never existed for him. He couldn't know.

With my mind frozen in time, I had agreed to pay.

I should have told him that night. I had no idea why I hadn't seen that at the time. Even after Nadia left me alone, when I had a moment to think, when the feelings started to poke their heads up to the surface. I could have told him then. I could have stopped the blackmail a hundred times by simply talking to my husband. I could have saved myself from all of this. I could have saved Justine and Kellyn, and maybe even Nadia.

Most of all, every moment I'd waited, I'd added to

Cameron's pain. When he found out I would rather ask his father for money than talk to him, he would …

Still, the tears didn't come. I'd thought they surely would now. The thoughts in my mind were the most painful I'd ever experienced. A small piece of me felt like I should be crying my heart out, but I couldn't. I could hardly believe this was happening to me. I felt like I was watching someone else's life unravel.

Could I be in a theater, watching a show that had nothing to do with me, too caught up, too invested in what was portrayed on the screen? How I longed for that to be true.

I poured a glass of wine and went to the patio outside my bedroom. It was the only place I could count on avoiding the eyes and voices of my mother and Nadia.

I took a sip of chilled white wine and closed my eyes. I listened to the trickle of water from the tiny waterfall built near the curve of the patio wall. I breathed in, trying to find the aroma of orchids. All I inhaled was the cool, odorless evening air.

Looking at the wreck of my life, I couldn't comprehend why I hadn't immediately told Cameron about Nadia. It was such a simple solution. Yet, as I began to imagine the words I would choose, it still felt utterly impossible.

I had to. There was no other tunnel out of this pit in which I was being buried alive.

With my eyes closed and the sound of the waterfall seeming to grow louder inside my head, I imagined a hundred different conversations, each one stalling as I failed to find any certainty about how Cameron might respond to the things I had to tell him. Finally, my mind exhausted from asking unanswerable questions, I opened my eyes.

I sipped the rest of my wine and tried not to think of anything. When the glass was empty, I went inside and got ready for bed, turned out the light, and slipped under the covers.

Cameron had gone out for dinner with his father, at Cameron's suggestion. It felt good to settle into sleep without him there, without the tension of wondering when he would ask about Nadia, without worrying that he would finally say, *This is it. I want her to leave now.*

As I drifted to sleep, I felt a tear run down my cheek and soak into the pillow. I wondered if I would never fall asleep in my husband's arms again.

A sound woke me, and I lifted my head slightly to look at the clock on the nightstand—1:14. Cameron wasn't beside me. What had I heard?

The door must be closed because the room was completely dark except for the pale green numbers on the clock. But I'd heard a distinct sound. It wasn't the remnant of a dream. Something felt different in our room. If Cameron were moving around, I would know. This wasn't someone walking around getting ready for bed.

I turned onto my back and was aware of a shadow beside me. I gasped.

"You're awake," Nadia said.

"Get out of here." I tried to push myself up to a sitting position.

Her arm shot out, and she gripped my shoulder, holding me down. "No need to get up. I'll be quick."

"You have no right to just walk into my room."

"I said I'll be quick." I felt something cold and hard brush my forehead.

"Don't be scared. It's my gun, but I know how to use it properly. The safety's on."

I was so cold my body began shaking.

Nadia tugged the blankets up to my neck. "There, that should be better. I just wanted to tell you, because you seem to keep forgetting—you're my mother. The only one I have now that my adoptive mother is dead. And you owe me a place to live."

"But—"

She touched the gun to my lips. "Shh. Let me finish ... Parents can't just cut their children out of their lives. You should know that. Parents are supposed to be there for their kids no matter what. So you can't just pretend I don't exist. You tried once, and you succeeded for a long time. Now I'm here to stay. For good."

The gun was gone from my face. I heard myself whimper. More than anything, I longed for Cameron to walk into the room, but the house felt thick with silence, the entire space occupied only by Nadia and me. "I don't understand."

"Yes, you do. And if you can't manage to do that, don't underestimate me. You can't keep secrets from me like you do from your husband. For example, I know Micah is my father. And if you don't find some love in your heart for me, you might end up like that heartless doctor."

"Nadia, please ..."

I felt the air move around me. I heard the bedroom door open and close softly.

I turned onto my side, my back to the space Cameron should have occupied. I was shaking, and I couldn't make myself stop.

I must have fallen asleep that way, because when I woke, Cameron was beside me, and it was morning.

34

NADIA

The day after I snuck into Ruth's bedroom and silenced her excuses with the nose of my gun, I thought Ruth would do something. I thought she would say *something* or pick a fight or try to force me to do what she wanted or ... I wasn't sure.

But maybe, after I thought about it, what ended up happening was her plan after all—sending my grandma to intervene. She'd done it once before.

It was Saturday morning, and when I went into the kitchen, it was obvious no one had been up yet—no smell of coffee, the counters spotless, the dishwasher empty because Ruth liked to run it, then put all the dishes in the cabinets before she went to bed at night.

Cheryl came sweeping into the kitchen through the back door as if she'd been watching the kitchen window, waiting for me to arrive. Her hair was brushed, and she was wearing lip gloss, but she was still dressed in a long silky robe that made her look like she was making a grand, movie-star entrance. She stood just inside the doorway, leaving it open behind her so the breeze moved her gown around her body.

"I'd love to take you out to dinner tonight. A granny and granddaughter dinner." She smiled, her face full of hope.

"Dinner would be nice," I said. "Are Ruth and Cameron coming?"

She laughed. "No. That's why I said granny and grand-daughter." She flowed toward me and kissed my cheek. "I'm really looking forward to this."

After that, I didn't see Ruth all day. When I checked the garage later, her car was gone. She must have snuck away while I was in the shower. She definitely did not want to see me. I wondered if she'd gone to figure out a plan with Micah on how to be rid of me. I also wondered what Cheryl wanted to say to me.

Even though I liked to say outrageous stuff to see what Ruth would do, the things I'd said to her in the dark weren't just a game. I meant them. She was the only mother I had, and I wasn't going to just move out. I liked living there, and it did sort of seem like it was her job to take care of me now. I'd spent my college years taking care of my adoptive mom, so it was only fair I needed some time to figure out where I was going in my life, even if I was a little old to think my mother still owed me a place to live.

Cheryl took me to a really nice Chinese restaurant. She let me order whatever I wanted, which did make me feel like a granddaughter getting a special treat. She ordered a Midori sour and suggested I should get a fun cocktail as well. I'd never even heard of a Midori sour, so I decided to try one. It was pretty good. We both ended up having two.

After the egg rolls and potstickers were gone, Cheryl waded into the speech that I knew was coming the minute she said she wanted to take me out to dinner. I thought it might be about holding a gun to her daughter's head, but it seemed that she didn't know anything about that. It was about her daughter, though.

"I know you're upset that Ruth wants you to get your own place."

"She couldn't care less if I have my own place. She just wants me out of hers."

Cheryl sighed. "Well, I feel terrible that I hurt your feelings when I talked to you about that a few days ago."

"Ancient history," I said.

"It's been bothering me."

"It's not your fault. You've made it really obvious you like having me around. She's the one who hates me."

"Oh, sweetie. She doesn't hate you."

"Yes, she does."

"You have to give her time."

"I think she's had way more time than most mothers get to bond with their children. Way, way more."

"The situation was unbelievably complicated. And giving birth at fifteen was really hard on her. I think anyone can—"

"Can you stop the patronizing nonsense? I'm not a little kid. There's nothing complicated about it except that my father is Cameron's dad. On that I agree—it's complicated."

She gasped. I guess it was a shock, hearing it so bluntly.

"I get it that she didn't want me when she was fifteen," I said. "And that maybe it was hard and confusing. But she's an adult now. I'm a real live human being, and she can't pretend I don't belong to her. She's in a perfect position to welcome her daughter into her awesome life, but she's made it really clear, over and over, that she's not interested."

Cheryl twirled noodles around her chopsticks. She kept twirling and twirling, letting the end flap out, then twirling again. She didn't try to raise the little ball of noodles to her mouth. It was making me want to bite them off her chopsticks myself. I twirled my own noodles and ate them.

"I think a lot of it is my fault," Cheryl said. "I told her it was best to give you up for adoption. And I told her it was healthier to forget it had ever happened."

"*It*?" I took a large swallow of my bright green cocktail.

"I meant being pregnant and having a child and ..." She waved her hand around, still holding the chopstick. A long noodle came unstuck and dropped to the floor, but she didn't seem to notice. "I didn't give her a choice. And I told her she would heal more quickly if she put you out of her mind entirely. So it really is my fault."

"You shouldn't blame yourself. She's a grown-up woman. She makes her own choices now. I see who she is, and you can't pretend she's this wounded little girl anymore."

"You don't understand." She placed her chopsticks across her plate. She picked up her water glass and took several sips. She shook it gently, letting the melting ice clink against the glass. Then she lifted it to her lips and drank the entire glass. "You don't know what happened."

It looked as if she was done eating, but I wanted more of everything. I spooned food onto my plate and swapped my chopsticks for a fork.

"I think you need to understand how complicated it was for Ruth."

"You keep saying that. I don't think it's complicated at all."

She put her hands over her face. At first, I thought she was crying; then I thought maybe she had a headache. Slowly, she took them away, but she didn't look at me. She spoke in a whisper so soft, I had to lean over the table to hear what she was saying. "Here's the thing. Ruth had a very hard time because she was ... she didn't willingly go along with it, I guess is the best way to put it. She had a lot to drink, especially for a girl her age, and he had sex with her, and she basically had passed out, I guess. And—"

"You guess?" I stared at her. She still didn't meet my gaze. I tried to think about what she was saying. I put down my fork. Now I wasn't hungry. Ruth was raped by her father-in-law? Before he was her father-in-law, but … I couldn't even …

"So it was a terrible time for her. Do you understand?"

"Yeah. I get that. It's awful. It's … But are you blaming an innocent baby for how she came to be? That's not right."

"I'm not blaming you for anything. I'm telling you to be patient with her. *Asking* you … I'm asking you to be patient with her."

"It doesn't sound that way. It sounds like you want something from me. It sounds like you told me an icky, creepy thing about your family so I would feel sorry for you. So I wouldn't be upset that my very own mother is trying to throw me out of her house and dump me in the gutter."

"I thought you were mature enough to understand how that would affect someone. That you might have some compassion for what she went through, and how that might bring up some traumatic feelings for her, even now."

"Do you want me to forgive you for not reporting your daughter's rape? Is that what this is about?"

"No! I already told you …"

We sat in silence for several minutes that felt a lot longer than minutes.

"It didn't seem like … we weren't sure at the time … well, I don't know. I just want you to try to understand what she's been through and try to be kind to her. She'll come around. I'm sure of it. She's a good person."

"I would expect her mother to think that."

"Please, Nadia. Will you think about what I've said?"

"Yes." I nodded slowly. "I'll definitely think about it."

She gave me a grateful smile.

She thought I meant that promise differently, and I wanted her to. What I would think about was that I now knew Cheryl was not on my side when things came down to it. She was team Ruth all the way. She might have wanted a granddaughter, but she thought her special daughter hadn't done anything wrong in how she'd treated me.

I excused myself and went to the restroom so I could think about everything she'd said to me. While I was staring into the mirror, wondering if I looked more like my mother or ... him, my phone buzzed with a text message. I looked down. The sender was just a phone number.

I opened the message.

Nadia—Micah here. I'd really like to get to know my daughter before I head back home. I've been remiss in not getting in touch sooner. Are you free to stop by my motel for a drink this evening?

The message had setup written all over it. I wanted to laugh at how stupid he was. I sure hoped I turned out smarter than my father. First, I already knew he and Ruth were figuring out a way to get rid of me. And now, thanks to Cheryl, I had double the inside scoop. This guy had drugged Ruth to get what he wanted. Did he really think I would have a drink with him? He probably had no clue I knew about that.

But it didn't mean I wasn't going. I was done with my granny dinner.

I went back to our table and saw that Cheryl was making another attempt at eating. Maybe now that she'd gotten all of that guilt off her chest, she had an appetite.

"Hey, I have something I have to do," I said. "I hate to ditch you, but it's important."

"But we just—"

"I really should go." I opened my purse. "What do I owe for my half?"

"Don't be silly. This is my treat."

"Thanks." I turned away.

"But I drove. How will you—"

"I already ordered an Uber." I smiled. "See you later, but probably not 'til tomorrow." I kissed the top of her head and went as fast as I could to the lobby.

Maybe Micah wanted to pretend he was longing to get to know me. That was fine. But I had a question for him. I didn't believe for a single minute that he had no clue Ruth was pregnant way back when. He was a family *friend*. He had to have known. So why didn't he try to take me in and include me with *his* family?

35

RUTH

I was grateful to my mother for taking Nadia out so Cameron and I could have the house to ourselves. I was close to panicked about how he would feel when I told him the truth and worried my mother wouldn't be able to keep Nadia away long enough. But I couldn't begin to imagine talking to him in a restaurant about these things. I couldn't do that to him. And I wasn't sure I could tell him everything if I risked being overheard or was worried about controlling my emotions for public scrutiny.

Despite all my imagined conversations, I simply launched myself into the middle without thinking. It was too much to sort out, too much to think I could control the flow or the outcome. He would have questions; he would have a multitude of reactions. I was walking into a firestorm, and there was nothing to do but face it head-on.

"There's something I should have told you a long time ago," I said. "After you digest it all, I'll explain why I didn't. I know my reasons are weak, and I know I've betrayed you, but here it is ..."

I felt his eyes on me with an intensity I'd never felt. He'd placed his fork on his plate the moment I said the words—*I should have told you.*

He held my gaze with a neutral expression, and I dreaded seeing it change.

"I got pregnant when I was fifteen. I gave the baby up for adoption and never had any contact. My mother thought that was the best thing, and I didn't see it any differently. Now she's found me. Nadia."

His expression didn't change. I felt my head spinning, sounds in my ears, like my skull was full of water. I wondered if he hadn't heard me. Was the loud rushing sound outside my head, some weather condition that he was also hearing, and my words had been drowned?

Finally, he looked down at his plate. He nudged it away from him, then looked at me again. "I don't know what to say."

"Say what you're thinking."

"I'm thinking that I don't know what to say."

"You must have some reaction."

"I don't understand."

"Which part?"

"Why you never told me."

"I ... you were away at school. And my mother home-schooled me so no one would know. And then I thought you'd look at me differently. And then things were so good with us it didn't seem important. And then your accident. It was always something. I know ..." I saw on his face how ridiculous it sounded. I also felt a tightness in my chest because even now, I was telling only part of the story. I was still lying. And the biggest lie of all was why I hadn't told him.

"How could I not know? I came home from school, didn't I? How could I not have seen you for six months? Nine months? I don't ..." He stared down at his plate again. "Who's her father?"

There was something in his tone that made me wonder, for the briefest moment, if he knew. But how could he? There was no way he could know, but he sounded uncomfortable, asking the question.

"I was ..." In that moment, I felt my mother's aversion to the word she never wanted to speak. There was something brutal about it. Something honest and not to be argued with. Something that left no room for discussion or explanation. I couldn't fall back on the easier euphemism. I couldn't cut him some slack at this point in my life. I'd come too far. "I was raped."

"Oh, my God." He shoved out his chair and stood. "Ruth, I'm so ..." He came around the table and put his hands on the sides of my face. He bent down and pressed his head against mine. "I don't understand why you never told me. I thought we told each other everything. I thought we knew every part of each other. I don't understand why you kept this from me. And now, all this time, she's been here. In our house, sitting at our table, looking at me. Why didn't you *tell* me?"

I was crying now. "It's so hard. It's so, so hard. I can't ..."

"But it's me." He pulled on my shoulders gently, trying to make me stand so he could put his arms around me.

I couldn't do that. Not until I finished, and he knew every last piece. I gently pushed him away from me. "I have to ..." My breath caught, and I wondered if I would be able to get the words out. It felt so huge. As if this boulder were inside me, and I was finally going to shove it out of my life, over the side of a cliff, ridding myself of the weight forever. At the same time, I was afraid I would destroy him.

"What is it?"

"The man who raped me ... the man ... it was your father."

A brutal cry erupted out of his chest. He stumbled away from me. "That's not ... no ... he can't ..."

Before he could say more, I began talking, rushing to tell him about that night. As quickly as I could get the words into a coherent order, I told him about the champagne and the compliments, the interested questions about my life, the stuff in my drink. And how my mother behaved afterwards.

He walked away from me as I talked, back to his end of the table. He collapsed onto his chair, picked up his wineglass, and swallowed the contents in a single gulp. He stood and went to the window, looking out at the backyard still soft with the last bit of light from the warm April evening.

"Why would you keep this to yourself for all these years? I ... it's not that I don't think you're telling the truth, but you've been in his house, you ate dinner with them, you invited him to my *birthday party*? I knew you felt chilly toward him, but ... I don't understand. Is this the whole story now? Is this everything? Or is there more?"

Of course there was more. I hadn't told him about the blackmail. I was utterly depleted, and I could feel his anger and confusion as if they were phantoms swirling around the room, wanting to take possession of the house. I felt as if one of them had its long bony fingers around my neck, pressing into my throat. I couldn't talk. Hadn't I said enough? Didn't he already think I'd hoarded my secrets, hiding my entire soul from him?

It was impossible to read him. I couldn't tell from the few strangled words he'd spoken or from the pained spasms crossing his face what he was feeling. He refused to say, and I didn't feel I had the right to ask.

"There's more?!"

He was shouting. I'd never heard him like this. It was the rage of a stranger. We'd raised our voices from time to time in arguments, become upset and angry with each other, but we'd never shouted, never lost control of our emotions in a way that turned us into the kind of person who lost all self-awareness, on the way to losing that last shred of self-control.

"It's so hard to explain. I blocked it out for so many years. For most of my life. I honestly didn't think about it for months at a time."

"*It*? You think of her as an *it*?"

I started crying, sobbing so that it was difficult to speak. "Not her. I didn't even know if the baby was a boy or a girl. I didn't mean I called the baby *it*, I meant what happened. The whole thing ... It." I gave myself over to crying for a few minutes. Finally, it began to subside.

"When she first came to me," I whispered, "she was ... combative, or defiant. I don't know how to explain it. And I was so shocked, absolutely, utterly in shock. She saw right away that I didn't respond the way she'd hoped, or imagined, maybe? I'm not sure. Anyway, I was scared. I didn't know what you'd think, how you'd feel. I knew I'd made an awful mistake. And it wasn't how I wanted to tell you."

"Apparently you didn't want to tell me at all."

"I always thought I might, at some point."

"But probably not. Since you waited half our lives." He glared at me.

"I ... She was so upset, and it went sideways so fast. She demanded fifty thousand dollars not to tell you who she was."

He kicked the dining room chair, shoving it against the table. The glasses trembled. "Now I get it. Now I know why she acts like she has a right to live in our house, why you've been so God-damned secretive and distant and impossible to understand."

"Oh, Cameron." I stood, wavering slightly, and stumbled toward him.

He stepped back.

"I'm so sorry," I said. "I was ... I don't want to make excuses ..."

"Then don't." He took several more steps back, then turned toward the entrance to the living room. "I'm going for a drive. I need to think, and I can't—"

"We need to talk."

"You had a lot of years to talk. And right now, the one thing I don't want is to hear you talk."

And then he was gone.

With tears running down my face, I dragged myself back to the table. I picked up the plates and carried them to the kitchen. I scraped the food into the trash. I poured the wine from my glass down the drain and corked the bottle. I washed the glasses and other dishes. By the time I was finished, I felt numb, and the tears had dried on my cheeks.

I got out a martini glass and a bottle of gin, the vermouth, and a jar of olives. I put ice in the shaker and mixed myself an icy-cold martini. I went into the living room and sat on the couch. I took a sip. I felt calmer. Resigned, maybe. I felt light and emptied of something I hadn't known was there. But I was scared out of my mind.

36

NADIA

I asked the Uber to drop me at Ruth's house so I could get my car. I didn't want to be at Micah's motel without a way to escape easily. Not that I thought I would be escaping anything necessarily, but it just felt like I would be trapped if I didn't have my car close by and had to rely on an app.

He'd told me to meet him by the swimming pool.

Once the sun went down, it had gotten cold fast. I shivered when I thought about sitting by the pool in a skirt and sandals that had seemed like an okay choice when I'd gone to dinner with my granny, but as I walked toward the garden entrance to the motel, I wished I'd taken time to change my clothes. I was glad I was wearing my hoodie.

Because it was cold, there was no one in the pool. And the patio area around it was circled with empty tables and chairs and lounges. Micah stood out like a bear lurking in the woods. Even sitting down, his height was obvious. He had on a dark jacket and dark pants, but surrounded by all that white furniture, his presence wasn't very subtle.

I walked down the steps from the garden to the pool. I unlatched the iron gate and stepped inside the fenced area, feeling slightly trapped already. I walked along the side of the pool about a third of the way to where he was sitting at a table that was nestled beside a concrete planter with tropical-looking flowers, the blooms almost supernatural yellow in the dim light.

It felt strange because I was so used to sitting at the opposite end, watching his room. This felt backwards, and I had this weird urge to suggest we should move to the other side.

"Hi, Nadia. I'm glad you agreed to join me."

"No worries."

He laughed. "I ordered you a gin and tonic. I know everyone likes those."

I didn't know how he would know that. It seemed like a big assumption. "Maybe," I said.

"You don't?"

"It's fine."

He lifted his glass. "To new connections." He waited for me to pick up my glass. "Aren't you going to toast?"

I picked up the glass and clicked it against his. He took a sip, and I set mine on the table.

"You don't drink?"

"I will. I just had a drink. I'm pacing myself."

"Ahh." He laughed. "Smart girl." He took another sip of his drink. "So, tell me a little about yourself, Nadia."

"What's the sudden interest after all these years?"

"I'd like to know more about the daughter I never knew I had."

"I don't believe that."

"Believe what?"

"That you never knew about me."

He took a few sips of his drink. "Still not having any?" He gestured toward my glass.

"In a minute."

He smiled.

"Believe me, I never knew you existed. Cheryl is a cagey woman. She didn't tell me her little temptress was pregnant."

"Temptress? God, she was fifteen."

"Yes, and I definitely regret that. But I had a lot to drink, as did she. Her own choice. And it was one of those in-the-moment things. We were drinking champagne. And she'd had champagne before. Cheryl allowed it. Ruth was a very mature young woman. Like you."

I felt ill, even though he didn't say it in a slimy way, it still made me feel like worms were crawling along my skin. "She wasn't a woman. She was a girl. I'm twenty-two."

"But mature for twenty-two. An old soul, you could say."

"How could you force yourself on a—"

"Hold on. I didn't *force* anything. She was dressed in a very sexy little outfit, and she was filling my glass with champagne and talking to me like we were on a date. She kept moving closer to me and, yes, flirting. I regretted it immediately, of course, but it takes two."

"She was—"

The iron gate slammed. I turned and saw Deanne striding toward us. Her long, blond-streaked hair was tangled across her face, and she was trying to brush it away as if she were fighting through cobwebs. She wore white, as she had at the party, so it was easy to see her coming as the small garden lights around the pool reflected off her clothes.

"What's this?" Deanne said.

"Go back inside," Micah said. "We're just ... she's a friend of Ruth's and—"

"I know who she is." Deanne's voice was sharp, and her tone made clear she wanted to be sure I knew I was scum on her shoe. "That hooker from your son's party."

I jumped out of my chair. My purse, still on my shoulder,

swung out and hit the table, rattling the glasses and sloshing gin and tonic onto the table.

Micah grabbed the edge of the table. "Calm down."

"I'm not a hooker!"

"I'm guessing a junkie too ... that was disgusting, leaving your blood all over our door. What the hell were you trying to do anyway?"

"I didn't—"

"I should have called the police right then. Who knows what diseases you could have." She laughed. "I have insomnia. Right, Micah?" She didn't wait for him to agree. "I saw you lurking outside our door. I heard you drop your booze and run away."

"I'm not any of those things."

She lifted her chin, glaring at Micah. "You couldn't keep your eyes off her at that party," Deanne said. "And this little slut was loving it."

I laughed. "You are so wrong. You have no idea who I—"

"Stop talking!" Micah slammed his palm on the table. "Let's all just calm down. Deanne, go back to the room. I'll be there in a—"

"I'm not going back to the room while you sit out here with this little whore and figure out where you'll hook up."

"I'm not!" I shoved her, and her ankle twisted, making her leg collapse like a strand of spaghetti. She went over sideways, crashing down without any chance to put out her hands to break her fall. Her head smacked against the concrete planter with an awful sound—like a walnut being smashed with a hammer. She slumped to the ground.

Breathing hard, I stepped around her and inched away, moving close to the edge of the pool.

"What did you do?!" Micah was out of his chair, stumbling around the table, then falling onto his knees beside

Deanne. He picked up her head as if it weren't even attached to her body, cradling it in his hands. He stroked the sides of her face with his thumbs and leaned close, as if to feel her breath on his lips. Then he pulled back suddenly, lifting his hands away from the back of her head. They were coated with blood.

"What did you *do*!?!"

I took a step back, aware that I was very close to the edge of the pool, but before I could turn, he was on his feet. He reached one bloody hand into his jacket pocket and pulled out a gun. Then he lunged toward me, the other blood-caked hand reaching for my arm.

I skittered away from the edge of the water and began running, twisting my own ankle as I made a sudden turn. Despite the sharp pain, I kept going. My sandals slapped the concrete, then skidded slightly on a damp spot. I continued skidding, then got my footing back and raced around the corner of the pool toward the iron gate. It took me too long to get it unlatched, and I could feel how close he was.

The gate opened, and I stumbled up the stairs to the garden. I heard it clang, and I hoped that meant he had to open it himself. I forced myself not to look back to see how close he was. I ran faster now, winding along the path, almost to the parking lot. When I was away from the buildings and flowering plants hemming me in, I ran as fast as I could in my slippery sandals.

I pressed my fob before I reached my car. I yanked open the door and fell inside, leaving my purse looped over my arm instead of wasting time putting it on the other seat. I didn't buckle my belt. I just locked the doors and started the car. I looked in the mirror for Micah and backed out. As I put the car in drive, I saw him in the rearview mirror.

I sped to the end of the parking lot, but once I was on the

city streets, I drove normally. My heart was pounding so hard I still felt like I was in a race, a slow-motion race, the kind you have in a dream where you have to go faster, but you can't because something is holding you back.

37.

RUTH

I'd only had two sips from my martini, but I'd eaten all the olives off the stir stick. The glass sat on the coffee table. I sat in the center of the couch, staring into the entryway at the front door, willing it to open, revealing Cameron's face. It had been two hours now, and my heart ached more as each minute ticked past.

Part of me wanted to down the martini and make another, not stopping until he returned. But another part of me knew that I wanted to be sober and ready to have the most important conversation of my life. Now the drink was warm, which helped go a long way toward defeating my desire for it.

I thought I heard a sound in the front yard. I picked up my glass and walked to the entryway. I looked out the window beside the door. The driveway was empty, the yard deserted. I turned and placed my martini on the shelf beside a black onyx egg Cameron had bought for me when we visited the Grand Canyon. I went outside and stood in the driveway, as if my presence there might draw him back home.

After a few minutes, I went back inside, leaving the door unlocked, hoping he would arrive any minute. I couldn't imagine where he'd gone. Was he driving aimlessly around the area? Had he gone farther, possibly to the beach or maybe to a bar?

I settled on the couch, staring into space, trying not to speculate.

My mother had returned earlier, telling me Nadia left their dinner abruptly before they finished eating, saying she had somewhere else to go. It no longer mattered, so I'd simply shrugged. She'd asked how it went with Cameron, and I'd shrugged again, annoyed that she thought it was any of her business.

She offered to keep me company until he returned, and I declined, but she refused to leave the house. She didn't think it was good for me to be alone. I didn't argue.

She was now sitting in the family room, watching TV with the volume off because I told her I didn't want the chatter of it. I could feel her waiting, as I was, her anxiety increasing on my behalf. I should have told her to wait in her own place, but there was something in me that was half-glad to have another beating heart in the house with me. When Cameron came home, she could easily slip out the family room door to the backyard and across the yard to the privacy of the guest cottage.

My drifting thoughts exploded out of my head as the front door slammed open. I jolted forward on the couch.

Nadia flung herself into the entryway, slammed the door closed, and locked it.

"I was leaving that unlocked for Cameron. He—"

"He wants to kill me!"

"What are you talking about?"

"Micah. He has a gun." She was panting. "He chased me all the way to my car. And I think I saw him get in his ... or maybe not. But he will. And he ..." She gasped for air, looking around wildly as if she thought he might be in the house.

My mother came into the room. "What's going on?"

"Micah," Nadia said. "Deanne. She ..."

I stood and moved out from behind the coffee table. "Sit down and catch your breath."

My mother joined her in the other armchair facing the couch.

"What happened?" I asked.

"Micah asked me to meet him for a drink. He said he wanted to get to know me better."

I doubted that. I felt a shiver run through me, thinking about his promise to find a solution to the blackmail problem. Maybe I should have ...

"Deanne came out of their room. She was beyond pissed. She misread everything and thought ... she was calling me a hooker! I shoved her, and she fell and hit her head." Nadia let out a panicked sob. "I'm sure she's dead because she was just lying there, and he was holding her head, and then his hands were all bloody. But instead of calling for paramedics, he started chasing me. And he had a gun. He thinks I killed her! On purpose. But I didn't! It was an accident. She was saying those things, and I just pushed her. I didn't mean for her to die!"

For half a second, my mother looked like she was going to be sick. She took a deep breath. "Okay," she said. "We should ... we need to call the police."

"But what if they don't believe me?" Nadia's voice was shrill with panic.

"We have to call them," I said.

The room was silent as none of us moved to make the call, each of us sorting through in our minds how to begin the explanation of what had happened.

I heard a key in the lock and felt all of the tightness in my heart unwind in a single breath—Cameron was home. I started toward the door, anxious to see his face, hoping I would recognize something welcoming there. The door swung open, and Micah stepped into the entryway, his face distorted with rage.

I inhaled sharply and moved backwards, glancing at my mother and Nadia as I continued backing away. "How do you have a key?" I cried.

As he closed the door, I saw the gun in his right hand. I glanced at Nadia and my mother—they were both holding their hands to their mouths, inching closer to each other.

He laughed without amusement. "Cameron gave me a key years ago. In case of emergencies." He stepped into the living room. "You need to come with me, Nadia. So we can discuss what happened."

"No."

"Yes." He took a few steps toward her.

"I'm not going anywhere with you."

He moved quickly, grabbing Nadia's upper arm and pulling her roughly to his side. She shrieked, and Micah tugged harder, causing her to whimper. "We need to talk about what you did."

"It was an accident!"

"You killed her. Ruth told me what a vindictive little bitch you are. You murdered the best thing that ever happened to me." As Nadia pulled against him, twisting around, trying to get close enough to kick him, he dragged her toward the entryway.

He had no right to call her that. She was vulnerable and hurting. He'd seen nothing of her good qualities. She didn't deserve that. Overcome, fear rushing through me with a force that I could hardly contain, I rushed across the room and grabbed Micah's wrist, forcing the nose of the gun toward the ceiling.

"Let go of her! What's wrong with you? It was an accident. We need to call the police."

"You weren't there. Did she tell you she smeared blood all over the door to our room a few days ago? Deanne knew it was a threat. She wanted to call the police, and I wouldn't listen to her!" His voice broke, and he paused, breathing heavily. "She killed Deanne in cold blood! She slammed her head into that planter box like it was a sack of garbage." He sobbed. "It was the worst thing I've ever heard. My beautiful, beautiful wife. I'm not letting this little monster get away with calling it an accident. So no, you don't need to call the police."

He and I struggled, his ability to get the best of me weakened by his attention to holding onto Nadia. He had no way to pry my fingers off his wrist without letting go of Nadia. But the size of him, the length of his arms, allowed him to keep us both far enough away that it was impossible to kick him or scratch at his arms or face.

After a few moments of struggle, I managed to wrench his arm in a way that caused him to groan slightly. It must have also caused him to loosen his grip on Nadia because a moment later she'd slipped away, and my mother was holding onto her.

Micah grabbed my hair and pulled. I screamed at the pain but held on. He threw me against the wall, and I saw my chance. The martini was sitting on the shelf. I grabbed it and flung the liquid at his face. As he turned away and put his hand to his eyes, the glass slipped from my hand and crashed to the wood floor.

I yanked the gun out of his other hand, but before I could get control of it, his eyes were clear. He bent over, grabbed the broken stem of the glass, sharp as a spear, and lunged toward Nadia, who was still wrapped in my mother's arms.

I looked for the safety catch like I'd seen on Nadia's gun. It was already off. I raised the gun toward Micah's back and pressed the trigger three times in a row. I couldn't stop. I had to be sure I hit him. But he was so tall, and his back so broad, it was almost impossible to miss. I saw him hesitate, then turn. He stared directly at me, his face blank with shock before he collapsed to the floor. I gazed at his body crumpled in a heap. Was it real? Had I done that?

The sound of the gunshot deadened my ears, making it feel like I moved in slow motion, as if Nadia and my mother were otherworldly creatures, slowly moving their mouths and bodies, but not talking. I moved as slowly myself, securing and dropping the gun, then taking Nadia in my arms.

Was this what it felt like to be a mother? I wanted to hold her for as long as I could. I wanted to smell her hair and feel her heartbeat and the rise and fall of her shoulders. I wanted to be sure she was alive, and I didn't care what happened because he had to be stopped.

He had wanted to kill my daughter.

38

Having Ruth hold me was the strangest feeling ever. I could feel her heart racing, thumping against my chest as she held me so close. Or maybe I was imagining that, and it was my own heartbeat. It felt kind of awkward. I felt like an adult but also a little kid. I felt like I wanted her to hug me but also like she was a stranger.

For a few minutes, or maybe a lot longer, it seemed as if time stopped moving. No one said anything, and then, maybe all at the same time, we realized we were standing there beside a dead body. I started to move back from her, and Ruth's arms slipped away from me, and we all sort of drifted toward the living room.

Ruth picked up her cell phone, and then I heard the operator's voice really loud, even though it wasn't on speakerphone, saying, *What's your emergency?*

While Ruth was trying to explain a really complicated situation so the operator could understand the important parts, the front door opened, and Cameron came into the house.

Before he even saw his father's body on the floor, he

jerked back, as if he knew something really bad had happened. He looked across at Ruth, wrinkling his forehead like he couldn't understand what she was saying into the phone, or why she was even talking on the phone.

Then he looked down.

He dropped to his knees, and I heard the crunch of his bones against the wood floor. A loud cry came out of him as he put his hand on his father's shoulder. Cameron shook him gently as if he were trying to wake him up, then cried out again. He grabbed onto Micah with both hands, shaking him.

His father's body moved slightly, turning so he was facing up. Cameron fell away, catching himself before he collapsed onto his back. He inched across the floor until his back was against the wall. He covered his face with his hands. His shoulders shook as he began crying.

I felt like I was watching a play that didn't have words. My ears still had a ringing tone from the gunshots that made Ruth's voice talking to the 911 operator sound far away. Cheryl hadn't said a word. She stood in the corner of the living room, her back shoved into the tight space, staring at Micah's body. Both her hands were curled into fists and pressed against her mouth. I wasn't sure if she was trying to stop herself from crying or screaming. Her face was twisted into an agonized expression, as if someone were pinching the tender skin of her neck. Cameron had cried out like he was in pain, then wept softly. None of them seemed to notice anyone else was in the room.

I felt like I was all alone, watching strangers. And mostly, I guess I was.

After that, it seemed like a switch flipped somewhere inside Cameron. He wiped his hands across his face, then wiped them on his jeans. He pushed himself up to his feet and walked into the living room. Ruth had finished her phone call. He put his arms around her, and they stood there, holding each other for a really long time. Such a long time I wondered if they were just going to stay like that when the paramedics or the police or whoever came to the house.

They had barely stopped hugging when I heard the sirens. I wasn't sure why they had sirens because it wasn't an emergency at all anymore.

Just before the police came into the house, I realized why that switch flipped in Cameron. And I realized why he held onto Ruth for such a long time.

She'd told him. She'd told him everything. So Cameron cried for his dad, but he couldn't help thinking—*good riddance*. Or something like that. Maybe he wasn't that cold. But he knew now what his father was.

Explaining everything to the police took a long time. I kept thinking about Cheryl and how she always said things were complicated. It *was* complicated, trying to tell them about me and my relationship to Micah, and that Micah was Cameron's dad. It was complicated trying to explain how Micah came in the house and how Ruth got the gun and how he grabbed that broken glass and went after me.

Telling them about Deanne and why I pushed her was really complicated. It was hard to know if they believed me, but they didn't not believe me, and they didn't arrest me. I guess that meant they believed me. Mostly. And who was there to say it was any different? They did say they would have to investigate the scene and look at the evidence and check for witnesses, but I didn't see how that would tell them anything different than what I had said.

After they asked us questions in the living room, they took each one of us into Ruth's office and interviewed us alone. Ruth was first, then Cheryl, then Cameron. I was last, which made me nervous, but maybe it meant nothing.

It took forever for them to interview the others. And while they did, another cop sat in the living room with the three of us who were not being interviewed, so of course, there was no talking. It was the longest bout of silence I'd ever lived through. And it gave me way too much time to think.

First, I realized I'd never gotten a chance to ask my father why he hadn't taken me. He probably would have stuck to his story that he hadn't known I existed. But it didn't really matter anymore. I was glad he hadn't taken me and tried to raise me. Even though my adoptive dad was having a hard time after my mom died, he'd been a good dad, a caring dad, and he'd kept us safe.

Too much thinking in the center of all that silence also led to worrying, which was not what I usually did, but I started reliving the whole night in my head.

Everything had happened so fast, it was already hard to remember some details, so that made me nervous about talking to them. What if I forgot and I said something different in my private interview from what I'd said in front of the others? What if what they said about Ruth shooting Micah was different from what I said? Would I send Ruth to prison? Did I want to send her there?

That made my thoughts drift to remembering how it felt having her save me from him. He really did want to kill me. His own daughter. Not that he really saw me that way. And I'm sure it was a shock finding out he even had a daughter.

But she saved me. She actually kind of put her own life on the line for me. Not that she was going to die, but maybe. And definitely she could end up going to prison if they decided she didn't have to kill him.

It was funny how police and other people would get to decide if she had no choice but to kill him. Like it was their call. Like they knew what she'd been through. Like they knew him the way she did and knew what he was capable of. Like they knew the fear or the gut instinct she felt in that moment.

But she saved me. It was almost embarrassing how good that made me feel.

Still, I was worried.

How much were they going to ask her about me? How far into this whole complicated story were they going to dig? I'm sure their own curiosity was going to take over if someone mentioned blackmail and a man who was the father of her husband and also the man who raped her, and that her daughter was also her husband's half-sister. It was all too weird.

What if they asked her a lot of questions about me blackmailing her? What if they found out I was living in her house and blackmailing her? They probably would because they asked to see all our IDs. And they knew I didn't live in California. And what if they searched the house? What if they found my gun?

And what if ... what if Ruth remembered what I had said to her in the middle of the night? How awake had she been? I didn't know why I'd been so stupid to think I had to scare her so much that I had to start talking about killing my mom's doctor. Ruth didn't have to know that. She was scared enough. It was my secret that no one else on the whole planet knew, and I'd gone and hinted about it to her. And a very big hint that was so, so easy for her to look up.

Was she really totally awake that night? Did she wake up in the morning and think it was a dream? Did she remember I was in her room at all? Or was she totally awake and remembered every word?

39

RUTH

It was two thirty in the morning by the time Micah's body was removed from our house. I wondered if I would ever be able to walk through that doorway again without picturing him lying on the floor. I'd never wanted him in my home, and then he'd unlocked the door and stepped inside as if he owned the place. Just as he'd acted as if he owned me all those years ago.

I couldn't tell anyone what had happened. This time, it would be my secret alone.

Shooting him had been the most satisfying thing I'd ever done. I didn't hesitate for a single moment, pressing my finger against that all-powerful trigger. I didn't give it a second thought when I did it two more times. It wasn't as if I needed those other shots to keep him from hurting Nadia. The police seemed to take those extra shots as the behavior of a novice in a state of absolute fear. I was, but once I pulled the trigger the first time, and it felt so smooth and easy, the fear evaporated. Then I simply wanted to be sure he was dead.

I aimed the gun to save Nadia, but I pulled the trigger to save myself.

Now I was lying in Cameron's arms, wondering how he felt.

It had been clear from the way he moved and the expression on his face when he first stepped through the doorway, before he saw his father's body, that he understood, at least to some degree, why I'd hidden so much from him for so many years. Then, when he held me, his arms felt so reassuring and promising as we stood there while I finished my emergency call, and while we waited for the wail of the sirens to separate us.

Despite my secrets and so many lies of omission, I could feel in his arms that we did have the connection I'd always believed we had. I could feel that he knew me well enough, that I hadn't hidden everything about myself from him. Somehow, those parts of me had seeped through, and he was aware that there were other facets to me, even without my spelling out the details.

Or maybe, because I was able to help Cameron when his body was so broken by the accident, he knew on some deeper, instinctive level that I knew what it was to be broken.

"I never thought he was the best father," he said. "Even when I was a kid. And you know how it was after my accident —walking out on me."

"Yes."

"But even before. I knew he cheated on my mom. I just never ..."

His arms tightened around me. Neither of us spoke for several minutes. I wondered if he'd drifted to sleep. I couldn't imagine sleeping. I felt as if the clock was moving toward three in the afternoon, not the morning. I wondered when I would ever be able to relax enough to sleep.

"I kept trying to believe there was something there, some part of him I could love. And I'm sure he must have loved me

... or cared about me. The world feels off balance, thinking that he's not in it. But ... what he did. I ..."

His body tightened as if all his muscles were turning to stone. "I wish I could have asked him about it."

I felt my own body tighten. Was there a sliver of doubt embedded like a shard of glass in his skin, invisible but sharp and painful? All he knew was what I'd said. Was he comforting me because he believed I'd suffered some trauma, but he didn't believe everything I'd told him? Did he want to hear his father's *side* of things? "What would you ask him?"

He groaned. "I don't even know. Maybe nothing. I guess I want to ask him everything—how he could do something so ... so heinous. At the same time, I don't want to hear his answer. Ever. So probably nothing."

His body still felt stiff. I had the sense he wasn't even aware he was holding me, that his mind was living out imagined conversations in an alternate reality.

"It feels unfinished."

For me, it was finished. Finally. But I couldn't tell him that.

"I'm just so deeply disgusted by what he did. And I feel ... ashamed, I guess, that he denied it and ..."

I felt him shaking slightly. I tightened my arms around him. He cried softly. Soon, I felt the moisture of his tears on my shoulder. It didn't last long, only a few seconds, but it was enough to unsettle me so that I felt I didn't want to say anything more.

He sighed deeply, half moaning. "And I wonder if there were other girls."

I inhaled sharply. In all these years, it had never entered my thoughts.

"But I'll never know that, and it doesn't make what he did to you any worse, or any less awful if there weren't. So I don't know why I mentioned it. I just … it was there, and I needed to say it."

We lay quietly. Soon, our breathing synchronized, and I felt the calming of that rhythm.

"I don't know what else to say except that I'm sorry he did that to you, and I'm sorry you couldn't tell me for all those years, and I'm sorry for how the coldness of the adoption affected Nadia. I'm sorry for the whole, awful mess. And I hope things can get better for you."

"They already have. It's such a relief that you know, and that you … I'm so lucky to have you."

"Me too," he whispered.

"We should try to sleep," I said.

"How are you feeling about Nadia?"

"I don't know," I said. "I suppose if she wants to stay, it might be a good thing. What do you think?"

"I agree. It could be good. For a while. Or maybe we don't put a deadline on it. We can take it one step at a time."

"We can," I said.

Then we lay there with our own thoughts. I'm not sure how long it took before we fell asleep.

We didn't wake until almost noon on Sunday. It was the best sleep I'd had in over a month. And it's possible it was the best sleep I'd had in nearly twenty-three years. I slept peacefully because I felt safe. Until Micah was dead, I hadn't realized I never really had felt completely safe in my own bed, even in my own body.

40

NADIA

I t was shocking how much everything had changed. Ruth and Cheryl, and even Cameron, were all treating me like a member of the family. Three strange days since Ruth shot my biological father, and I felt like I'd been whisked away to life in a magical castle.

I wasn't sure how I felt about all of it. I'd walked into the Wellness Center less than two months ago, planning and truly wanting to punish her. It wasn't as if I'd suddenly lost all those feelings about my mom not getting the help that might have saved her life. I still saw her face in my dreams, her skin sinking into her skull as her body slowly gave up trying to fight the cancer eating at her from the inside. I still heard her voice saying she would be okay, promising I would be okay, even though she couldn't possibly know that for sure.

It was so confusing, I tried not to think about my feelings. I tried to think about how amazing the food was and the really nice, elegant house and their interesting conversations about good health and plans for the Wellness Center and what their vision was and where they had issues they needed to address and how they could make things better. They were always talking about how they could make it better.

On that third day, when Ruth was doing her morning ritual with the insulated coffee mugs, she asked me if I could get any time off work to come to the Center with her. "I want to properly introduce you to Justine—to tell her who you are. I want to explain everything to her."

I stared at her face, her eyes looking back at mine as if this was a normal, everyday activity. It was another brick in the wall of strangeness. "She doesn't like me."

"I think she misunderstood you ... and that's my fault, of course. Because I was lying about everything."

"Yeah. Sure."

"So you can get some time off?"

"I guess."

It was easy enough. But I wasn't sure Justine would suddenly think I was an amazing person just because Ruth said so, just because I was her daughter. Ruth's hopes were too high, and I wanted to tell her that, but she seemed convinced, so I went along to see what would happen.

I was sitting on the couch in Ruth's office when she brought Justine in. Justine immediately stopped in the doorway. Then she took an actual step back. "What's this about?"

"I have some things to tell you," Ruth said.

"I have a client in fifteen minutes."

"This won't take long. I need to clear things up. First, I wanted to let you know that Nadia is actually my daughter. And that was the reason for all the weird things I've been doing, all the lies, and I'm really so sorry for that. I ..."

The look on Justine's face was one of total disbelief. Like she thought this might be another game on my part. As if maybe there was some way I could trick Ruth into thinking she'd had a child. "Your *daughter*?"

"I had a baby when I was fifteen. It was a closed adoption —private. I didn't even know my baby's gender; it was—"

"You didn't know her ... how could that be?"

"My mother wanted it that way. So when Nadia showed up, I was so shocked and overwhelmed. I ..."

Justine stared at her, then at me, then back at Ruth.

"I'm sorry for what I put you through. I had never told Cameron any of this, so knowing she was here was terrifying. I just ... I handled it all really badly. So badly. I lied to everyone." Ruth choked back a gentle sob. "To Cameron, to you. And I'm really sorry."

Justine nodded.

Then Ruth told her all about Micah and why she never told a soul about having a baby. She told her about shooting Micah and about how Deanne died and the police, and about her and Cameron working things out.

Justine didn't say anything. She made little upset sounds, but that's all. She stared, nodding, her eyes looking so big and kind of dazed, almost like she was drugged.

"I just wanted to say—no more secrets," Ruth said. "No more lying."

Justine looked like her head might explode. "I don't know what to say."

"It's a lot."

"It is, and I don't know what to think."

"And I also want to say, I really respect you for raising a child by yourself. I think you already knew that, but wanted to say it again because it's different now, isn't it?"

Justine nodded.

"I hope you'll think about giving me another chance. And Nadia too."

"I don't know if—"

"Not right away. I know I hurt you. I know Nadia messed with your head."

"Yeah, sorry," I said. She didn't look at me. I wasn't sure if it sounded honest, and I wasn't sure if it even was honest, but I thought I should say something. And maybe it was partially honest. Maybe it would become the truth after a while.

"Anyway," Ruth said, "I hope after some time goes by, in the future, when you've had some room to breathe, to think about it."

"Okay. Sure. I really appreciate you telling me all this. It must be hard."

"Not really," Ruth said. "It feels pretty good." She walked to the doorway, where Justine hadn't moved more than a few inches. She didn't seem very inclined to forgive, but it was a lot to ask. A bit of a shock, a big shock, actually. Justine had spent all that time thinking things were one way, and suddenly they were completely different. You can't just change how you think about people that fast.

"Can I give you a hug?" Ruth asked.

"Um, sure."

They gave each other a long hug. After Justine left, Ruth didn't say anything to me. I felt like a bit of a stuffed toy sitting on her couch. So I took out my phone and started playing a game. I wondered if she would ever tell Justine about the blackmail. I wondered why Justine didn't bring up my gun, but I guess she had too many other things to run through her mind.

41

The police provided an update on their investigation to let us know that the drink sitting on the table by the pool at Micah and Deanne's motel contained Rohypnol. This gave credibility to Nadia's story that shoving Deanne had been a justifiable reaction because clearly Micah, and possibly Deanne as well, was threatening her with something criminal in mind.

We learned this in the evening just as we three women were sitting down for dinner.

Cameron had gone to the Giants game with some friends. Seeing him head off to a baseball game in his fan gear made me feel more alive than I had in weeks. It was the first sign that we might be returning to a normal life. It would definitely be a changed life, depending on what happened with Nadia, but still a normal life, if there is such a thing.

I'd made a vegetarian lasagna and green salad for dinner. My mother had picked up fresh sourdough bread, and I'd opened a bottle of red wine.

Something had been nagging at me since my long, soul-cleansing, late night talk with Cameron. I'd thought that experiencing his support and comfort might allow me to finally let go of my anger toward my mother for not acknowledging what Micah had done to me. I thought maybe with Micah dead, and no more secrets, it would matter less.

But it had been the opposite.

And tonight, with Cameron gone, I planned to confront her. Again. Maybe it was wrong to do that in front of Nadia, but somehow, I had received an unexpected rush of courage from her presence.

Talking to Cameron and hearing his perspective made me realize I'd been kinder to my mother and more accepting of her horrific *mistakes* than she deserved. I'd buried my own feelings and shoved aside my own needs for too long. I'd done everything she wanted so she could carry on pretending Micah was a dear family friend. She'd forced me to treat the man who raped me with respect, and I was only now beginning to recognize how that had damaged me.

I took a few sips of water and turned my attention to my mother. She was on her second serving of lasagna, diligently wrapping strands of cheese around her fork.

"I need to ask you something," I said.

She didn't look up.

"You've never given me a straight answer for this, and I really need to know. After everything that's happened, I hope you will."

The room felt suddenly quieter.

My mother let out a loud, contented sigh. "I'm really enjoying my lasagna." She looked up and beamed a smile at Nadia and me. "It's so nice to have my daughter and granddaughter here, eating dinner together. I never dreamed ..."

"Why was your very first thought when I told you that Micah drugged me and had sex with me, to suggest that I seduced him?" I felt strong asking that question. I could thank Cameron for that. I owed him so much. It felt like he and I had a circular support system. I'd helped put him back together when his body was so badly broken, and now he was doing the same for me with the damage that had been done not only to my body, but to my heart and mind.

A look of annoyance settled on my mother's face. She glanced at her plate, clearly wanting to finish her lasagna.

"He drugged me, and you refused to believe that. The police report we just received confirms that's his go-to trick."

"Are you suggesting he was going to assault his own daughter?" my mother cried. "Is that what this is about?"

"No. But he said he would *find a solution* if Nadia kept asking for money. I think he was planning to let her fall in the pool and drown ... or something like that. I don't know. I never will. Maybe I'm wrong. That isn't what I want to talk about. I was only reminding you it isn't the first time he's slipped a drug into someone's drink. What I'm saying is you didn't believe me. You *refused* to believe me."

"Why are we talking about this? He's dead. It's all over. Cameron knows, and your marriage survived ... all this ..." My mother waved her hand erratically in front of her. "And now ... you have your daughter. The rest is in the past. You need to let it go."

"What I need is for you to not tell me how to deal with a traumatic experience that you pretended didn't even happen to me. You not only pretended it didn't happen, you *blamed* me!"

"I don't understand why it matters now that he's dead."

"It matters to me! Even after I told you what he did, you socialized with them. You invited Micah over to dinner every time Sylvia went to visit her sister, like it never happened."

"He was ... they were our friends. What did you want me to do? You ended up with Cameron, so it all turned out for the best."

"I want you to call it what it was! He raped me. And your first instinct was to blame it on me."

Nadia was staring at my mother as if she'd never seen her before. The entire time my mother was talking, Nadia's gaze had been boring into the side of her face.

"What's wrong?" Nadia asked.

Without turning to look at her, my mother muttered, "Nothing."

"Your face is so red," Nadia said. "Like you're ... blushing." Nadia pressed her fingertips to her mouth. "When Ruth shot him you were so ... I couldn't figure out why you looked so *weird*, as if ... did you ... were you in *love* with him?"

My mother's face turned blood red, so red, I thought she might be having a heart attack.

"You made Ruth give me away so it wouldn't mess up your *love affair*?"

My mother pushed back her chair. She stood. "I don't know why you want to talk about a man who's dead. Why do you want to dig up something so upsetting that happened over twenty years ago? You have a beautiful life. It doesn't matter anymore." She went to the glass door that led from the dining room to the backyard and opened it. She stepped outside and walked quickly across the yard, leaving the door standing open behind her.

I stared across the table at Nadia.

Memories from those years flooded my mind.

From that night—my mother and Micah opening a bottle of champagne. Micah raising his glass for a toast. Saying something about feeling at home, at last. I couldn't remember exactly. I remembered him telling my mother her headache had spoiled the evening, that he'd waited weeks to be with her. Other memories came rushing in—lying in my bed, hearing them talking and laughing late at night. Waking before dawn to hear Micah's car pulling out of our driveway. I remembered how many times there were other families around when Micah and Sylvia and Cameron and his brother came over, but when Micah came over because Sylvia was out of town, it was only him.

My mother didn't want to believe he'd raped me. She *couldn't* believe he'd raped me. So she told herself her fifteen-year-old daughter had seduced her lover. It was the only story she could live with.

As we cleared the table, Nadia was eager to talk about my mother and Micah, but I brushed her off. I asked her to finish cleaning up the dishes. I went outside and breathed in the cool evening air. I walked to the guest cottage and knocked on the door. It took a long time for my mother to answer. She knew why I was there.

I kept it simple. "You need to find a new place to live. You should have plenty saved by now. And you need to do it quickly."

Without giving her a chance to speak, I returned to the kitchen. I poured two glasses of wine, placing one on the counter. Nadia turned from the sink and gave me a questioning look.

"I'm going to sit on the patio outside my bedroom, if you want to join me," I said.

I walked slowly down the hallway to our bedroom and out through the sliding glass door. I sat down and took a sip of wine. It was several minutes before Nadia arrived, looking nervous, as if she wasn't sure she'd heard my invitation correctly. She settled in the chair beside me.

Strangely enough, she read my mood and didn't talk. I think she understood that I no longer felt the need to escape to my private patio in an effort to avoid her curious eyes. I listened to the waterfall and felt the presence of Nadia next to me. I realized my home felt like it would soon become my own for the first time ever.

EPILOGUE
NADIA

Ruth had sucked me into their extreme healthy lifestyle, and I actually liked it. I didn't miss meat, and I was really getting into yoga. I was pretty good at it too, even though it's probably not supposed to be a competitive sport. The only funny thing in all their super-healthy living was they sure liked their wine with dinner.

Every weekend Ruth and I went hiking while Cameron took off on long bike rides with a friend of his.

I'd never been hiking, and I never really understood the point, but I was starting to like it. I liked being outside where there weren't a lot of people and no cars and streets and noise. I liked feeling all my muscles working, and that it took most of my concentration to pay attention to where my feet were going, which made me forget about other things floating around in my head. Most of the time. Except when we reached level places in the trails, and then I sometimes started overthinking. Ruth didn't want to talk while she hiked, and that was fine. We talked enough at dinner or when we were resting beside the pool after swimming laps.

For all the things she and I talked about, there were a few

things we did not talk about, and there was one huge thing that screamed at me every time I looked her in the eye.

My gun.

The night Micah had been shot, while the police were plodding through all their questions and I had too much time to think, I decided I needed to find a better hiding place for my gun. I was seriously considering whether I should get rid of it, but at that point, I still didn't know what might happen, so I wasn't quite ready to do something that drastic. I still might need it just to feel safe if I ended up in a weird situation, or if Ruth decided to take back the money she'd paid me, or if Cameron decided I didn't deserve to keep his father's cash.

A hundred different things could happen, most of them things I probably couldn't even imagine right then.

At first, I was thinking I would hide the gun in my car. But if the police came back with a search warrant because they didn't believe Micah had been trying to kill me, they would probably search my car after they finished with the house. I thought about somewhere in the yard. I closed my eyes and tried to picture all the potted plants, all the shrubs, the pathways, the tiny gardens clustered outside the floor-to-ceiling windows of some of the rooms. It seemed too risky.

I finally decided maybe I could get a safe-deposit box. The bank employees weren't allowed to look at what you put into those, and even though I wouldn't have the gun close by, I also wouldn't get caught with it. The police seemed like they believed what I told them had happened with Deanne, but you never know. And I still wasn't sure where I stood with Ruth. Or Cameron, now that he knew all about me.

It was better to move the gun away from me, but not get rid of it.

After the police left and Ruth and Cameron and Cheryl had all gone to bed, I dragged my backpack out of the closet. I unzipped it and pulled out my hoodie and journal and the other things stuffed in the top. I shoved my hand inside, but the bag was empty. I lifted it up, shocked by how light it was. I turned the bag upside down, shaking it as if that violent motion would make my gun reappear out of nowhere.

I searched the closet floor. Did I forget and put it in my suitcase? I opened my suitcase and dug through all the pockets. I lay on my stomach and felt under the bed. I shoved my arm between the mattress and box spring, even though I knew it wasn't there. I sure hadn't hidden it, and no one would take it and hide it right where I could find it. Still, I searched the entire room. The gun was not there.

Ruth was way ahead of me. She didn't want the police finding that gun either. Or maybe she didn't care about that. Maybe she was so upset after I tried to scare her, she took it then. There wasn't really time after she killed Micah. I didn't remember her leaving the room, unless she'd gone to the bathroom, and I hadn't noticed?

She must have done it ages ago. Was she still scared of me? Was she only pretending to be nice now but sleeping with one eye open, as they say? Did she just want to make sure I couldn't get the upper hand?

Climbing a steeper part of the trail now, I felt the same crawling feeling in my stomach that I had that night when I wondered if she would tell the police about my gun, if she would tell them I had blackmailed and threatened her. Did she want me to ask what she'd done with it? I was sweating, my head starting to ache, trying to keep up with her. She was in fantastic shape, and I always felt like I was hurrying to catch up when we got to the steeper areas.

As I had every single day, probably three or four times a day, since that night when I realized she had taken my gun, I tried to figure out if I should ask her.

Was she holding it for blackmail against me? But for

what? In case I did something else she didn't like? Then she would turn it over to the police and tell them I'd made some crazy comment about a doctor in Washington State who was punished? Did she remember what I'd whispered to her in the dark that night? Had she figured out what it meant? It wasn't as if I'd said I *killed* that doctor. I'd said Ruth would be punished. But maybe, if she took the time to do some research, that was really clear. Maybe I had totally given myself away.

Or did she get rid of it to keep me safe? Did she hear me and understand perfectly well, and she was trying to protect me? Had she destroyed the evidence so they could never charge me with murder?

Did she *know*? Did my mother love me enough to be able to keep the secret of knowing I committed murder? Or had she fallen back to sleep that night, scared, but forgetting what I'd said because she wasn't really awake? Maybe she only took the gun because she didn't want me to have it.

As we continued climbing, the sun on our backs, I wondered if I would ever tell her or if I needed to keep that secret to myself for the rest of my life.

A NOTE FROM THE AUTHOR

Thank you so much for choosing to read *The Secret She Kept*. I hope you enjoyed reading the book as much as I loved writing it.

This story went through so many evolutions that the original idea has a very vague resemblance to what you just read! Ruth and Cameron did have a good marriage that was disrupted by a young woman named Nadia, but originally Nadia was a pawn in someone else's game. Once she took charge of her story, I fell in love with this hurt, slightly bitter, but vulnerable and ultimately hopeful heroine, and I knew Ruth would too.

I want to take a moment to give an enormous thank you to Brian Lynch and Garret Ryan at Inkubator Books. Their belief in my writing, their unique, passionate approach to developing and shaping a story, as well as their investment in getting the word out to readers has changed my writing career in amazing ways.

A special thank you to my editor, Line Langebek. She sees characters through a lens that's very much like mine. Sometimes, brainstorming and revising my outline with her feels like talking to my alter ego.

I'm also very grateful to Sara Henry for her detailed copy editing and Pauline Nolet for her careful attention to the little things. And finally, thank you to Claire Milto, Stephen Ryan, and the rest of the team at Inkubator Books for their stunning support in preparing my books for publication and getting the word out to readers with creativity and style.

Reviews are so important to us authors. If you could spend a moment to write an honest review on Amazon, no matter how short, I would be extremely grateful. They really do help get the word out

Best wishes,

Cathryn

www.cathryngrant.com

ALSO BY CATHRYN GRANT

The Woman In the Dark ◆ *The Woman In the Cellar*

The Woman In the Photograph ◆ *The Woman In the Storm*

The Woman In the Taxi ◆ *The Woman In the Church*

The Woman In the Shadows

SUBURBAN NOIR NOVELS

Buried by Debt

The Suburban Abyss ◆ *The Hallelujah Horror Show*

Faceless ◆ *An Affair With God*

THE HAUNTED SHIP TRILOGY

Alone On the Beach ◆ *Slipping Away From the Beach*

Haunting the Beach

NOVELLAS

Madison Keith Ghost Story Series ◆ *Chances Are*

Jealousy Junction

SHORT FICTION

Reduction in Force ◆ *Maternal Instinct*

Flash Fiction For the Cocktail Hour

The 12 Days of Xmas

NONFICTION

Writing is Murder: Motive, Means, and Opportunity

Made in United States
North Haven, CT
21 January 2023

31401748R00178